Out of the Gutter

Karol Tiler

PublishAmerica
Baltimore

ISBN: 1-4241-4186-9
PUBLISHED BY PUBLISHAMERICA, LLLP
www.publishamerica.com
Baltimore

Printed in the United States of America

To my sister, she knows who she is.

Remember, I'll always be there so we can share our secrets.

Many things in life cannot be explained:
The death of an infant, the loss of a job, the rebellion of a child,
the desertion by a loved one, or any number of circumstances beyond our control.

Have you ever wondered *why did this have to happen to me*?
God can help us with those "Why?" questions.

Karol Tiler

To Ruth.

much Love.

Karol. (Florida 2004)

Understanding the Dialect

Each country has its own language. Within that country, each state or city has its own accent or dialect.

In the United Kingdom, some dialects are harder to understand. For example, Liverpool, Birmingham, Cornwall and Yorkshire.

Yorkshire folk have a habit of cutting their words short. The list below will help you, the reader, understand the meaning of certain words:

Yer	You or Your
Fer	For
Yer'll	You will
Mam	Mom or Mother
Snot Nose	Snooty
Oy	Jewish Exclaimation
Nowt	Nothing
Bloomin Ek	Exclaimation, Oh Boy, Can You Believe it? Etc
Ob Nobbin	Associating with
Aint	I Am Not
Teckin	Taking
Somat	Something
In The Club	Pregnant
Moochin	Moping or Miserable
Mek	Make
Side	Clear the table
Wot's	What's
Yer've	You Have
Ignorin	Ignoring
Yer Gonna	You are going to
Ter	To

Gypsophelia	Foilage that accompany flowers in a bouquets
Ferget	Forget
Ta'ra	Goodbye
Owt	Anything
Bide	Wait/Mind
Ape'orth	Affectionate word for Silly
Ta'	Thanks/Thank You
Haggle	Barter
Brew	Cup of Tea
Side	Clear
Lurch	Stagger
Soppy	Soft
Gis	Give Us
'Un	One
Bairn	Baby/Child
Mash Tea	Make a cup of tea
Jar	Glass
Mite	Small child
Goes Down	Sent to Prison
Top it All	Above all Else
Flit	Move House
Mucky	Dirty

The radio gave time checks every ten minutes. Tina Martin stood in the cold kitchen, combing her hair and drinking a pot of tea.

"God how I hate this place," she said to herself as she looked around with disgust. Every worktop that you could see, was heaped with junk.

There were old newspapers, empty bottles and old car parts on the floor. The sink full of dishes from the previous day stood in a bowl of cold greasy water.

There was mildew all along the windowsill, and the window was so filthy, that you had trouble seeing out of it.

The cracked mirror that hung on a nail above the sink wasn't too clean either.

The floor covered with lino was cracked and dirty.

Tina stepped from the kitchen into a room that was no better and sighed. The table was covered with a newspaper that served as a tablecloth and in the middle of the table stood sauce and vinegar bottles, dirty mugs, plates and overflowing ashtrays.

The fireplace was filthy, and every corner of the room piled high with rubbish. The only "woman's touch" was a dirty vase containing plastic flowers that stood on the windowsill.

The rest of the house was the same. The bathroom and toilet were filthy. The bedroom stank of stale sweat, the bedding on the beds had not been changed for weeks if not months, and dirty clothes were piled in the corners of the room.

The whole house reeked of stale tobacco, cooking smells and unwashed bodies.

Tina hated the smell of smoke; she had never smoked and she had no intention of starting.

The radio said the time was eight o'clock. Tina took her coat from the peg behind the door and walked out of the house.

The smell of fresh air hit her nostrils. Even though there was a slight frost and the cold stung her nose and made her eyes water, it was better than what was behind her.

She stepped into the back yard and this, too, was overgrown, and littered with bits of oily cars and bikes.

At the end of the street, Tina stopped and took shelter from the cold. She waited here for her friend Rose. Every morning they would walk to work at the printing factory to make maps.

As she stood waiting, Tina reflected on what her life had been like since her parents had divorced when she was eight years old.

Being the eldest of three it had fallen upon her to look after the others. Her father was a violent man, and once too often had come home drunk and kicked her mother out of the house for no reason other than his tea had not been ready on the table. Regardless of the fact that he had drank all the housekeeping money away the previous night.

Her mother was terrified of him when he was drunk; he thought nothing of kicking her out of the home, but the last time he had done this, she had been too frightened to come back for the kids.

Shortly after this incident, he had brought another woman to the house and told them that she was their new mother; years later Tina found out that they had never married.

Her stepmother was a dirty, lazy harridan. She never attempted to keep the house clean, but still managed to produce three more children.

They moved house a few times and it was always the same; the house would remain presentable for a few weeks and then things began to slide.

Tina did her best to keep the house clean at the weekends, but felt that she was fighting a losing battle.

She was waiting for the day when she would be old enough to leave home, but she was only fifteen, so, she had to stick it for a while longer.

Tina saw Rose coming along the road. As she got nearer she said, "Hi."

"Hello, you look fed up."

"I am."

"Why?"

"I can't stand that house much longer, I hate having to go home each night?"

"So what's new?"

Tina smiled. "Yes, what's new?"

They started walking towards work and Tina thought back to when she had been at school. She had hated it, but her attendance at school had been one hundred percent, because she had hated being at home even more.

Ten minutes later, both girls walked through the gates along with everyone else to "clock on."

The job was OK, but Tina wanted something else. Something that would lift her out of the slum that she was living in.

Her wages were just two pounds a week and out of it, her stepmother gave her ten shillings back. It didn't leave her very much.

She was always hungry and cold. Her clothes came from second-hand shops; she was sick of living the way she was, and if she could work her way out of this mess, she would.

Her idol was Marilyn Monroe, and people said that she had a look of her. Maybe someone would come along and think she was pretty, enough to take her away from all this and make her rich, but for now she had to work and only her dreams kept her going.

Her friend Rose was only a little better off than she was, but at least her clothes were clean and she did have stockings and proper shoes to wear.

Rose had no ambition; all she wanted to do was get married, have her own home and family.

There was nothing wrong with wanting these things, but Tina had seen too much poverty to want to be stuck in a rut.

Tina and Rose worked steadily at their bench putting sheets of the maps together until nearly tea break.

When it was time, between them they would carry the big rack with handles on round the factory and collect everyone's mugs. The youngest workers had to make the tea for everyone else in the factory.

Wholly, they were a good-humoured lot who worked in the factory.

Rose looked forward to this part of the day because she fancied one of the lads that worked in the packing department. He had ginger hair and his name was Kevin. Everyone called him Spud, his last name being Murphy. Tina never understood the connection until years later.

He was old at eighteen, and he played in a group in the pubs. Around this time, when groups were becoming popular, such as The Beatles, Gerry and the Pacemakers and suchlike, most boys were forming their own groups and hoping to follow their success.

Kevin was the same; his group played in the hope that someone would discover them.

"Ta, Rosie," he said as she blushingly handed him his tea, and then carried on handing the rest of the tea out.

The women in the factory were loud and coarse. They had little happening in their own lives so they talked about everyone else's.

If you were not there, they would talk about you, and if there were nothing for them to talk about, they would make it up having little regard of the trouble it could cause.

This was why, for many years later, Tina said that she would never work with a bunch of women again.

One of the women called Ivy was in charge of the women's section.

She had bleached blonde hair and wore very heavy makeup; when she wanted to talk to her friend Elsie, she had to shout above the noise of the machinery.

"You know that silly cow that lives next door ter'me, well she got a right thumpin' last night she did."

Tina shook her head. Ivy came across so righteous and at the same time, she was so two faced, everyone knew that she had been having an affair with Cyril the foreman for the last three years.

Elsie shouted back, "Why, what did she do?"

"Locked him out she did; when he couldn't get in, he ranted an' raved and kicked door. She had to let 'im in, then he thumped her."

"The poor cow," shouted Elsie, "she should get out."

"Where can she go with eight kids?"

They both stopped talking when Tina and Rose came back, but Tina and Rose had heard it all anyway.

The only other girls that were anywhere near their ages were Yvonne and Anne. Both had left the school that Tina and Rose had attended the previous year.

The year they had been working had made a big difference, turning them into knowledgeable young women where the opposite sex was concerned.

Yvonne was pretty with short, dark hair, but she had an awful problem with body odour. Tina and Rose wondered how she ever managed to get a date with the boys.

Anne had a squint and was very plain. She was tall and had no figure to speak of; she left the factory six months later when she found herself pregnant, with no boyfriend or husband in evidence

One day was very much like another, going to work and coming home, going out on Saturday nights, but having to be home by nine p.m.

Life was monotonous and Tina felt like fifty instead of fifteen.

She did not dislike going to work the way she had disliked school, but even if she did, she would still go because it meant she was not at home.

She could not even have the luxury of a regular bath; their bath was in the kitchen covered with a worktop, and like everything else in the house, it was always full of dirty pots and pans, and anything else that needed a place to stand.

Tina kept herself clean by giving herself wash downs every day, and once a week, she would go to the public baths. The water was hot and the towels were rough but clean, the biggest bonus was that she had privacy.

She tried not to be on her own in the company of men; she thought that they were all after one thing, and they usually proved her right.

When Tina was thirteen, her "uncle" had been staying at the house. He wasn't really her uncle but a long-time friend of her father's, and they all had to call him uncle.

One day, she was in the kitchen having a wash. She was unable lock the door as it was broken. Tina thought she was alone in the house, so she was very surprised when her uncle walked into the kitchen, and saw her stood without a stitch of clothing on.

He grabbed hold of her and fondled her breasts, grabbed her hand and put it to his crotch; her faced burned with embarrassment.

She punched him out of the way and ran upstairs. She vowed to make sure she was never on her own with him again.

Her father was another matter. She suspected "that side" of marriage had ceased between him and her step mum.

One night he asked her if she wanted to go to the cinema; this was unusual and out of character. An Elvis Presley film was showing and Tina wanted to see it. When he said he would take her, she had been surprised but did not think anything wrong.

She really enjoyed it, but on the way home her father had stopped the car and told her what he wanted; he also told her that if she said anything, no one would believe her, and the authorities would put her away.

This had gone on for two years; she couldn't refuse to go out with him or her stepmother would wonder what was wrong.

She would not have believed her if she had told her. The only person she could tell was Rose.

"I don't know what to do," Tina said

"I'd kill him," answered Rose. "Threaten him, call his bluff, you could tell the police you know."

"No one would believe me."

"They would."

Tina was too scared until one night her stepmother had gone to bingo; she and her father were alone, and Tina felt sick with fear.

"Come here," he said.

"No, I don't want to."

She felt a stinging blow at the side of her head and Tina stood up. "You ever touch me again and I'll go to the police."

"They won't believe yer, I'll tell them yer a liar and they'll lock yer up."

"Well if they do, then I won't be here for you to do what you want with me will I?"

Tina stormed from the room and went to bed. She closed the door and wedged a chair beneath the door handle.

Her heart thumped and her head ached as she sat fully clothed on the bed waiting.

She woke next morning still fully clothed and cold, but she had not been disturbed. She told herself that she would leave as soon as she could.

Over the next two years, life changed very little for Tina and Rose, both now seventeen.

Rose had been out with a few boys; her burning passion for "Spud" had quickly subsided when she had gone out with him one night and he thought she owed him something for buying her a Cherry B."

She was now dating a boy called Douglas, Dougie for short.

Tina didn't get out much; when she wasn't working, she was cleaning at home, although it seemed to make little difference.

She had been out a couple of times with a lad who came round each Sunday afternoon with the ice cream cart.

Tina had felt flattered that he had shown an interest in her, but the second date ended two hours after it had started when he had tried to force himself upon her.

One day Tina and Rose were in the local Wimpy bar when Tina said, "Rose, do you think I'm pretty?"

"Course, I wish I looked like you."

"Then why is it that all the men I come into contact with are only out for one thing? Why don't they get to know me instead of trying to get to know my body?"

Rose sighed and said, "Maybe you give out the wrong signals."

Tina's faced burned. "What do you mean by that?"

"Don't get yer knickers in a twist; you've never been loved, and you've a lot to give. You cry out for love, but your innocence shines through and the men you meet think they can take advantage of you. It's not your fault I know, but with your looks you're not going to find it easy. Someone will always try to use you and you're just too quiet to fight back."

"You're wrong, Rose, I'm not quiet and I won't be used; if I do make anything of myself it will be because of hard work, not because of how I look or the favours I do for people."

Six months later Rose announced that she was pregnant and that she and Dougie would have to get married.

"What did your mum say?"

"Not a lot, I think she'll be glad to see the back of me. Our Gordon's working so she won't miss the money I give her, but I think she wants me room."

Rose's dad had walked out a few years ago, and with six kids to feed, her mum took in "lodgers." Well that's what she called them.

"So," Rose was saying, "will yer stand up for me at the register office?"

"Course I will, when is it?"

"Four weeks time. Dougie's making the arrangements when he comes back."

"Why, where's he going?"

"He goes on holiday next week."

"On holiday, lucky him, why doesn't he save his money and use it for your honeymoon?"

"He goes with his mates every year to the Isle of Man TT Races; it was already booked and paid for, so I can't say 'owt."

Tina sighed. "What a start for you, Rose, no money, you pregnant and he's going on holiday, don't you want anything more from life?"

"Only to be happy with a house of me own and a couple of kids."

"Mm," said Tina, "if it stops at a couple of kids."

Tina and Rose finished their shopping. They arranged to meet the following day and said goodbye.

They walked away in opposite directions. Tina walked past some offices and noticed a sign in the window.

YOUNG LADIES WANTED FOR MODELLING AND IN-STORE DEMONSTRATIONS. MUST BE AGED BETWEEN 17 AND 20, APPLY WITHIN.

She found a pen and paper in her bag and wrote down the number; she told herself that she would call first thing Monday morning.

Tina was excited all weekend about the note she had in her bag and could not wait for the start of the week.

On Monday morning she clocked in at work; at tea break she went out to the pay phone by the gate and dialled the number written down.

A woman's voice answered, "Good morning, may I help you?"

"Yes, I'd like some information regarding the advert in your window."

"Would you like to make an appointment for an interview with Mr Ableson?"

"Yes, when shall I come?"

"Would tomorrow at ten-thirty be convenient?"

"Yes, I'll be there."

Tina gave the woman her name and hung up.

She would have to make up an excuse for leaving work early. Maybe she could say she was going to the dentist or something, and if she said she would go back to work afterwards, it should be OK.

At lunchtime, she told Rose about the appointment.

"It sounds a bit dodgy to me, Tina."

"How can you say that, you don't know any more about it than I do. I've got to get away from home; if it means working hard for a few years, then I'll do it, but I'm going to have something to show for it."

"You could always get married."

"No thanks, not yet. When I do, he will have to be something special. My experience tells me that men are out for what they can get, and I won't be the one giving it to them."

"They're not all the same yer know," said Rose.

"The ones I know are."

That night Tina locked herself in the kitchen, boiled a pan of water and washed her hair, rolled it up, then washed herself.

She took a bag and put her best blouse and skirt in it. She would take them to work with her and change before she left for her appointment.

Tina used the nailbrush to tidy up her shoes. The suede on them had gone scruffy, but they had only cost her £1 at the market; they would have to do.

She had no stockings to wear but thought it would be OK. She decided she would have an early night.

Her brother and sisters were already in bed and her stepmother was down the street with Mrs. Gallagher who was about to produce her tenth child; her father was at the pub.

Tina went to bed; her head was full of the possibilities that could come out of the interview the next day.

She heard a door bang and the heavy footsteps on the stairs told her that her father had come home from the pub. It didn't sound as if he was sober either.

She heard the footsteps stop outside her door and the handle turned. Tina held her breath and pretended to be asleep.

She was aware of the strong smell of beer and his hands began pulling at the bedclothes.

"C'mon," he slurred, "gis' a kiss."

"Go away," she hissed.

"C'mon, I need lovin', yer mam's a cold bugger."

"Go away or I'll scream, and she's not my mother."

Tina felt a stinging blow at the side of her head, the bedclothes pulled off her, and then he was grunting on top of her.

She struggled and tried to push him off, but he was too heavy for her. Her hands touched the side of the bed as she felt around. She grasped the nail file she had on a little table, swung her hand down and the nail file embedded in his shoulder; he let out a scream and fell to the floor.

"You bloody bitch, yer'll pay for that yer will," he screamed.

She sat up and pulled the bedclothes over her, her head still ringing from his blow. He raised his fist again and she quietly said, "You do, and I'll be out of here and down the police station. I'll have you locked up within the hour."

"They won't believe yer," he sneered.

"Oh yes they will when I show them the bruises."

He crawled to the door. "Don't yer say anything."

"It's you who has the explaining to do; you make me sick." She sat a long time after he had gone, now shaking and the tears coursed down her face.

Tina made her way to the bathroom where she emptied the contents of her stomach. She washed herself as best she could with cold water then returned to her bed, but she could not sleep for the rest of the night.

Next morning when she looked in the mirror she saw the side of her face all swollen and bruised; she combed her hair forward, hoping it covered the bruising.

When she went downstairs, her stepmother was at the table with a pot of tea surrounded by a cloud of smoke from her cigarette.

"Tea's mashed," she said to Tina.

"Thanks, how is Mrs Gallagher?"

"Another girl, that makes seven." Mrs Gallagher had previously given birth to three boys and they had all been still born, so she kept producing babies in the hope that the next one would be a boy and alive.

"Did yer hear yer dad come home last night?"

"Yes, he was drunk as usual."

"Did he say anything?" she asked.

"No I was in bed."

"He's gorn the 'ospital, said he banged his shoulder; must say he looked rough."

Tina shrugged her shoulders, picked up her bag and left for work. She waited for Rose as usual, and when she arrived told her what had happened the night before.

When Rose saw her face she said, "Yer've got ter do something, Tina, report him."

"No, I'll get my own back, you wait and see."

They arrived at work and Tina kept herself busy. At break time, she went to the toilet and tried to make herself respectable. She left work at ten o' clock, it gave her plenty of time to get to her appointment.

She arrived at the building and entered the office area. She saw two other girls waiting, and her heart sank.

They looked very glamorous compared to her; their clothes were immaculate, and they wore stockings.

Their hair and makeup were perfect. Tina felt like a down and out beside them.

Their appointments were before hers, but they didn't seem to be in the office very long before they came out again, and then it was her turn.

She entered the room. Mr Ableson was short, fat and he sat behind a large desk; the air hung heavy with the smoke from the fat cigar he had in his mouth.

"Come in, come in, I don't bite," he said.

She walked over to the desk and he looked her up and down critically.

"What can I do for you, my dear?"

Tina nervously cleared her throat. "I saw your advert in the window and would like some details of the work you have?"

He looked at her again and the silence that followed made her feel very uncomfortable. She looked down at her hands in her lap and didn't meet his gaze.

"Brush your hair back."

She brushed back the side opposite the bruise.

"Now the other side," and she did hesitantly.

"What is this?" he asked kindly.

Tina felt the tears start to prick her eyes. "I had a knock yesterday," she answered.

He pressed the buzzer on his desk and the woman from the outer office came in.

"Lilly, bring us some coffee please."

He looked at her again and said, "I need girls to work in the big department stores promoting products for various clients. I also need girls to do modelling."

Tina looked at him. "I don't take my clothes off for anyone."

"I never asked you to," he answered. "The modelling is for catalogues, very respectable."

"Oh," she said.

The woman called Lilly, brought the coffee in. When they were alone again he said, "Do you want to talk about it?"

Tina was not used to kindness and sympathy, and before she knew, she was sobbing.

He handed her a large white handkerchief; she told him some, but not all of what had taken place the night before.

When she'd finished he said, "When your face has healed I can use you, but the last thing I need is an interfering father who keeps bruising your face."

"Is the work guaranteed to be regular?"

"Yes."

"Then I'll find somewhere to live and pay my way."

"Are you sure this is what you want, Tina?"

"As sure as I wish him dead. I can't stand the hovel that I call home; with or without this job I'd leave in any case."

He nodded. "I may be able to help you; come back and see me tomorrow."

"I have to work you know, I can't just take the time off."

"You won't lose by it; leave your job at the end of the week. You start working for me on Monday."

"What's the catch?"

"Tina, there is no catch."

"No one does something for nothing," she said.

"Neither do I, you'll pay me back out of what you earn. I'm just helping to you get started, trust me."

"I trust no one. I'll accept your help, but I'll pay you back."

"Fine, Tina, that's fine, I'll see you tomorrow."

She nodded and left the office. Tina was apprehensive but elated at the same time. She would show them, she'd be someone one day.

She didn't want to go back to work so she wandered around the town looking in the shop windows at all the fashions, wondering if someday she would model clothes like them.

Tina enjoyed the day. It was a luxury to take a day off work and not have to worry about losing money.

Eventually she wandered back to the factory and waited outside the gates for Rose; it would be clocking off time soon.

When Rose came out of the gates she said, "What happened to you? Why didn't you come back to work?"

Tina told her about Mr Ableson and what he said.

"Sounds too good to be true to me."

"Rose, just be happy for me. I know it sounds too good to be true, but you have to start somewhere. I tell you what though, I will earn respect and no one will ever use me again. I can't wait to live on my own, I won't be going work tomorrow either."

"You'll lose your job, Tina."

"I don't care. I was leaving at the end of the week in any case."

"But we'll still see each other, won't we?"

"Of course we will, silly, you're the only friend I've got."

"Good, Dougie goes away at the weekend and I'll need some company."

"I'll meet you outside work tomorrow night."

"OK, why don't you come and spend the night tomorrow? Mum's going to her sisters, they're going to a wedding on Saturday, I'll be on my own and we can keep each other company."

"Great, I'll look forward to it; anyway see you tomorrow, Rose."

They parted company and Tina made her way home; as she let herself in the house, the smell hit her.

The house was dirty and smoky as usual, and everyone sat in the one room.

"Tea's in the oven," her stepmother called out to her.

When Tina took the plate from the oven, the egg and sausage had set hard on the plate; she tipped it in the bin and added the plate to the dirty pile at the side of the sink.

"Haven't you done any housework today?" she asked.

"No, I've not had time."

"Why, what have you been doing?"

"I've been down at Mrs Gallagher's looking after her kids."

"We could do with a bit of that charity here," said Tina.

Her father who sat in a chair in the corner said, "Watch yer mouth. Who do yer think yer are wi' yer igh and mighty ways; yer gonna come a cropper one day, girl, just wait an' see."

"Why, because I don't like living in filth?"

"We've give yer a good 'ome we 'ave," said her stepmother, "yer should be grateful."

"Grateful," Tina shouted, "you haven't got a clue any of you."

Her father rose from the chair. "I said watch yer mouth."

Tina quickly left the room and went upstairs. She took her clothes from the drawer and put them in a holdall; everything she owned fit into the one bag.

She decided that she'd go to Rose's house that night; even if she had to sleep on the floor, it would be better than here.

Tina went downstairs and her father said, "Where yer goin'?"

"To Rose's. She's asked me to stay for a couple of nights."

"Yer not goin'," he said.

"Why?"

"Because I said so, she's a slut."

"No she's not, she's my friend."

"She's in the club."

"What's that got to do with it?"

"She'll lead yer into 'er ways."

"She has no ways, she was just unlucky; anyway it's what she wants, and she's getting married in two weeks' time."

"I don't want yer turning out like her."

"What are you worried about? That someone will get what you can't have," she shouted.

He lunged forward and punched her in the face. Her stepmother left the room. "Shut yer mouth."

"I'll have my day with you," she told him, then turned and left the house.

That will be another bruise tomorrow, she thought to herself.

She knocked on the door at Rose's house and her mother came to the door. "Hello, Tina love, come in."

"Thanks, Rose said I could stay a couple of nights from tomorrow. Could you put me up tonight?"

"Of course, love, I'll put Jesse in with our May and you can have her bed."

"I don't want to put you out, I'll sleep on the floor."

"You'll do no such thing, have yer had yer tea?" she asked.

Tina shook her head. "I'm not very hungry, thanks."

"Just try a bit, it's only stew, but it's hot."

21

"Thanks very much."

Tina sat down at the table and, even though the house was crowded, it was clean and warm. Rose came into the room, "Hello, Tina, what's wrong?"

"Nothing, I just wondered if I could stay tonight and your mum said it would be OK."

"Come upstairs, I'll show you where you'll be sleeping." Rose looked at her mother. "Shall I put Jesse and May together, Mum?"

"Yes."

"Thanks again," said Tina to Rose's mum.

"It's OK, love, stay as long as yer want."

When they got upstairs Rose said, "Have you had another fight?"

Tina nodded her head. "You'll be OK here," Rose said.

When Tina went to bed, she slept better than she ever had done and woke up feeling refreshed; she looked better than she had done of late, apart from the bruising on her face.

She went downstairs and the room was clean and warm. Rose's mum had tea, toast and eggs on the table.

"Come and have some breakfast, love," she said.

"Thanks, Mrs Hirst, I'm not very hungry."

"Yer not in the club as well are yer?"

"No fear."

"No I didn't think so, got more sense I dare say, not like our Rose."

"It's what she wants though isn't it?"

"What do you want, Tina?"

"I'm not getting tied down, I have ambitions; in fact I have to see Mr Ableson today and he's going to help me."

"Be careful, love, there's a lot of funny folk out there."

"I know, but I have to try."

"I'll always be here if yer need somewhere ter go."

"Thanks." Tina found that she was hungry after all. She could not remember when she'd last sat down and eaten breakfast.

Rose popped her head round the door. "Right," she said. "I'm off, see you back here, Tina, good luck."

"Thanks, Rose."

Tina helped clear away the dishes and then said she would go get herself ready. Mrs Hirst looked at her and said, "Yer know, I was your size once, I've a dress upstairs I think would fit you. Why don't you try it on, Tina, it's no good to me."

"Are you sure?"

"It won't go near me and our Rose is expectin', come on."

They went upstairs to the bedroom and she took the dress covered in a polythene bag, from the wardrobe.

The dress was simple cut, in dark blue and it fitted Tina like a glove. It was better than anything she'd ever had.

"There yer are," said Mrs Hirst. "I have a pair of shoes that goes with it."

Tina's eyes filled with tears. "I don't know how to thank you."

Mrs Hirst put her ample arms around her. "No need to, lass, I've known yer long enough and I know what it's been like fer yer."

Tina looked at her. "Oh not everything, our Rose don't say much, but I can read between the lines. We aint got much, but we're decent, Tina. Just you go and get that job, give yerself a chance."

"Thanks," she said and, without a backward glance, left the room and the house to see Mr Ableson.

When Tina arrived at the office, there were three other people waiting. Lilly, the woman she had seen the previous day, looked up and smiled at her. "You have to go straight in, Tina."

"Thanks," she replied.

She knocked at the door and walked in. Mr Ableson sat, as usual, behind his desk, surrounded by cigar smoke.

"Ah, Tina, come in, come in," he said. He got up and took her hand. He looked at her and said, "Well, that's an improvement from yesterday," he smiled, "apart from your face."

"I can't help that, I was born with it."

"No, my dear, I was referring to the bruising."

"Oh, yes well, I stayed at my friend's last night and I can stay until something else turns up."

He looked at her. "Tina, if you work for me, you are going to have to trust me, will you do that?"

"I'll never trust anyone completely."

He sighed. "Well I guess I'll have to accept that. I won't ever tell you wrong though."

"Why are you being so nice to me, Mr Ableson?"

"Call me Solly, because I like you. You are young and fresh, and hungry for work. We can make improvements. I know that if I look after you, you will pay me back and work well. It's an investment. I am firm but fair. Too many people exploit young girls, but not me. You can trust me, Tina, I know you are hurting, why I do not know, perhaps one day you'll tell me. But I promise to be fair with you, and you have to promise to do right by me, do we have a deal?"

"What do you mean do right by you?"

"Òy, did I not just say that I would not tell you wrong? What I mean is, I will get you plenty of work. I will be your agent, now does that sound good to you?"

"Yes." She nodded.

"Right, first we'll get some things sorted out for you and do the paperwork later."

He handed her a piece of paper with a name and address on.

"This lady has some nice rooms, clean and warm. Her one fault is that she'll make a fuss over you like a mother hen. If you take the room, your rent will be paid by me."

"No thank you, I'm not being kept," she interrupted.

"Listen to me, let me finish," he said. "It will be paid by me until you are receiving regular wages, then what I've paid out, I'll take back; call it a loan. I'll also open a bank account for you and put some money in. you'll need working capital."

He walked to the door and called for Lilly.

She came in and he handed her a cheque for £200. "Go to the bank; take Tina with you. Open an account in her name and then give her the cheque book; this should cover it."

He handed her another £200 in cash. "Take her shopping and make her look presentable; come back here at four o' clock."

He looked at Tina. "I'll have the contract drawn up and all this money listed on a separate document that will be paid back from your earnings."

"It'll take me a lifetime to repay this lot, Mr Ableson."

"Solly," he said. "No it won't, you'll earn this and more in the first month you work for me, is that OK by you?"

Tina nodded her head; all this money she could earn. Previously, her wages had been two pounds a week. Something would go wrong and spoil it, she was sure.

She looked at Solly. "The woman who owns the rooms, does she know of the arrangements?"

He nodded. "She'll look after you, Tina, she's my sister." He smiled and she didn't feel as nervous as she had been at the beginning of the day.

Solly threw some keys on the desk. "Take the car, Lilly, it'll be quicker."

"Thanks." She turned to Tina. "Come on, I like days like this."

"Do you do this often?"

"No I don't, you must have something special for Solly to help you. Believe me, Tina, you can trust him as if he were your own father."

"I hope not," she replied.

"What was that you said?"

"Nothing, it doesn't matter."

First, they went to see the rooms that Solly had sent her to; they were in the Temple Newsome area. This area was predominantly Jewish, and the houses were big and expensive. It was a nice part of Leeds, very quiet and respectable.

They found the address and stopped in front of a large Victorian terraced house. They climbed the steps and rang the doorbell.

A woman opened the door; she was small and her grey hair tied in a bun. She greeted them warmly.

"Come in. Solly has rung me already; he said you would be calling. I'll show you the room."

The room was at the top of the house. They climbed three flights of stairs to get there.

The room turned out to be rooms. The sitting room was very large and furnished comfortably. Leading off from the living room was the bedroom; this was as big as the living room, had lots of cupboards, a dressing table and a large bed.

Tina had only ever dreamed of sleeping in a bed this big. The luxury was the real sheets and blankets on the bed, not the old army coats she had been used to.

When she opened the door leading from the bedroom, she saw a bathroom. It was small, but to Tina, it was luxury. She would be able to have a bath whenever she felt like it.

The overall thing that struck her was how clean everything was. Coming back from the bedroom into the living room, there was a small kitchenette concealed behind a curtain. It had all she would need to make drinks and meals.

Tina could not believe what she saw; it was luxury compared to what she had been used to. A rich person's home she would have called it.

"Is this all mine?" she asked.

"It is if you want it, dear."

"Do I want it? I can't wait, when can I move in?"

"You can move in as soon as you're ready."

"Oh thank you, Mrs…"

"You can call me Hilda, would you like to move in today?"

"No, I have to sort some things out. Will it be alright if I come tomorrow?"

"Whenever it suits you, dear, here are the keys."

"We may as well have your shopping delivered here today, Tina, it will save you moving it twice," said Lilly.

Tina nodded. "Thank you so much. I'm really looking forward to moving in."

"You're welcome. Solly said you needed somewhere, and he said you were a good girl, so that's good enough for me."

Tina thanked Hilda again, and then she and Lilly left to go into town to start their shopping.

Lilly knew which places to buy clothes. They bought dresses, skirts and blouses, shoes, stockings and some underwear.

Tina had never had so many clothes, or dreamed of ever owning so many. They went to the bank and opened a bank account, and when Tina put the cheque book into her bag, she couldn't help wondering if it was all a dream.

Things had certainly happened quickly in the last couple of days, maybe a little too fast, and she was afraid someone would come along and burst the bubble.

They finished their shopping and returned to the office. Solly had the contract ready and Tina read every single word before she signed.

When she'd signed the contract, he said, "I suggest you don't go back to your old job. Take a week to rest, get something done with your hair, and give those bruises time to heal. Why don't you move into you new rooms and contact me after the weekend. Lilly will arrange for you to go to a beautician. They will give you a makeup case and show you how to apply it. I'll see you back in office in a week's time; in the meantime, if you need anything call me or Lilly, is that clear?"

"Yes, thanks very much. I don't know what to say."

"Just get some rest, work hard for me and you'll not look back, Tina. You have a lot of potential. At the moment you are very pretty, but with a little help you will be beautiful."

Tina returned to Rose's a little bewildered. She had left home that morning wearing secondhand clothes, and had come back with a brand new wardrobe, money in the bank and somewhere decent to live.

Yet, she still had the uneasy feeling that something would go wrong, and it put a dampener on what should be the happiest day of her life so far.

Rose came in from her day at work. "How did you get on?"

Tina sat round the table and told them of the events of the day.

"It sounds fantastic," said Rose, and her mother agreed. "It sounds as if you have fallen on your feet."

"I have, and I'm not returning to the factory. Will it be OK if I stay here tonight? I'll be moving into my new place tomorrow."

"I thought you were staying anyway," said Rose.

"What about yer things at home?" said Mrs Hirst.

"I've already brought all I had," replied Tina.

"Yer mean that's all you've got?"

"Yes, and it's all I want. I won't wear the clothes again, but I'll keep them to remind me of who I am and where I came from."

After tea, things became a little chaotic, as all the family tried to get ready at once for their trip. Two hours later, they were all ready to leave.

Now Tina and Rose had the house to themselves; the silence was deafening. The two girls sat in front of the fire and Tina went over her day again not quite believing that it was all happening.

"I'll go with you tomorrow to help you settle in your new place if you want?"

"If you want to, but Rose, you have to promise me one thing. You have to swear not to tell anyone where the house is. That last thing I want is for any of my family finding out where I am."

"You don't have to ask me that, love, you know I wouldn't do anything to hurt you."

Both girls went to bed early. Even this was a pleasure, because usually there would be a mad scramble to use the bathroom first.

When they got to the factory next morning, Tina went to the office to see the owner.

"Mr. Wrigley, I just came to tell you that I am leaving, I have another job."

"I will be sorry to lose you, Tina, does the new job pay better than I do?"

"Yes it does, and hopefully it will lead to better things, and allow me to move away from here."

"Well, you are a good worker, but far be it for me to stop you moving on. Who is your new employer, Tina?"

"Solly Ableson," she replied.

"Well good luck to you, you could do a lot worse. I know he will do right by you. I have known Solly for many years. Give him my regards when you see him. If you ever change your mind, your job will be here for you."

"Thank you, Mr. Wrigley, I just need to ask a favour, can Rose Hirst have the day off?"

"She can, but she won't get paid for it."

"She will, if she says she's sick."

Mr. Wrigley laughed out aloud. "You're a crafty young bugger, Tina, I suppose I have no choice. Yes, alright, and for your cheek, I'll pay her."

"Thank you very much."

Tina went outside and told Rose of the conversation she'd had with the boss, and that she had got her the day off work with pay.

"How did you manage that?"

"When he said he wouldn't pay you, I told him he would have to if you went home sick."

"What did he say to that?"

"He called me a crafty young bugger and that for my cheek he would pay you."

Together they went to her new place in the luxury of a taxi. Hilda met them at the door.

"There you are, love, some parcels arrived for you so I've put them in your room."

"Thanks very much."

She went upstairs and opened the door, and was surprised to see the room filled with flowers. Hilda was behind them. "They're from Solly to say welcome."

"They're beautiful," said Rose.

Tina went into the bedroom, opened the parcels, and hung each item in the wardrobe.

"I wish I was as pretty as you," said Rose." I could do with some of this."

"I thought you were only interested in homes and babies," Tina remarked.

"I think I could adapt to the change; if you ever need an assistant, call me will you?"

"What about your baby?"

Rose looked at her, and for the first time, she thought that maybe she had been hasty in wanting to have a baby so young.

"Oh, I want my baby, of course I do. I am just saying if it's ever possible, I would help you, and try to make things better for me. Do you think me selfish?"

"No, I think for once you are being sensible. If ever I need help, you will be my first choice."

They finished unpacking and spent the day in the rooms, Tina still not believing that this was all hers.

Over the weekend, Tina returned home to tell her father and stepmother she had found somewhere else to live and she was changing her job.

"Ungrateful bugger," said her father.

"We need yer money," said her stepmother.

"Then you'll have to work or let my room out; that is, if you can get anyone to rent it," said Tina.

"We've never been good enough fer yer," said her stepmother.

"She get's that from her mother, she was a slut; yer'll end up like her."

Tina did not want another row, but she wasn't going to listen to them both going on.

So she retorted, "She was too good for you, and it was you who kicked her out, remember. You probably did her a favour."

"Yer'll be sorry," spluttered her father, "I'll make yer pay one day."

"Not if I make you pay first, and at least I'll be able to sleep at night and not have to worry about fighting you off."

Her stepmother looked at her and then her father. "What does she mean?"

"Ask him," said Tina, "but I doubt you'll get the truth."

Before anything more was said, or another outburst from her father, she left.

The transformation in Tina over the next week was unbelievable. She had plenty of rest, the bruises faded and with some proper food her skin improved.

She was able to bathe in the privacy of her own room and she took two baths every day. She had her hair re-styled and the beautician showed her how to apply her makeup to make the best of her features.

The beautician also gave her a large box full of makeup, creams and oils.

At the weekend, she called Solly, and he told her to be in his office at ten o' clock the following Monday.

Rose visited her a couple of evenings during the week. She said she was looking forward to Saturday when Dougie would be back from holiday.

On Saturday night, Tina had a bath and was relaxing with a book; she was just thinking about an early night when the telephone rang.

Solly had insisted she have one for her safety. Every time she saw him, she expected him to say it was pay up time and ask her to do something she did not want to do.

But Solly wasn't like that, and he intended to show her that there were some decent people in the world, as he suspected that she had not met many.

She picked up the phone to hear Rose on the other end.

"Tina, are you busy?"

"No, why?"

"Can I come round?"

"Of course you can, you don't need to ask, you know that."

"I'll be there in a little while."

A short while later Rose was at the door and Tina could see at once that there was something wrong. "Come in. What's wrong?"

"It's Dougie."

"Has he been in an accident?"

"I wish he had. You know he goes to the T.T. races every year? Well, apparently last year he met this girl over there. Her name is Doreen. She lives the other side of the town. When he came back last year he continued to see her."

"What, while he was seeing you?"

"Yes, but that's not all, she's pregnant, and her parents are insisting he marries her."

"And is he going to?"

"Yes," cried Rose.

"What about you? What are you going to do? You're pregnant and you were supposed to be getting married next week."

"No I'm not, he's not arranged anything."

"Oh Rose, what are you going to do?"

"Become one of the fast growing number of single mums," she cried.

Tina was full of sympathy for her friend, and this episode just confirmed what she thought about men. "What does your mum say?"

"I never knew she possessed such a colourful vocabulary. What she said about him is unrepeatable. She said we'd manage."

"If there's anything I can do, just let me know."

"Thanks, I hope yer didn't mind me coming round, I just had to get out of the house."

"Rose, we've been friends for most of our lives, I'll always be here for you, and you can come here anytime you need to get away. Do you want to stay here tonight?"

"No, I'll be alright, I just needed to tell someone. I'll see yer tomorrow."

"You will, Rose. Take care, and I'm really sorry."

Next morning Tina showered and applied her makeup. Then chose her clothes with care. When she looked in the mirror, she was pleased with the effect. She left the house and made her way to Solly's office.

As she walked into the outer office Lilly looked at her and smiled. "Well, you look nice. Go in, he's waiting."

Tina said thanks as she opened the office door. He sat and looked at her for a few seconds before he said anything.

"So the swan blossoms from the ugly duckling. Come, sit down." He smiled.

She sat opposite him. "I like it when I'm right."

"Are you always right?"

"No, but when something comes along and I think it has potential and I'm proved right, it's nice. I knew you were pretty, but this morning you look beautiful.

"So, tomorrow I have a job for you. You have to be at the Town Hall at ten o' clock. I will meet you there. You are going to have some promotional photos taken and they will be put into a portfolio. This will be your bread and butter, Tina, we show them around and you get your work from them."

He then told her she could have the rest of the day off. She left the office and went to meet Rose for lunch.

They went to a café in town and they ordered lunch. Tina told her about her morning. Then she said, "Are you feeling OK, Rose?"

"Yes, why?"

"You look tired."

"I'm not sleeping very well. I'm worried what will happen when I have to stop work to have the baby. It doesn't seem fair to burden Mam."

"Don't worry, Rose, I'll help you all I can."

"I know yer will, but it's not your responsibility."

"You should go to court. Dougie should be made to pay towards the baby."

"I can't do anything until it's born."

"We'll work it out."

Rose looked at Tina. "How will I be able to get another job with a baby to look after. Me mam has enough on without taking on anymore?"

"I'll see what I can do. You never know, if things take off I may need you and Solly can pay you a wage from what I earn."

"Thanks, Tina, I don't know what else to say."

They left the café and Rose felt a little more optimistic. She knew Tina would be there for her, just the way she would always be there for Tina.

The following morning Tina went to the town hall where she met Lilly, Solly and a couple of photographers.

She spent the next three hours in various parts of the building, being photographed, wearing different outfits. When they had finished, the photographers told Solly the photos would be ready the next day.

Solly told Tina she could take the rest of the day off and he would see her the following morning. "I'll ring you if things change."

She went home, changed her clothes and then she went to go meet Rose for lunch.

Tina waited at the gate and met Yvonne coming out of work. "Hi, Tina, thought you would be at the hospital?"

"Why?"

"Rosie, she fell at work this morning an' they took her to the infirmary."

"I've been working. I'll go now, what time did she go?"

"'Bout eleven."

The infirmary was only five minutes away. When she reached reception, she asked what ward Rose was on.

The nurse told her. Tina thanked her and followed the signs to the ward.

As she made her way down the corridor, she was met by Rose's mum. "How is she?"

"I don't know, love, I'm still waiting to hear."

They sat waiting together. Eventually a doctor came towards them,."Mrs Hirst, you can see your daughter now. I am afraid she has lost the baby. She's a little weak, we'll keep her here a couple of days. She's young, she'll be OK."

They went into the room and saw Rose, looking almost as white as the pillows under her head.

"What happened?" asked Tina.

"I slipped, and then I had pains. I've lost the baby."

Her mum took her hand. "Don't worry about it, Rose, all you have ter do is get well."

They stayed another half hour and then had to leave.

"I won't be coming back tonight, love. I have ter see to the others," she said.

"I'll come back and see you later on," said Tina.

When she left, Tina went into town. She bought some fruit and flowers. As she paid for them, Tina thought how different things were now.

Only two weeks ago, she would have had to think twice about buying a sandwich. Now she had the money to buy things for her friend.

She went to another shop and bought some toiletries and a couple of pretty nightdresses. She knew Rose did not own any decent ones and would appreciate them.

Rose had slept most of the day, but was sitting up in bed when Tina returned to the hospital. "How do you feel?" she asked her.

"Empty," replied Rose.

"Here, I know you need these."

She opened the packages. "Thanks, Tina, they're lovely, but you shouldn't have."

During the time Tina was there, they talked about the baby and Rose said, "Don't think me too hard, but it may be a blessing; now I won't have to worry about working."

"I'm going to ask Solly if he can use you, it'll be easier work than the factory."

"That would be great, Tina, but don't worry if he has nothing."

"OK, I have to go now, but I'll come and see you tomorrow."

When Tina left the hospital she went straight home, had a bath and had just made a cup of tea. When the telephone rang, it was Solly.

"Tina, I've a job for you, day after tomorrow. You have to go to London with Lilly for a fashion show; one of their girls has dropped out."

"But they've not seen me yet."

"No matter. You'll have to travel back the same day though, I need Lilly in the office."

"I could always go by myself," she said.

"It's just not done, and when the work starts coming in regular, I'll have to get someone to travel with you. Someone who will be able to handle bookings, and help with travel arrangements and accompany you on jobs."

"Solly, I know someone who could do all that. I'd pay for her myself. It wouldn't cost you anything."

"No way, Tina. Anyone who takes on the job will go on the payroll. Why, who do you know?

"My friend Rose."

"The pregnant Rose?"

"Not anymore, she lost the baby yesterday and now she needs a break and a new job."

"I'll think about it. Anyway Lilly will call you with the details and I'll see you later."

"OK."

The next morning Lilly rang and said she would pick her up at seven-thirty the following morning.

Tina spent the day getting her things together, then went to see Rose who was out of bed and looked much better.

They had moved her to another room, and she was talking to another woman who had also lost her baby.

"Hi, you look a lot better."

"I feel better. They said I can go home today. Have you been working?"

"I have to go to London tomorrow," Tina said. She said she had spoken to Solly, and he said he would think about giving her the job, but nothing was definite.

"Tina, that'd be great. You know, I really don't want to go back home at the moment, would you help me look for somewhere to live?"

"But you'd have your mum to look after you, Rose."

"I know, but I'd really like to be on my own."

"You could come and stay with me."

"I couldn't do that, Solly's paying your rent."

"Only until I start earning, then I'll pay him back; you'll be welcome."

"Thanks, I really could do with the break."

Later that day, Tina took a taxi back to the hospital to collect Rose. They detoured to her home and picked up a few things before going back to Tina's house.

Rose's mum was understandably concerned that Rose wouldn't be going straight home, but she understood when Rose explained she had enough to do without playing nursemaid.

When they arrived at Tina's, Rose unpacked and Tina told her to help herself to whatever she needed while she was gone the following day.

"We will be back tomorrow night. Solly wants Lilly back in the office as soon as possible."

They spent the rest of the evening just talking and then Tina said she was going to bed because she had to be up next morning.

"Thanks again for letting me stay. I hope things go well tomorrow for you."

Lilly was at the door at seven-thirty the next morning. They drove down the motorway, stopping for breakfast on the way.

They made good time and reached London by eleven-thirty.

They went straight to the London Fashion House where, for the next six hours, Tina and Lilly worked nonstop.

Tina walked up and down all day showing outfits to select clients, having to change her clothes numerous times. They finished working at six-thirty, and Tina was exhausted.

People began to leave, and as Tina and Lilly were packing up to go, a funny little man walked over to Lilly and said, "Lilly, you can tell Solly he's found a little gem with this one. His fee is in the post and we'll definitely use her for all our bookings."

"Thanks, Abe, I'll pass on the message," said Lilly.

They left the building, stopped and had some supper, then headed back up the motorway for home. Rose made a hot drink for her before going to bed.

The following day, Tina stayed in bed until after ten. She was still tired from the previous day.

At lunchtime, Solly called. "Tina, do you feel like coming into the office to see the portfolio of the pictures we did the other day?"

"Yes, I'd love to, Solly. I'll be there in about an hour."

"I have to go into the office to look at the photos, Rose. Do you want to come with me?"

"No, I'll stay here if you don't mind. I'll see you when you get back."

"OK, I won't be too long. See you later. Bye."

When Tina saw the photos she was surprised, very surprised. The photos she was looking at made her look very pretty.

"I can't believe this is really me."

"With this portfolio the work will come rolling in. By the way, I've deposited a sum of money into your bank account."

"Why?"

"It's what you earned yesterday, less my commission of course."

"Fine," she said.

"Do you want to know how much?"

"How much?"

" A thousand pounds."

"That much?" she exclaimed.

"Yes, it's big money out there for looking pretty. Now, about your friend, if a lot of work starts coming in for you, I won't be able to release Lilly each time to go with you.

"Your friend can do the job, but she'll have to learn about appointments, travel arrangements, negotiate prices and generally keep the wolves at bay, and be loyal to me in case one of these smart snot nose operators wants to move in and take you over. For this she will be well paid, but the hours are long."

"She can do it, Solly."

"Words are no good to me, Tina, results talk. Now, when will your friend be ready to start work?"

"She's out of hospital now, and she's staying with me a few days because her house is a bit overcrowded. I thought it would be OK."

"Yes, yes, but your flat is only a base, you'll be travelling quite a lot, I hope."

"I think she'll be ready in a few days' time."

"Good, if it's alright, I'll visit this evening and have a chat with her; meanwhile, you stay by the phone. I have something lined up for you. If it comes off, it'll pay well and you could combine it with a holiday; you still look a little pale yourself."

Tina rushed home excitedly to tell Rose what Solly had said. They spent a relaxing afternoon, and at seven o' clock Solly turned up.

Tina gave him a drink and he told Rose exactly what he had said to Tina earlier in the day.

Rose could hardly believe her luck. "I can be ready to start work Monday," she said.

"Good," replied Solly. "Be in the office nine sharp. Lilly will work with you each day showing you the ropes until she feels you can do the job on your own, and don't worry, you'll be on the payroll straight away. I'll get Lilly to open a bank account for you."

"I haven't left my job at the factory yet," said Rose.

"You have now," replied Solly. "I know old John Wrigley, I'll call him and explain; now get some rest and I'll see you Monday."

"Thanks, Solly, I'll not let you down," she said.

"You better not." He shook his head and then said, "Òy, not only am I paying well, but I have to be a benefactor to the world's poor." As he left, he was smiling and waving his hand.

"Goodnight, girlies."

"Night," they answered in unison.

When he had gone, Tina and Rose talked late into the night, mainly about their good luck.

"Just think," said Rose, "if you hadn't seen the advert in his window, we would still be clocking on at the factory."

"Yes, now do you still think it all sounds dodgy?"

"No," Rose said sheepishly.

The following morning, Solly rang Tina and said he had another assignment for her. It was local at the John Lewis store so she would not have far to travel.

She had to go to the top floor and model the new fashions for private clients. It's not really glamorous work, but it paid. She was to arrive at eleven a.m. and finish at four p.m.

Tina found the store and when she had found the floor, the manager set her straight to work. The time passed without her ever being aware of it.

When the day was over, she realised how tiring walking up and down could be, and when she got home, Rose had made tea of which she was grateful.

Solly rang her later that evening. "Hi, how did it go?"

"Fine," she answered. "It was hot and tiring, but I enjoyed it."

"Good, there's a cocktail party tomorrow night; it would be good for you to be there. Take Rose with you if she's up to it. There'll be a few influential people there and I'll be there about nine p.m."

"OK, Solly."

She turned to Rose and said, "We have been invited to a cocktail party tomorrow night. There will be some people Solly wants me to meet."

"Good, I hope you have a nice time."

"I said WE, that means you as well."

"I've nowt to wear and I'll show you up."

"No you won't, and you can borrow something of mine."

"Are you sure?"

"Yes, now come on, let's have an early night."

They went to bed and slept well.

The next day they did some housework and some shopping, then came back, had some tea and thought about getting ready for the party.

When they were dressed, Tina helped Rose apply her makeup. "We brush up well don't we?" Tina said.

Rose laughed a little nervously. "Yes, I'm not used to hob nobbin'."

"You don't have to say much, Solly will be there to talk to you. Come on, you'll be OK."

When they arrived, someone took their names as they went through the door. He said, "Oh yes, Solly's girls," and let them in.

Tina and Rose looked at each other as someone put a glass of wine in their hand. Rose took a sip and pulled a face. "I'd rather have had a beer."

Tina laughed at her. "You'll get used to it. You can't really drink beer in a place like this."

"Why not? The men do."

They both stood in a corner like wallflowers and watched people behaving in a pretentious way, putting on an act, laughing for effect and talking as if they had a mouth full of plums.

As they stood watching, they saw Solly making his way towards them. "Are you two OK?"

"Yes, thanks," answered Tina.

"Have you had something to eat and drink?"

"I don't like wine. I don't suppose I could have a beer?" Rose asked.

Solly laughed. "I don't see why not, I'll get you one." He turned to Tina, "I want you to meet two friends of mine. They tell me they have a lot of work they can put your way. One of the jobs is in Portugal. Rose is ready to start work now and she could go with you."

"I've never been out of Leeds, never mind the country," said Rose.

"I'll get Lilly to arrange passports for you; anyway come and meet these people."

He led the way over to the other side of the room and interrupted a group of men.

"Mike, I want you to meet Tina and Rose. Tina has just joined us and I'd like some work for her."

Mike was tall, about forty-five years of age, not handsome, but rugged; there was something about him that was attractive.

"When are you coming to work for me, Tina?" he asked.

"She's not," said Solly. "She's ours." They carried on with their conversation. Tina and Rose continued to look around at the other people who were there.

"They're not my kind of people," said Rose.

"No, but I reckon we can earn a lot of money."

"I think we need to watch people like these. They'll think we're naïve and stupid and if we let them, they'll take advantage of us," said Rose.

"By their standards we are naïve, but no one will ever take advantage of me."

They stayed a while longer then went in search of Solly and told him they wanted to go home.

"I'll get you a taxi," he said.

The taxi arrived within ten minutes; they said their goodbyes and left.

Twenty minutes later they arrived home; they both were very tired and without any delay went to bed.

On Monday morning, Rose went to the office with Tina.

"I feel ever so nervous. I hope I don't let you down, Tina."

All the previous week, Rose had worked closely with Lilly, who had been kind and patient, and at the end of the week, Lilly had told her she would be fine. Lilly told Solly that Rose was a fast learner and that she would do well; anything else she needed to know, she could pick up as she went along.

Tina worked throughout the week. Rose managed all the arrangements, and Solly said how pleased he was with her.

Tina was surprised to learn that she had earned over two hundred pounds in one week and that was after Solly had taken back a percentage of what she owed him.

He had not wanted to take anything from her, but he knew she would not have it any other way.

Rose was overwhelmed with the amount of money she put into her bank account at the end of the week.

Solly called her into the office. "How are you feeling, do you think you're up to going with Tina on assignments?"

"Yes, and I know I can do it well."

"Good, I'll call round home later and discuss the work that's coming up in Portugal."

"I've said it before, Solly, I won't let you or Tina down."

He nodded his head. "I'll see you both later."

Later in the evening Solly turned up. Tina poured him his usual whisky that she kept there for that purpose.

"Right," he said, "the trip to Portugal is on. Over the coming week, we will sort out passports for you both. You will need to take enough clothes for three weeks. All you have to do is get on the plane, there'll be someone to meet you at the other end and show you where you will be staying.

"You'll need to see Lilly first thing in the morning for passport photographs, and she'll need all your details. I know it's Sunday, but on Monday morning, she'll have to go to Liverpool to the passport office to collect them. If we rely on the post, there is no guarantee they will arrive. Be at the office at eleven. Lilly will be there. Right, girls, I'm off." He eased himself from the chair, said goodnight and left.

When Solly had gone, both girls looked at each other then shouted with delight and hugged one another.

They couldn't believe they were actually going out of the country. They talked late into the night, and when they went to bed, sleep still eluded them. They could not believe things were going so well for them.

Next morning, they went to the office to find Lilly waiting for them. She sent them off to have their photos taken, and when they returned to the office, she sat with them and filled in all the forms.

"OK," she said. "I'll see you Tuesday morning and go over all the details." She handed them a list and said, "You will need to get these few things for your trip."

Over the weekend, Tina and Rose shopped for what they would need, and spent some time with Rose's family who were all as excited about their trip as they were.

On Monday morning Tina and Rose spent the day wandering around the town. They bought some things, had a meal and then returned home.

They decided to go to bed early. Both girls had not slept much the night before.

Tuesday morning they arrived at the office early. Lilly had their passports. Solly told them they would be travelling on Saturday, and that they would need to be at the airport by nine a.m. They would fly to Faro airport and someone called Antòine would meet them.

He and his wife Alicia would put them up for the duration of their stay.

The rest of the week they spent relaxing and shopping. On Friday night, Tina and Rose went to bed early, and were up and ready to leave by seven the following morning. The taxi arrived to take them to the airport. It took them half an hour to get there, so they had plenty of time.

When they had checked in their luggage, they looked in the many shops, had coffee and discussed the people they saw walking around the airport, wondering where they were going and what they were doing as they waited for their flight.

Eventually their flight was called and they boarded the plane. They found their seats and, as they sat down, Rose looked at Tina. "I don't think I want to fly, I've never done this before."

"It's too late now, you'll be OK," she answered.

The plane took off and once they were in the air, Rose relaxed and she enjoyed the flight.

Four hours later, the plane touched down in Fargo. As they stepped from the plane, the heat hit them. "Bloomin' ek," said Rose "It's hot here."

They went through passport control and collected the luggage, and as they went to the exit, a line of people stood waiting with various names written on pieces of cardboard. Tina saw her name and walked over towards the man. "That's me, are you Antóine?" she asked.

"Si, Si," he replied. What Solly had failed to tell them was that Antóine and his wife spoke no English whatsoever.

Antóine took them outside. He loaded their luggage into the tiny car. He told them his village, called Ferragudo, was an hour's drive away. They settled back and took in the scenery as they drove through winding narrow roads. At one time, Tina feared they would drop down over the edge of the road into nothingness.

Finally the car stopped. By now it was dark so it was difficult to see their surroundings. They entered the house and Alicia greeted them in the only way she could, nodding her head and smiling.

Antoine and Alicia occupied the whole of the ground floor. He took them upstairs, put their cases in the doorway, smiled and went downstairs.

Tina and Rose looked round; the apartment was cool and clean. There were two bedrooms, a kitchen, sitting room and bathroom. Up another flight of stairs, there was a sunroof.

"This is fantastic," said Tina. Rose just nodded in agreement.

They were both tired. There was nothing they could do until the morning, so they went to bed.

Next morning, a woman came to the apartment and said her name was Paolo. She spoke good English and she suggested that they get a phrase book.

"You may not learn to speak the language fluently, but it will help you a little. If you need help with anything, just let me know."

Tina and Rose thanked her and when she had gone Tina said, "Shall we take a walk round the village, try and get our bearings?"

"OK, when do you start work?"

"Someone is supposed to contact me tomorrow; meanwhile, we have today to settle in and look around."

The houses stood on a sloping hill. Some painted white, whilst others were blue. The story was, the higher up the hill you lived, the richer you were.

This seemed to be true, because over the time they were there, and looked more closely, they saw that the houses at the bottom of the hill were little more than shacks. The higher up you went, the better the design, and if you had a flat sunroof, you were wealthy.

They followed the winding path down to the harbour. There was a little supply store, an inn and a fish restaurant called Jamie's Bar. Whilst they were there, it became a favourite place to eat.

The village was tiny and you could walk the full circle in thirty minutes. They returned to the house, collected their swimsuits and spent the rest of the day on the beach.

In the evening, they went to Jamie's to eat, and by the end of the night, they felt as if they had known him for years. He was friendly, and insisted on refilling their glasses with the local wine. At first, Rose pulled a face at the taste, but after consuming three glasses, she said it was good.

The girls said goodnight to Jamie, and left somewhat tipsy and full of giggles to go up the hill. This caused them to laugh even more as neither of them was sober.

Next morning, Tina was making breakfast and Rose complained her head hurt when the telephone rang.

The call was from a designer called Michos. Tina would be working for him and he arranged to pick her up in one hour.

"What will you do while I'm working?"

"I'm coming with you of course, make sure these foreign men don't get any fancy ideas. After all, I am supposed to be working with you, taking care of any arrangements."

"We have an hour to get ready before Michos arrives."

"I think I can manage that. Why did you let me drink all that wine, Tina?"

"I thought you liked it."

"I did, but not the hangover that comes with it."

Michos arrived and drove them out of the village to his studio in Albufera. He said they would be working each morning and finish by lunchtime. He said no one worked in the afternoon because it was too hot.

Over the next three weeks, Tina worked between three and four hours a day. They would spend the rest of the day on the beach or exploring the neighbouring villages. Early evenings they would walk along the harbour and see the old fisherman who sat on the wall mending his nets and singing. Occasionally they would eat at another bistro, but mostly at Jamie's, and they would take their wine up to the roof and watch the sunset.

Three days before they returned home, Michos asked Tina and Rose if they would have dinner with him and another designer, a Dutchman named Ben.

The food was good and Michos and Ben good company. Tina saw a different side of Michos. He was so serious when they worked together, but socially he was very amusing, regaling them with some of his escapades and adventures.

Michos arranged for a taxi to take them back to the village and Tina thanked them both and promised to stay in touch when she returned home. Her work had finished and for the remainder of their stay, she could do what she wanted.

The day arrived when they would be leaving, and again, Antòine would take them to the airport. They said goodbye to Alicia, then made a detour to where Paolo lived and said their farewells. The holiday had gone so quickly. Tina had enjoyed the work and they were sorry to have to leave, but vowed they would return.

Both girls were rather subdued on the return flight. They arrived back in England feeling cold. It was very late when they arrived home and they were so tired, all they managed to do, was make some tea and fall into bed.

Tina slept better than she had all the time she had been away. But what an experience she'd had. She had met some lovely people and had a wonderful time.

The ringing of the telephone woke her next morning. Solly called to say he had spoken to Michos and he was full of praise about her work. He had asked Solly if he could buy her contract.

"No way," said Tina. "We had dinner with him one time and that's all. I trust you, Solly, but I don't trust other men. If you sell my contract, I'll go work back in the factory."

"Don't worry, I won't sell your contract. I've had good reports and I'm pleased how Rose has fit in. Both of you take the weekend off and I'll see you first thing Monday morning."

Tina and Rose spent the next day just relaxing. That night Rose said that she was going to see her mum to slip her a few quid. "Will you be OK, Tina?"

"Of course, give your mum my love."

When Rose had gone, Tina decided to have a bath and then relax with a drink. She was listening to some music when she heard her doorbell ring. She got up. "I suppose that's Rose, she'll have forgotten her key again," she said to herself.

As she opened the door, she was knocked off her feet and the door slammed shut. She gazed up and saw the drunken, leering face of her father.

"Yer bitch," he slobbered, "too good fer the likes of us now aint yer?"

"How did you find me?" she said, struggling to get to her feet.

"I've bin watching the place fer ages. I got friends an' they told me where yer was."

"Leave me alone, I don't owe you anything."

"Yer high an' mighty, yer need tecking down a peg or two. Modellin'," he sneered, "nothing but a' 'igh class whore."

She turned from him, and as she did, felt a stinging blow to the side of her head. He pushed her, and as she fell, she felt her robe ripped from her body.

Suddenly he was above her and undoing his pants.

"No" she cried, "where's your decency?"

"Yer like yer mother, she was a slut, she thought she was too good fer me."

"She probably was," said Tina, then she realised she should have kept quiet, because the next thing she felt was the punch across her mouth. As she blacked out, she felt a searing pain rip through her.

How long she was unconscious for, she did not know. She started to come round and was aware of a voice in the distance and gentle hands trying to lift her.

"Tina, answer me, are you OK, what happened?"

Through the fog, she started to focus and tried to lift her head. Her lips felt swollen and she could not speak; the pain was so intense, she nearly lost consciousness again.

She was aware of gentle hands lifting her and bright lights, then she remembered nothing more. When she did come round, it was to see a dim light. Rose sat at the side of the bed holding her hand.

"Tina, what happened, the police are outside. Solly is beside himself with concern. Who did this?"

Tina shook her head; a tear trickled down her face. "I can't say," she managed to mumble through her swollen lips.

"Was it someone you know?"

Tina shook her head and the tears would not stop. The doctor came in, gave her an injection and she drifted off into oblivion.

When she opened her eyes again, Rose was still holding her hand, her head resting on the side of the bed. Tina's head and face felt the size of a football, her body ravaged and felt as if on fire. As she moved, Rose sat up.

"It was him, I know it."

"I'm not saying," said Tina.

"Well I am," answered Rose.

"No don't, there'll come a day when I'll get him back. Just now, he has lots of friends who will cover for him, but believe me, he won't get away with it."

"You have to tell 'em, Tina.

"No, let me deal with it in my own way."

When the police came into the room, they were very sympathetic and asked her if she knew who had attacked her. All she would tell them was that she had opened the door and been taken by surprise.

As they left, Solly came in and he winced at what he saw.

"Tina, Tina," he said, taking her hand, "what can I do to make you feel better."

"Find me somewhere else to live, Solly, and no one must know about it."

"Do you know who did this to you? If you do, you must tell them."

"No, I can handle it," she said as the tears started falling once again.

"Don't upset yourself. Rose and I will sort things out," he sighed and kissed her gently on the forehead. "I'll be along later, Tina, try to get some rest," he said. He then left the room.

Rose, who was still sitting at the side of her bed, said, "What will you do now, Tina?"

"I don't know yet. I'll have my day, go after Solly, help him find somewhere to live, but you must tell no one, not even your mum."

Rose nodded her head. "OK, you get some rest and I'll come back tomorrow."

By now, Tina was exhausted. She closed her eyes and let sleep overtake her.

When Rose walked outside, she was surprised to see Solly waiting for her. "Would you like a lift home?"

"Thanks, Solly," she said as she got into the car.

"She knows who it was doesn't she?"

"Yes, but she has to tell you, it's not my place."

"I just want to help."

"Then let her decide what she wants to do. We'll be there for her if she needs us."

"Life is not fair," he said.

"No one ever said it was," she answered. "Some have more than their fair share of troubles, and Tina is one of them."

"Yes, but some will fail and fall by the wayside. Tina is one of those who will fight for what she believes in."

They arrived home, and as she got out of the car, he said, "I'll give you a ring in the morning, Rose. Just tell me, was she just beat up?"

"I'm not sure, we will have to see if she wants to tell us. I'm not going to ask her."

He nodded his head. "Fine, I'll call you in the morning, goodnight."

As Rose let herself into the flat, she heard the phone ringing. She picked up the receiver and heard her mother on the other end.

"Rosie, where have yer been?"

"To the hospital, Mum."

"Why, are yer hurt?"

"No, but Tina is."

"Why, what's 'appened?"

"When I came home I found her all beaten up."

"Who did it?"

"Don't know."

"Are yer sure, Rosie?"

"Can't say anything until Tina says."

"Was it that dirty bugger, her old man?"

"Mum, just leave it."

"I'll tell you what, our Rose, if it was him, he better watch out. There's a lot o' folk round here likes Tina, an' he'll have to look over his shoulder."

"Mum, calm down, I'll ring you tomorrow when I know a bit more."

"OK, luv, you tek care."

Rose decided to take a shower and have something to eat. When she had finished, she made sure the door and window were locked, and then went to bed. At first, she could not go to sleep, all she could think of was what Tina had gone through.

Eventually, she did sleep, and woke next morning slightly later than she had meant to. She had just finished dressing, when Lilly arrived to take her to the hospital.

"Solly can't face it. He's very fond of Tina, and he's quite upset about all this."

"I know, he was quite upset yesterday," answered Rose.

They arrived at the hospital and went to the ward where Tina was. She looked to be asleep, but turned her head towards them as they stopped at her bed. Her face all bruised and swollen looked much worse than when Rose had seen her the previous day. The nurse who had followed them in said they could only stay a few minutes.

Lilly gasped when she saw Tina. She took her hand. "Tina, do you need anything, love?"

Tina shook her head. "I just don't want to go back to the flat when I get out of here."

"Don't worry about it. Solly's taking care of things, just let Rose know if you need anything else. Have the police found out who did this?"

She shook her head, knowing they never would unless she told them, and she would wait and handle things in her own way.

Tina was in hospital for a week. By the time she was ready to leave, Solly had found her a new place at the other end of town, and with Rose's help, had moved everything in.

The only other person who knew about the place was Lilly. If anyone else wanted to know where she was, they would have to go through her or Solly.

When Tina was released from the hospital, Solly and Rose arrived to take her home.

Tina was very quiet on the journey, but when she saw the place Solly had found her, she was very pleased, and more so when she had looked round inside.

The flat was lovely, very spacious and very new. Solly had taken care of all the furnishings while Lilly and Rose had worked on the decoration.

When she had unpacked, he said he must get back to the office.

He kissed her forehead. "Get some rest, I'll call you later," then he left.

The problem was, he really did not know what to say to her. He felt sorry for her and was angry that she had been hurt. He knew she knew who had done her harm, she just wouldn't say.

When he had gone, Tina looked around while Rose made her a cup of tea. "Are you OK?" she asked.

"Yes. You know, being in hospital has given me time to think, Rose, and I've done plenty."

"Don't go doing anything that'll get you into trouble."

"By the time I've finished it won't matter."

Rose didn't know what she meant by this.

It was another three weeks before Tina was ready to work again. When she did, she threw herself into everything she could. After a month, Solly said that she should slow down a little, that she was doing too much.

"I don't want to slow down. I have to work."

He reluctantly agreed with her, but nevertheless, he cut her workload down a little, and he expressed his concerns to Rosie. Rose said she would keep an eye on her.

A few days later Rose woke, and heard Tina throwing up in the bathroom, concerned she got up and went through to her.

"Are you OK?"

"No I'm not, and if it's right what I'm thinking, then I need to find someone who can help me."

"In what way?"

"Why else do you think I have morning sickness?"

"Do you think you could be pregnant?"

"Yes and someone's going to pay."

"So he did rape you," Rose said softly.

Tina nodded her head and Rose gently put her arms round her friend. Tina was shaking and her head was cold and clammy. By now she was weeping softly.

"I know someone who will help," said Rose.

"When can I see them?"

"I'll see Mum today."

"She mustn't know."

"I think she's already guessed. I didn't tell her. You have a lot of friends, Tina, let them help."

"Just get me this person."

"Will you think what you're doing first."

"I don't need to. I don't want anything that belongs to that animal."

Rose nodded her head. She got ready and left the house. While she was gone, Tina had a shower, then made a cup of tea. By this time, she felt a little better. Rose came back an hour later.

"I can take you to a woman, but she said if you say anything, she'll deny she has ever met you."

They left a short while later and went to the area where Rose had lived. They stopped in front of a house. From the outside, it looked very respectable. They knocked at the door and it was opened by a woman who was clean and tidy and knew Rose.

"Come in," she said.

She told Rose to wait in the front room. She took Tina through to a back room. Rose sat and waited. About fifteen minutes had elapsed when the woman returned with Tina.

"Now remember, take one tablet when you get home and one in the morning. Stay close to home for the next forty-eight hours and you should be OK."

Tina handed her some money. "Thank you," and the woman let them out into the street and closed the door quickly.

When they arrived home, Rose asked Tina what the woman had said.

"Nothing, she just examined me, told me I was in the club, which I knew and you heard the rest."

Tina went into the kitchen and took the first of the tablets.

She felt a little shaky, so the rest of the day, she stayed at home. By ten o'clock, nothing had happened and she and Rose decided to go to bed. Tina slept until about six-thirty; she went to the bathroom, took the other tablet and went straight back to bed.

She slept and woke two hours later doubled up in pain, the bed soaking with sweat.

Rose heard her moaning and came to her bedroom. When she saw her she said she was going to get the doctor.

"No, don't do that."

Rose was worried and quickly left the room. Tina lost all track of time and had no idea know how long she lay, only that the pain was getting unbearable. She heard a door close, then Rose came back into the room and she had someone with her.

Tina felt a cold flannel on her face, but she was so racked with pain she was barely conscious.

Suddenly, a searing red-hot pain ran through her body. She felt as if her insides were being torn from her body. There was a sudden gush of water and the pain started to recede. Her whole body ached.

She must have passed out for a short while. When she came to, she was aware of feeling cool and clean, and her nightgown was being changed, She recognised the voice of Rose's mum, Mrs Hirst.

"The bastard, he won't get away wi' this."

She drifted away and slept. When she opened her eyes again, it was quiet and dark but she could see a thin ribbon of light under the door.

Her body ached and she dare not move for a while. The door opened and the figure of Mrs. Hirst came in and stood by the bed.

"'Ow yer feelin', luv?"

"Like I've been kicked by a horse," she replied.

Mrs. Hirst nodded her head. "A nice cuppa will do the trick." She moved to the door and shouted, "Rosie, mek us a cuppa, nice and strong, none o' yer dishwater muck."

Rose went from the room into the kitchen to make the tea. Mrs Hirst sat on the bed and took a hold of Tina's hand.

"Now, love, I think you ought to tell me about it. Yer've had more than yer fair share of troubles in the last two months to last yer a lifetime, and believe me, I know 'bout trouble."

Tina's eyes filled with tears. This was a new feeling; she had never known the love or warmth of a mother, and this was the closest she would get.

She shook her head. "I can't, Mrs Hirst."

"It won't go no further, less you want it to, but let me tell you what I think. For years you've 'ad to put up with that dirty sod that calls his self yer dad, an' I don't know how he's got away wi' it.

"I think it was him found out where you were an beat yer up, an by the looks of things, that's not all he did. An' wot's she doing 'bout it?" The SHE was referring to Tina's stepmother.

"I never told her," replied Tina, "I doubt if she would have believed me anyway."

"Yer mean she didn't want to know. I'll tell yer this, I love me kids, Tina, but I wish I had a daughter like you, yer pretty, work hard and a good girl."

"Not anymore I'm not, I'm what you call spoilt goods and no man wants that, but to be honest, I don't want anything to do with men either."

"Eh, lass, wait an' see, one day yer might meet someone who'll respect yer, and then yer'll feel different."

"No I won't, all the men I've ever met have been after only one thing, and if you don't give it, they take it. But not anymore, they won't."

Mrs Hirst sighed "Someone will bring him down one day, are yer gonna tell the cops? Yer ought to yer know. They should lock him up an throw away the bloody key."

"No, Mrs. Hirst, I'll handle this in my own way. It may not be tomorrow or next week, but I'll know when the time comes."

"Listen, duck, wot yer said 'bout all men bein' the same. S'not true yer know, my Gordon's always had a soft spot fer yer, but he's always kept it quiet, him being a bit older like. (He was thirty.) An' he wouldn't harm a hair on yer head. Would yer like him ter move into yer spare room, ter keep an eye on you an' our Rosie?"

Tina shook her head. "No thanks, Mrs Hirst, I don't want anyone to know where we are."

"Our Gordon would cut his tongue out first, love. He's not a violent man, but when he hears about this, yer dad will have ter watch his back."

Tina sighed. "Stuck up he called me, he said I was stuck up like my mother."

"Yer mother was a good woman, Tina, always clean an' smart, kept the house neat as a pin. Yer didn't have many clothes an' she used ter wash them out every night. She never had owt, he made sure of that, but she knew how ter hold herself. She would put up wi' his drinkin' and womanising an' his temper, an' that's why she left, well to be honest, he kicked her out."

"But why did she leave me? She knew what he was like."

"She loved yer, girl, she must have had her reasons; yer'll find out one day."

"Well I'll tell you this, Mrs Hirst, I'm sick of my life, and no one is going to come round and wave a magic wand to make me a princess. So, I'm going to work, I'll work so hard and make something of myself. I'll not spend the rest of my life like this, I'll pull myself out of the gutter if it's the last thing I do."

"I know yer will, Tina love, yer've got guts, more than I would have had in your circumstances. But while yer going to the top, don't ferget yer friends on the bottom will yer. No matter how high someone climbs, they always need their friends, and I'll always be here if yer want me. I'll stand in fer yer mother, that's if yer want me o' course."

Tears ran down Tina's face. "Thanks, Mrs Hirst, I'll remember that."

"Yer've bin good to my Rosie, so it's the least I can do. She's had her fair share of trouble lately, what with that bloke leaving her like that. I didn't want her left in that factory. Yer a carin' lass, Tina. Yer young, but yer have an old head on yer shoulders. Well I'll go now and let yer get some sleep, but if yer want me, just send our Rosie."

She got up, kissed her cheek and left the room. Tina wasn't used to such displays of affection and this caused her tears to start again.

She lay for a long time just thinking. She was tired but couldn't sleep and when the morning came, she had come to the conclusion that she would have to pull herself together and get out and start work. But no one would ever use her again, of that she was certain.

After three days, she was ready to go to work again. Rose and her mother had been wonderful and she would never forget it.

They had shown her what being a part of a family was like, something she'd never known.

The morning she was going back to work, she was up bright and early. She was dressed and drinking tea, when Rose walked into the kitchen.

"Well," said Rose, "you look like you're going somewhere."

"I am, work."

"Are you ready?"

"As ready as I'll ever be."

"OK, I'll go with you. See if Solly has some work and we'll go over the details."

"You do like this job, don't you, Rose?"

"Yes I do, and it's all thanks to you."

"Right then, when you're ready we'll get going."

"I'll be ready in ten minutes. By the ways it's Mam's birthday tomorrow. I have to get her something nice. We always have a bit of a do, not much like, but I never miss it."

"I'll get her something too."

"You don't have to."

"I know, but I want to, and you can take it to her with yours."

"I won't, you can take it yourself."

"It's a family do, I'm not invited."

"Yes you are."

"I don't know, I might just stay here and have a quiet night."

"Look," said Rose as she came from the bedroom, "do you like having me to stay?"

"Yes. You know I do. Why?"

"Well, if I go without you tomorrow, I'll be hung, drawn and quartered, and then you won't have me around."

Tina laughed. "Okay, if you're sure, now are we ready?"

Rose nodded and they left.

They entered the office and Lilly looked up. "Hello, girls, I'm pleased to see you, and so will he," she nodded towards the shut door of Solly's office.

"Work's piling in and I think he's a little worried. Are you well now, Tina?"

"Yes, raring to go."

The office door opened. "Who's panicking, I never panic," and his face broke into a wide grin when he saw Tina.

"Well, my dear, it's good to see you back, and you look as if you mean business."

"I do, tell me what you have for me?"

He took her into the office where they spent the next four hours going over work schedules. There was enough work in for a month, and Rose was going to have her work cut out making all the arrangements.

Tina was happy. The more work she had the better it was. It would keep her from thinking about recent events. She would never forget, but she could try to put it to the back of her mind.

It was late afternoon when they finally left the office. Both girls decided they would go shopping for the birthday gift for Rose's mum. It was a novelty they didn't have to shop in the market anymore.

"This will suit Mam," said Rose, picking up a red dress from a rail.

Tina looked at it and shook her head.

"Don't you like it?"

"Yes, but I think the colour's wrong for your mum."

"What do you suggest? I don't have the knack of choosing the right thing like you have."

"I suggest we look at the rack over there; the colours are more subtle and the styles will suit your mum better. That one's too young."

They spent a few minutes looking through the rack. "This looks nice," said Tina as she picked out a nice blue dress. It was simply cut and very plain.

"Yes it does," agreed Rose.

As they were talking, an assistant not much older than they were, walked over towards them. "I think you'll find something more suitable in the bargain rails downstairs. This floor is more for our select clients."

Tina looked at her. "How do you know I'm not buying this dress for just that type of client?"

Blustering, the assistant said, "I don't, but…"

"But nothing. We have every right to shop here. If you don't like it we'll take our business elsewhere."

"Tina."

She heard her name called, and turned to see who it was.

Striding towards her was the department manager, Mr. King. "I thought it was you, having problems?"

"Hello, Mr. King, nothing we can't handle. Your assistant here thought we would be better off in the bargain basement. I was just telling her different."

"Bargain basement?" He turned to the girl. "Tina models our top fashions, and when she's here, you'll give her the same courtesy you give our other clients, is that understood?"

"Yes, Mr. King," the girl answered.

He turned to Tina. "Do you need anything else, my dear?"

"No, I know what I'm looking for, I'll find it."

53

He smiled and said he would see her again and walked from the floor. When he'd gone, the assistant was helpful, but her manner was very aloof.

"We'll take the dress," Tina said. "I saw some lockets with a blue stone in, would you show me those please?"

The assistant gave them the lockets to look at and took the dress away for wrapping.

"Blimey, you came back at her a bit strong," said Rose.

"Serves her right for being snooty. Our money's as good as anyone else's. No one will look down on us again, Rose."

Rose looked at her friend; even though Tina's face had shown no emotion, there had been a hardness about her manner, a hardness that she had not seen before.

Maybe it was an isolated incident, thought Rose, and she pushed it to the back of her mind. "This will go with the dress," Tina was saying.

"Tina, you can't pay all that, it's too expensive."

"Rose, your mum is the only person who has ever shown me real love, and she's never asked for anything in return. I think it's a small price to pay."

Rose smiled and nodded her head. Now she was sure that the hardness she had just seen Tina display, had been a one off.

Happy with their purchases, they left the store and were walking down the road when they met Rose's brother, Gordon.

"Hello, you two, where have you been?"

"To get Mum a present," said Rose. "Where are you going?"

"I've just done the same, and now I'm going to get a cup of coffee. Why don't you both come with me?"

Although the question was for both of them, his eyes were looking at Tina. "Great."

"I don't think I will," said Tina.

Gordon looked at her. "It's only a cup of coffee, Tina, not a date."

Tina felt her face burn with embarrassment; after all he was only being polite. She agreed and all three of them made their way to one of the many coffee bars in the town.

They found seats while Gordon got the coffee. When they were all together he asked if they had much work coming in.

"It's picking up," answered Rose. "We've a lot of work scheduled for the next month."

"I envy you, I wish I could travel in my work instead of being stuck in an office, but you have an advantage over me," he said to Tina.

"What's that?"

"You're prettier." They all laughed. When they had finished their coffee, Tina got up and said they would have to go.

"Will we see you later at Mam's?"

"I wouldn't miss it," she replied.

When they had gone, Gordon sat a while. He knew Tina had suffered some hard times lately, but how she had suffered, he had no idea.

He had always had a soft spot for her. He knew he couldn't push it; if he did, any chance he had of getting close to her would be blown.

Later at home he gave his mum his present and said that he'd seen Rose and Tina in town, and they would be here in a little while.

When they did arrive, all Mrs Hirst could do was laugh and then cry when they gave her the gifts.

"Oh! I don't deserve all this."

"Why not, Mum, you've done enough for us in your time."

They enjoyed themselves that night. There was plenty of food and drink put on by the neighbours. Someone started a sing-song.

Tina had never known a family so close, and she realised what she had missed with her own family.

All too soon, they had to leave. Tina and Rose still had some details to sort out for the busy time they had ahead of them.

Over the next month, they worked flat out. Rose had settled into the job and was looking after things very well.

At the end of the month, Solly told them to take a few days' break. "You girls have worked hard this last month, you need a break."

For the first two days, all they did was sleep, bathe and eat. On the third day, they felt a little more relaxed.

"Why don't we go out somewhere?" said Tina.

"Where to?"

"Let's go into town, do some shopping and have a meal."

"Sounds good to me," said Rose.

They spent the next hour getting ready, and then took a taxi into the town. They made a decision that when they had done with their shopping, they would go to one of the many wine bars that had opened recently.

Both girls really enjoyed the morning. They found a bar and walked in; it was very busy with the lunchtime trade.

Rose went to the bar for their drinks while Tina found a seat. When Rose returned with the drinks, she said she would go to the toilet before having her lunch.

Whilst waiting for her return, Tina let her eyes wander around the bar. Her eyes met another pair of eyes that seemed to be studying her.

She quickly looked away and saw that Rose was coming back. They spent an hour in the bar, but all the while, Tina had the uncomfortable feeling someone was watching her.

She looked around, but couldn't see anyone looking.

They finished their drinks and left the bar, walked down the road trying to decide where they should eat. Tina still felt uncomfortable, and it was only when they got into a taxi to go home, that she felt safe.

When they were getting ready for bed, Tina said, "I had a feeling that someone was watching us today, but I didn't see anyone, did you, Rose?"

"No, but I'll start looking around when we're out."

Nothing else caused Tina to remember that day and the uneasy feelings were forgotten.

Over the following two weeks, the girls worked long hours. At the end of another long day, Rose said to Tina, "Do you mind if I go out tonight?"

"Of course I don't mind, you should go out more often, is it anyone I know?"

"You may remember him. It's Steve, the lad who was in charge of changing all the backdrops when we did the Harrogate show."

"I thought he was getting a bit friendly."

"He's nice, Tina. A bit different from the rough and ready blokes we knew when we worked at the factory."

Tina laughed. "Yes they were rough. It's funny, when you work somewhere like that, it all seems so normal until you move away. Have a good time, but don't do anything you're likely to regret in three months time."

"No fear, I've learned my lesson. What will you do tonight?"

"I'm more than happy just to relax and have an early night. This last two weeks have been hard."

Rose spent the next hour getting ready for her date. When she had gone, Tina relaxed in the bath. She put on her robe and was reading, when the sound of the doorbell penetrated the silence.

"Hello?"

"Don't worry, Tina, it's me, Solly."

Tina pressed the intercom and let him in.

"What's wrong?" she asked as she let him in.

"Nothing, I worked late and didn't feel like going straight home."

Even though Tina had worked for him, and knew she could trust him, his answer put her on her guard.

He saw the look on her face. "You've nothing to worry about, I only want to talk and maybe have a drink. The only time I get to talk to you these days is when it involves work. Where's Rose?"

"She's gone out with someone she met when we worked in Harrogate."

"Good, she's worked out very well hasn't she? In fact both of you have done well. I'm glad I followed my instincts regarding you, I have done us both a favour."

Tina smiled and poured him a drink.

"You know, Tina, I worry about you, especially after what happened. Have you had any more problems?"

"No, things have been quiet, but then, no one knows where I am."

"You can't hide yourself away forever. Let me deal with whoever it is? Then you can start living your life as you should be."

"I'm fine, Solly, really. I'll deal with things in my own time and in my own way."

"That's all very well, but while you're hiding away, you're missing out on having a normal life."

"No I'm not. I have more than I've ever had in my entire life. I don't need anything else."

He sighed. "OK, but if you do need anything, promise you'll let me know? I want you to know that I care about you, Tina. I don't want anything from you except for you to be happy."

"Thank's. I'll remember that."

He stood up. "I'll go now, thank you for your company."

"Thank you," she said, and gave him a friendly peck on the cheek. "I'll see you tomorrow."

"No you won't. It's Yom Kippur, a Jewish holiday for us, so it'll be Tuesday before I'm back in the office. If you need me or have any problems, contact Lilly."

"I will, Solly, and again, thank you. Have a happy Yom Kippur."

When he had gone, Tina was just thinking of going to bed, when Rose arrived home.

"Hi, have you had a good time?"

"It was OK."

"Just OK?"

"Yes, just OK," Rose answered. She couldn't tell her that Steve had spent the whole date asking questions about Tina, and she wondered if he had used her to get information.

Every time Rose had changed the subject, he would turn things around and still insist on asking more questions. Rose became a little suspicious at his motive and began feeding him false information.

When she told him that she wanted to go home, he asked where she lived. She told him not to worry, she would take a taxi home.

This seemed to upset him and he became sullen. When her taxi arrived, he didn't bother to see her inside or make another date.

Tina's father was a bit of a rogue and he knew so many people, Rose couldn't risk him finding out where they lived. All she wanted was to protect her friend, and she'd do it one way or another.

"Are you alright?"

Tina's voice brought Rose back to reality.

"Yes, why?"

"I just spoke to you, but you seemed to be miles away."

"Sorry, I suddenly thought about work on Monday, and wondered if we had everything ready."

"Don't worry, I'm sure you've thought of everything. You know, Rose, I'm not conceited enough to think I'll make it to the top with this modelling. All I want is to work hard and make as much money as I can. Then if anything happens and this job should finish, at least I'll know that we're secure for the future."

"Yeh, I know what you mean. I still want to get married and have kids, but the next time, I'll do it the right way round. By the way, I heard Doug got a baby girl. I've sent them a card."

"You didn't, did you?"

She nodded her head. "Yes I did. Believe it or not I really did love him and I suppose I still do."

"I don't know why after the way he treated you."

"Maybe that's life and circumstances haven't fallen on my side of the fence.

"That's what I like about you, Rose, you're so forgiving, but a bit soft. Just be careful, don't let people use you. Come on, let's go to bed. I'm tired. Oh, by the way, Solly called tonight. I think he's lonely. He told me he wouldn't be in the office until Tuesday. It's Yom Kippur."

"Yom Kippur, what's that?"

"Jewish New Year, time of atonement, you're meant to make peace with family and friends. Can you ever see me doing that? I'd like to find my mother, find out what she was really like."

"You might do one day."

Rose hoped she would. Tina needed someone to love and have love in return. So far, her life had been work, living in a pigsty and fighting to protect herself.

Over the last few months, Rose had seen a change in her friend. She had built an invisible screen round her. People had said she was stuck up or above herself, but she knew it was Tina's way of protecting herself from any more hurt.

Rose knew a different side of her. She knew Tina as being gentle, kind and considerate. She would help anyone. She was just making sure she would not be taken for granted ever again.

Tina had no close friend other than Rose. She knew lots of acquaintances but allowed no one to get too close to her.

Solly, true to his word, kept them supplied with plenty of work over the next six months. By this time, Tina had repaid all that she owed him and had a healthy bank balance.

At the same, Rose had saved money. She made sure that she took care of her mum. She bought her nice clothes and put food in the cupboard so that she did not have to go out to work.

On the surface, things appeared to be fine, but underneath, things were bubbling. Something was going to happen, what, she had no idea, but it had been too quiet for too long, and it gave her a sense of foreboding, a very uncomfortable feeling.

At times, Tina still had the feeling that someone was watching her. She was very aloof with people, keeping them at bay. Rose, Lilly and Solly were the only ones she would allow to get near her.

One night Tina and Rose went to a party. They were all advertising people and agents looking for new talent.

Tina was talking to Solly when someone approached them and introduced himself as Ged. Immediately, her guard was up.

"Who do you work for?" he asked her.

"She works for me," Solly replied.

Ged asked Tina about herself. She didn't like him, and Solly sensing this, stayed close. Tina only gave him information she wanted to give.

Having been to several of these get-togethers, Tina knew the regulars, but she had never seen him before.

Ged asked her other questions and Tina refused to answer.

His smile turned into a sneer. "Look, I'm only making conversation to be polite."

Tina smiled. "And I'm only talking to you to be polite. But that doesn't entitle you to know my life story."

"That's a bit of a high and mighty attitude isn't it?"

"It's my privilege."

He grabbed a hold of her wrist and quietly said, "That might work with others, but not with me. You are no better than them you left behind, in the hovel you grew up in. I know more about you than you think. When you see your old man, tell him payment is due, and if he doesn't pay up, I'm gonna' start takin'."

While all this was going on, Solly was talking to someone else. Suddenly he was back at her side. "What's going on?"

"Nothing," replied Ged. "Just having a conversation with Cinderella here."

Solly looked at him and then at Tina; he saw the pallor of her skin. "Well I think the conversation has just ended. I don't know who you are, but I think you ought to leave."

"I'm going." He looked at Tina. "Tell him." Then he walked away.

"Tell him, tell him what?"

"Nothing. It was a message for my father. Why he thinks I have contact with him, I don't know. Anyway, I'm tired, Solly, I think I'll go home."

"I'll get Rose," he said.

"No, don't do that. She has her own life to lead, not live it around me. She works hard and deserves some fun."

"Let me take you home then."

"No, Solly, I can't hide away forever. Just get me a taxi, I'll be fine."

When the taxi arrived, Tina said goodnight. She didn't want to spoil the night for Rose by asking her to leave early.

As she walked out of the door to get into the taxi, she thought she heard someone say, "Bitch." She looked around, but could not see anyone.

Once she was safely home, Tina poured herself a drink, and she sat down and thought about what had taken place.

How had he found out who she was, and who was he? Tina wondered what her father was involved in now. Not that she cared, unless it involved her, then she worried.

She decided that it was time to pay a visit to her old home. She would lay her cards on the table and tell him how it was going to be.

If he chose to ignore her, then she would have him locked up, and it would be for a very long time. Tina felt sick at the thought of it but she had to do it.

It wasn't very long before Rose arrived home.

"Why didn't you say you were coming home?" she asked.

"I don't need you to hold my hand all the time."

"Solly said something about a fella bothering you."

"Solly has a big mouth. I can handle things, I don't need a nursemaid ALL THE TIME."

Rose looked hurt. "I was only concerned for you that's all."

Tina realised she had been unkind to her friend. Why had she spoken to her the way she had?

"Look, Rose, I'm tired. I had no right to speak to you that way, I'm sorry. I think I'll go to bed."

"I really do care about you, Tina." She walked over and gave her a hug. "I have so much to thank you for, I think of you as my own sister."

Tina smiled at her. "I'm sorry, I shouldn't have taken things out on you. I'll see you in the morning. Goodnight."

"Night."

Tina went to bed but sleep eluded her. She kept going over in her mind what she would say to her father the following day when she returned to the streets she had grown up in.

She tossed and turned and it was a very long night. She heard the clock strike six and got up, went through to the kitchen and made a pot of coffee.

She bathed and dressed, felt so sick she couldn't eat anything. She was just about to leave when Rose came into the room.

"You're up early, where are you going?"

"To see someone. I won't be long."

"Tina, where are you going? Look, if you're in trouble I need to know."

"No, you don't need to know," she snapped.

"If anything happens to you, I need to know where you've been."

Tina sighed. "I'm paying him a call."

"Who?"

"My father."

"Why?"

"Because until I do, I'll never have any peace. That man last night was

61

looking for him. I don't want to be involved. I'm going to tell him that if I have any more trouble, I'm going to the police."

"Do you want me to come with you?"

"No, I have to do this on my own."

Rose nodded. "OK, if you need me, you know where I am."

Tina left the house. She caught a bus back to the area she used to live in. As she walked down the street, her heart was thumping so loudly, she was convinced that other people could hear it.

She looked around her and realised how much of a slum it was. She knew it had always been this way, but now that she no longer lived here, coming back made it so apparent.

She stopped in front of the house, took a deep breath and opened the gate. The garden was still littered with rubbish, old bits of car and bikes.

Nothing changes, she thought to herself.

The windows were still filthy and curtains hung on nails. She opened the door and the stale smell of cooking, tobacco and dampness hit her, causing her to gag.

Dirty newspaper covered the table where dirty mugs, empty milk bottles and overflowing ashtrays stood.

The fire was blazing, but the hearth itself was filthy. Her father sat reading the newspaper, her sister Susan, who was four years younger than Tina, was reading a magazine.

Her sister had always been a madam. She had been allowed to wear makeup from a very young age, but when Tina wore makeup, her father said she looked a tart.

Susan never had to be in for a certain time, and had been allowed to do more or less whatever she wanted. Tina had always wondered why.

The police had arrested her twice, on suspicion of soliciting, but they had not been able to prove it.

She also went shoplifting with her friend Leverne and it was only luck that had prevented them from getting arrested.

A slut in the making, but her dad thought the sun shone from her backside. Tina had her own thoughts on that score too.

Her father didn't noticed Tina as she walked into the room, but Susan looked up. "Well look what the cat's dragged in," she said.

Her father looked up and half rose from his chair. "Wot the hell have you come for? Come snivellin' to me have yer?"

She looked at him in disgust. "No, you're not that lucky. Someone gave me a message for you."

He looked at Susan.

"Go out a minute," he told her.

"I'm stopping here."

"I said go!" he yelled.

"Why can't I stay?"

"Because I said so," he yelled again.

She stomped out, banging the door behind her. She stood in the yard and lit a cigarette.

"Make it quick, unless you're offering somethin' else," he sneered.

Tina took a deep breath. "Someone called Ged said you owed him, and if he doesn't get paid, he said he'll come collecting. Now I don't know what you're mixed up in and I don't really care, but this part of my life is over. If I continue to be threatened and get any more hassle, I'll go to the police and have you locked up."

His face was like thunder and he raised his fist.

"Go on, people know I've come here and they're waiting for me to go back."

"You got no proof," he said.

"Oh yes I have. After that last time, and your bastard I got rid of, I vowed you'd never hurt me again, and if you tried, you'd be sorry."

He looked at her. "How bout givin' yer old dad a bit of cash eh? I'll make sure yer left alone."

"I'll give you nothing."

"Why? Yer can afford it."

"Yes, but I've worked for it."

"'How, on yer back like yer mother?"

"No, I'm not like Susan, I earned it by being respectable. Something you know nothing about."

"What, layin' on yer back fer some Jew boy wot's older than me. Is that what yer call bein' respectable?"

"You have a dirty mind; it's not like that."

"What do yer do when he comes round? Give 'im shows with yer dyke friend?" he shouted.

"You have a filthy mind, you don't know how to respect anything. But I'm telling you this, if anything happens to my friends, and I suspect you're involved, I'll shop you to the police."

Susan came back in from the yard. "Have you upset him? Why don't you just go?"

She looked round the room and then at them both. "I'm going. You know, you two are suited, you deserve each other."

"What's she mean, Dad?"

For once in his life, he was stuck for words.

Tina turned on her heels and left, the smell of the house clinging to her. She couldn't get home fast enough to have a bath, wash her hair and change her clothes.

Rose was waiting for her when she got back.

"Everything alright?" she asked.

"Yes, nothing to worry about. I'm going to wash the stench off me and change my clothes."

"But you did that before you went out."

"Yes and I'm doing it again. There's a certain smell in my nose I have to get rid of."

The next three months flew by. Tina was in great demand, and she had very little time for herself.

One morning Lilly and Rose were in the office as Solly arrived. He looked very pale and was out of breath.

"Are you alright?" Lilly asked him.

"Nothing to worry about. I have bad indigestion, my sister's cooking will kill me one of these days. Get me some tea, Lilly. I'll see if that works."

"You should get a check up, Solly, you haven't looked good for some time. You overwork, overeat and over drink," she told him.

"Òy, Òy, Òy. Don't go on, Lilly, just be a dear and get the tea."

The tea did not help him and he came out of his office two hours later. "I'm going home, Lilly, will you do the banking tonight?"

"Yes, of course I will, I'll give you a ring later."

"Don't fuss, woman," he said as he walked out.

Lilly looked at Rose. "That's the first time in twenty-five years I've known him leave the office early. Can you take the money to the bank for me, I'll go and have a word with his sister Hilda, not that he'll thank me for doing it, but I'm going anyway."

"Yes, I can do that, don't worry," Rose said.

Rose left the office and took the money to the bank. Later, sat on the bus going home, she idly flicked through the bankbook and saw that there were regular payments each month to a Mr. Martin.

Now, it may have been a coincidence that it was the same surname as

Tina's, but if it wasn't, why was Solly paying thirty pounds a month to Tina's old man?

Rose arrived home before Tina so she started to prepare their evening meal. Shortly after Tina arrived home, they started talking about what they had done during the day.

"Solly went home early today; he didn't look very well. Lilly said she was going to call and have a word with Hilda, ask her to keep her eye on him."

"Maybe I should call and see if he's feeling better," Tina said.

Rose looked at her. "Tina, I did the banking for Lilly today. Did you know Solly's paying your dad thirty pounds a month?"

"Are you sure?"

Rose nodded her head.

"No I didn't, but I'm going to find out why."

She had a drink, quickly changed, and without stopping to eat, left the house.

She arrived at Solly's house and rang the bell. He came to the door and Tina was surprised to see him looking so ill.

"Hello, Tina, what's wrong?"

"I should be asking you the same question. How do you feel?"

"I feel much better It was only indigestion, over-indulgence at our Hilda's. Would you like a drink?"

She nodded and sat down while he went to get her drink. When he returned he sat in the chair opposite her.

"Solly, I'm going to ask you something. I want a truthful answer and I won't be put off. Why are you paying my father thirty pounds every month?"

"How do you know that?"

"I just do, and it wasn't Lilly who told me."

Solly sighed. "He came to see me and asked me for money. He said that you would be left alone if I paid it. I think a lot about you, Tina, and thought it was a small price to pay for your safety."

"How much have you paid him so far?"

"It doesn't matter," he replied.

"It does to me, Solly, I'd like to know."

"One hundred and twenty pounds so far."

Tina reached for her bag, took out her cheque book, and wrote out a cheque and gave it to him.

"Here, now you're paid back. Don't make any more payments to him, Solly. He's not your problem."

"You don't have to repay me."

"Oh, but I do. Do you understand? I won't have things any other way, and there'll be no more money paid to that man."

Solly looked at her. "Tina, do you trust me?"

"Yes, why?"

"Do you like me a little?"

"I'm very fond of you."

"But do you love me?"

"No, Solly, I don't," she said as she stood up to leave.

"Please, Tina, sit down. Hear me out. I have a proposition to put to you, and before you give me your answer, just think about it will you?"

Tina sat down. "I'm listening."

"I have always had a soft spot for you. You're very young and I worry what could happen to you when I'm not around."

"Are you ill, Solly?"

"No, but I'm not getting any younger. Tina, I want you to marry me."

"What?"

He held up his hand. "Hear me out. If you marry me, I want nothing from you, but I can make sure that you are cared for. You can live here but have your own set of rooms. All I ask is for some companionship from you. I love you, Tina. I know you don't love me, but just to have you here under any circumstances, is enough for me."

"Solly, I don't know what to say."

"Don't say anything, just go home and think about what I have said. There's no time limit, just give me your answer when you've decided."

Tina got up, kissed his cheek as you would a child and walked to the door.

"If the answer is no, don't worry, it won't change things between us."

She smiled. "I'll think about it."

Tina didn't go straight home. Instead, she took a taxi to her old district. She didn't go to the house, but to the local pub where she knew her father would be at this time of the day.

She heard him before she saw him, propping up the bar with some of his cronies.

Tina walked over to the bar and he turned and leered at her.

"Well, well, what brings you here? Fancy a bit of rough do you?" he said, grabbing her wrist.

"No, I came to tell you to enjoy the little you have now, because there will be no more handouts."

"It's nowt ter do wi' you."

"Oh yes it is, because all the money you've had up to now, I've repaid. That's the last you will ever get."

"You slut." He was just about to give her a thump, when his hand stopped in mid-air.

She looked up to see Gordon standing behind, holding her father's hand, preventing it from reaching its target.

Gordon let go and walked to her side. Taking her arm he said, "Come on, you shouldn't be in here."

As they walked towards the door, her father shouted, "No, you should be down the docks."

When they were outside, he turned to her. "Why do you keep coming back, Tina? He only hurts you each time you do."

"I have to let him see that he doesn't frighten me anymore," she answered.

"You still should be careful. Come on, I'll take you home."

"No, it's OK, I can manage."

"Look, there's no way I'm going to walk away and let you go home alone. You needn't worry, I'm not going to tell anyone where you live."

Tina nodded her head in agreement and they walked towards the bus stop. They got on the bus and travelled in silence, and she thought how sweet he was. Gordon was lost in his own thoughts, how much he loved her, but didn't want to tell her in case he frightened her away.

Eventually they arrived at her door. "Thanks, Gordon, it was good of you to come all this way with me."

Glad to be some help. I heard some ugly talk so please be careful. If you ever need me, you know where I am." He turned and walked back towards the bus stop.

Tina let herself in and Rose met her at the door. "Where've you been? I was worried. Solly said you left his place ages ago."

"Don't worry, everything's going to be alright." She told her where she had been and that Gordon had seen her home.

"I'm glad he was there."

"So am I," Tina replied. She had been more frightened than she cared to admit.

"I'm going to bed. Goodnight, Rose, see you in the morning."

"Goodnight."

Tina didn't mention anything to Rose about Solly's proposal. She wanted to think about things before she said anything.

She slept very little that night. She was fond of him but she didn't love him. Would it appear that she was just using him and taking advantage of him?

Would he stick to his word and only want her company.

Tina could not sleep and got up about four a.m. She was still sat at the kitchen table when Rose got up at eight o' clock.

"You're up early."

" I couldn't sleep."

"Why, what's on your mind?"

There was no other way to say it, so she just came right out and told her. "Solly proposed to me last night."

Rose always reverted to her old way of speech when she got excited. "Wot, get married, but yer don't luv him."

"I know, but I'm fond of him."

"Yeh, but does he know that?"

"Yes he does. When I told him, he said that I could have my own rooms. All he wanted was my company, and he loves me."

"Bloomin' hell, yer can't turn 'im down, Tina. A chance like this won't come again."

"I know, but will it be fair to Solly? Will he come to want more in the end?"

Rose took her hand and said, "So far he's done everything he said he would. I reckon that if you could trust anyone in this world, it would be him, apart from me that is."

"So do you think I should accept?"

"You'd be a fool not to. Just think how safe you'd be."

"Right, that's that then."

"Yer mean yer gonna do it?"

"I suppose so."

"Good fer you."

"Rose, don't say anything to anyone else until I've seen Solly."

They got ready, left the house and went to the office. Lilly was already at her desk.

"Morning, Lilly, is he on his own?" Tina asked her.

"Yes he is, are you alright, Tina?"

"Fine," she said as she walked towards Solly's office.

Rose sat at her desk and Lilly said, "What's to do? She looks serious."

"She'll tell you," Rose replied.

Solly was behind his desk as usual, surrounded by a cloud of cigar smoke.

"Morning, Tina, nice to see you, is everything alright?"

"Yes. Solly, did you mean what you said last night, I can have my own room?"

"Anything, Tina, you can have anything."

"OK, I'll marry you. But it has to be a quiet affair. I don't want any fuss."

He took her hands in his. "You won't regret it, Tina. You'll see. Can we tell Lilly and Rose the news?"

She smiled and nodded.

He took her arm and guided her to the outer office. Lilly and Rose looked up.

"Tina and I are getting married."

Lilly walked over to her. "It's about time, I was getting fed up of seeing him mooching round this office. When's the day going to be?"

"As soon as I can arrange it." He looked at Tina. "If that's OK with you?"

She nodded her head.

"Good, I have some telephone calls to make. Lilly, give her some money. Rose, you can take her shopping. Choose something pretty for your wedding."

"I have my own money, Solly," Tina said.

"Yes, I know you have. Please allow me to do this as a wedding present. It would make me very happy. Will you all have dinner with me tonight to celebrate?" he asked.

They all said they would. Lilly handed Tina an envelope. When she opened it, she was surprised to see a wad of notes. When she counted them there was five hundred pounds.

"Solly, I can't accept all this."

"Why not?" he asked. "Half of it you earned anyway."

As she slipped it into her purse, she thanked him, and left the office with Rose.

"I need a drink."

"Let's go for coffee."

"I mean a drink, Rose. I didn't have coffee in mind."

"But its only eleven o' clock."

"So, it's not every day I agree to get married."

They found a wine bar open and went in. Tina went to the bar and got them both a glass of wine.

Tina drank hers in one go and then ordered another one. Rose took a sip of hers and pulled a face. "Ugh! I'll never get used to this stuff. Are you having any regrets, Tina?"

"No, but I still won't be owned by a man."

"Tina, let your guard drop a little. Solly will be good to you; he'll treat you well."

"I know, but when I'm faced with love or practicality, the latter wins every time."

"One day you'll find true love and then you'll really soften up."

"Why should I love any man? All I've seen is they cause you hardship, and you have a baby every year until you're old before your time. No thank you. I reckon the arrangement I'll have with Solly is the best I can hope for, and it suits me fine."

Rose sighed and finished her drink. Tina drank hers and stood up.

"Come on, we've some shopping to do. By the way, are you going to be my bridesmaid?"

"Try stopping me," replied Rose.

They visited many shops before Tina found something that she thought would do. The dress was a soft material in a coffee colour, with shoes to match. She chose a hat and gloves in white.

Rose chose a pink dress, shoes and hat. By the time they had bought makeup, it was rather late so they called it a day and went home.

Tina and Rose had arranged to meet Solly and Lilly in town at a restaurant they all knew.

Lilly was already there when they arrived. "Hello, girls." She turned to Tina. "You've made Solly very happy. You know he will never hurt you. I've always had a soft spot for him myself, but I was never anything other than a secretary to him."

Tina touched her arm. "Lilly, I'm sorry."

"Sssh, don't be. I never expected anything else. I'm just glad it's you he's marrying and not one of those silly empty headed girls we get passing through."

Just then Solly arrived. "Hope you're all hungry?" he said as they walked into the restaurant.

Lilly had made the reservations earlier in the day so they were expected. The waiter took them to their table immediately.

Solly ordered champagne, and when they all had some in their glasses, he raised his. "I'd like to thank Tina for agreeing to marry me, and hope that I can make her happy."

Lilly cleared her throat. "I'd like to say that I'm happy for both of you."

They drank the champagne, and Solly took a box from his pocket and passed it to Tina.

"Tina, will you accept this?"

In the box lay a beautiful sapphire and diamond ring, and her eyes filled with tears.

"If it doesn't fit we can change it," he told her, as he took the ring from the box and put it on her engagement finger. It did fit, and it was beautiful.

"Thank you, Solly, it really is a lovely ring."

"It's for a lovely girl," he replied. "Now here are the arrangements. I hope they suit you."

"I have booked the Register Office for next Thursday at ten-thirty. After the ceremony, we'll go to Paris for a long weekend."

She looked at him. He took her hand. "Everything's going to be fine, Tina, I promise."

She smiled and nodded.

"What's happening about your flat, Tina?" Rose asked her.

"It's your home also. I thought you would want to stay on there."

"Oh I do, thanks. I was hoping you'd say that."

"You've been loyal both to me and Tina, Rose. I'd like to repay that loyalty."

"I don't need no payin', Solly. Tina's my friend and it's lucky for you that I like you."

They all laughed. Solly nodded towards Lilly, and she handed Rose an envelope.

"What's this?"

"Just a little security for you," replied Solly.

Rose opened the envelope, and it was the deeds to the house.

"My sister Hilda has sold me the house. I've given it to you on the condition that Hilda lives out the rest of her life there."

"Oh Solly, how can I ever thank you? Imagine me owning a house." She got up and kissed him. They all laughed.

He blushed. "Just continue to be there for Tina if she ever needs you."

"That goes without sayin'. But you didn't have to buy the bloody house to make sure." Rose stopped and apologised for swearing, and they all laughed again.

Tears filled her eyes. "Thanks, Solly."

"You're both good girls and deserve some happiness."

The rest of the night went well. They all laughed and joked, had some more to drink, and by the time they were ready to leave, were all a little merry.

Solly made sure that Tina and Rose got home safely. Lilly took a taxi.

Over the next few days, Tina questioned herself on more than one occasion if she was doing the right thing.

Suddenly, it was Wednesday night, and she would be getting married the following morning.

All her things except the things she would need, had been taken to Solly's.

"Are you happy, Tina?"

"As happy as I'm ever going to be."

"Tina, most girls I know would be happy to be in your shoes."

"I know, but it just feels as if I'm going to work. I feel no different."

"It's great, you'll have everything you want. Do you remember what you once said? You would work hard and lift yourself out of the gutter. Well, I think that time has come, don't you?"

"Yes, but it doesn't get rid of the major problem. I'm still working on that. Believe me, he'll rear his ugly head again." (He, meaning her father.)

"Tina, he can't ever hurt you again," said Rose.

"He won't get the chance, not if I have anything to do with it."

Rose stood up. "Come on, let's have a drink and go to bed; you have a big day tomorrow."

Surprisingly, Tina slept very well and only woke up when Rose came into the room with a cup of coffee for her.

"Mornin', Tina, well it's not rainin', the sun's shinin'."

"Thanks, Rose."

Tina drank her coffee. By the time she had bathed, packed the remainder of her belongings and dressed, it was time for her to leave for the register office.

Rose came back to her room. "Are you ready?"

"Ready as I'll ever be."

"You look lovely."

"You don't look too bad yourself."

Rose suddenly said, "Wait, I nearly forgot something." She dashed from the room and returned with a posy of roses, carnations and gipsophelia.

"Solly sent them for you."

Tina smiled. They climbed into the waiting taxi that Solly had ordered. Soon after, they arrived at the register office. As Tina stepped from the taxi, she saw Rose's family and a few friends waiting for her to arrive.

Tina looked at Rose. "Well, you didn't want your family to come, and I thought you should have someone, so I asked them."

Tina smiled. "Thanks, it was nice of you to think of that."

They went inside, and Solly was waiting for her.

He smiled when he saw her. "You look lovely."

"Thanks for the flowers."

Within fifteen minutes, they left the register office as man and wife. Someone took photos, and as they ran to the car, someone threw confetti over them.

Solly arranged for a small reception at Roundhay Park Mansion. It was a grand building owned by one of his friends, and he had been delighted to let them use it.

As usual, Rose's family made it into a real knees up and made the day thoroughly enjoyable.

As they were dancing, several guests came over and wished Tina and Solly well.

At one point Gordon came over to where Tina sat. He took her hands in his.

"Congratulations, Tina. You deserve to be happy."

Tina thanked him and smiled, but he noticed the smile didn't reach her eyes.

"If you ever need a friend, day or night, I'll be there. All you have to do is call me."

"Thanks, Gordon, I'll remember that." Then someone came and whisked her away to dance.

Rose was talking to her mum. "Our Gordon is a sad man today, He's loved her a long time."

"I know, Mam, but Tina has had too many hangups to see it. Still, as long as she's happy, that's all I ask."

"Ay, she's a fine lass, and deserves some happiness."

Soon it was time to leave for the airport. Lilly offered to drive them, so they thanked everyone and left.

Solly took her hand. "I want you to be happy, Tina."

"You should have some happiness too," she replied.

"I have all I want in you."

They flew to Paris, and he took her to see all the sights. He was attentive and very considerate, trying to anticipate all her needs.

73

In their hotel room, they had separate beds. He said he would stay downstairs in the bar to give her time to get ready for bed.

When he came into the room, he went into the bathroom to undress. He came through to the bedroom, turned out the light and kissed her on the cheek before he got into his own bed.

"Goodnight, Tina, thank you for making me so happy today."

"Goodnight, thank you for today and bringing me here."

Over the next four days, they did everything. They went sightseeing, did some shopping and ate in the finest of places. Solly, true to his word, made no demands on her, and asked her for nothing.

The time flew and soon it was time for them to return home, Tina knew that Solly was someone she could trust completely. She had also seen another side of him, the loving, gentle and considerate side.

Tina did love him in her own way. Kissing him on the cheek was of no hardship to her. She doubted if she would ever be able to give him her body, or give it to anyone else for that matter; she was too scarred mentally for that.

They arrived back in Leeds and went straight to Solly's house, hers as well now.

They opened the door and it felt warm. Someone had been in and lit the fire, and had left them something to eat.

There was a note on the table. Solly picked it up. "Welcome home, love Lilly," he read.

"That was nice of her."

They unpacked, put everything away, and sat and ate the meal Lilly had left for them.

Later Solly showed her the room that was to be hers, and as they were going into the office the following morning, Tina said that she would have an early night.

Solly was reading the paper. "Look." He showed her the paper; it reported the news of their marriage.

"Oh no, do you know what this means?"

"Yes, but you don't have to worry, Tina. If he contacts me, he'll get his answer."

She could not help but worry.

For the next year, things carried on pretty much the same. Rose continued working. Tina worked the fashion houses and stores.

Solly kept his word and their arrangement worked well. Tina felt safe and secure, and yes, she felt loved.

Her affection for him grew into love. The contact between them had gone from a kiss on the cheek, to holding him in her arms and kissing him on the lips. Yet they still slept in separate beds.

One night Tina lay awake. She was cold and could not sleep. She slid out of her bed and crept in beside Solly.

"What's wrong, are you OK?"

"Nothing's wrong," she answered. "I'm cold and can't sleep."

He put his arms around her and held her and that's how she slept.

After that night, Tina moved into his bed. Solly didn't do anything other than just hold her.

On their first wedding anniversary, he arranged to take Tina, Rose and Lilly out to celebrate.

They went to a restaurant and had a lovely meal. Everyone had a good time. When it was time to leave, Lilly drove Rose home.

Solly and Tina had drunk quite a bit of champagne. When they got home, they went through the usual routine before getting into bed.

Solly held Tina in his arms, and kissed her. As he did, she suddenly felt a warm feeling spread through her body and a tingling sensation in her stomach. She had never felt it before and she pulled away.

"Let me love you, Tina," he said. "I promise I will never hurt you. If at any time I did, all you have to say is stop and I will. Just let me show you what a pleasure it is to love someone."

Because she was slightly tipsy from the drink, it had given her a little Dutch courage. Tina nodded her head, and with some apprehension, removed her nightgown.

"Tina, you're lovely and it's a pleasure to look at you in this way."

He took her into his arms and ran his hands gently over her body. At first, Tina held herself rigid, but as his hands gently caressed her body and rested on her breasts, she began to relax.

He ran his hand down her body and it rested on her soft mound, and the warm feeling spread right through her body.

He took her nipples into his mouth and gently suckled them like a baby being breastfed. This caused her to moan with the pleasure she began to feel. Tina had never experienced anything like this before. She never thought that lovemaking could be like this. All she had ever experienced was rough and brutal handling.

He rolled above her and gently spread her legs, little by little, he gently entered her, stopping each time in case he hurt her.

Tina was lost in the passion that she was feeling and thrust herself up to meet him. The feeling was new, and as she reached the climax, she screamed with pleasure, causing him to fill her with his own seed.

Afterwards he said, "Tina, thank you so much. I really love you."

She cried in his arms. "I never realised that it could be like that. I love you."

So was born the love between a girl and a man old enough to be her father.

They had been married for one year, and tonight, they had at last consummated their marriage, and it has erased from her mind all thoughts of love and sex being sordid and dirty. It was wonderful if it was with someone you loved.

As they went into the office the following day, Lilly said, "Well you two look radiant this morning."

Tina looked at him knowingly, winked at Lilly and walked into his office.

Tina and Rose left the office to go to an assignment. When they were outside, Rose turned to Tina and said, "What's happened?"

"What do you mean?"

"Well there's somthin' different, yer like someone who's in love."

"Well I am married to him, Rose."

"Yeh, but you didn't love him."

"But I do now." She smiled.

"Well good fer you, it's about time." She hugged her and said, "Tina, does that mean what I think it does?"

Tina nodded her head. " It was wonderful. He was so loving and gentle."

"I knew it would be OK."

Tina couldn't wait for night-time when she and Solly would be alone again, and she welcomed bedtime. He was always so gentle with her and showed her different ways of love and pleasure. She never thought that she would allow any man to touch her the way she let Solly. He used his mouth on every part of her body, always bringing her to new heights of pleasure.

Rose was also seeing someone regularly, but for some reason, she kept quiet about it and Tina did not ask.

One night, Tina and Solly were in town and they stopped off at a wine bar for a drink. As Tina looked around, she was surprised to see Rose tucked away in a corner deep in conversation, with the famous Dougie. They did not see her because they only had eyes for each other.

Tina sat as far away as possible so they would not see her if they looked up. Rosie had always loved him, and it was obvious that she still carried a torch for him and no one else would compare. Nevertheless, he was a married man, and it could only lead to more heartbreak. Still, it was none of her business, and she would not say anything, unless Rose did.

A couple of weeks later, Rose said she was going out for the night.

"Anyone I know?"

"Oh, just someone."

"Dougie?"

A deep blush coloured Rosie's face. "You know?"

"I saw you a while back."

"You never said anything."

"None of my business. But would you like it if someone did it to you, Rose."

"He said his marriage to Doreen was a sham."

"Is he ready to prove it to you, Rose?"

"What do you mean?"

"Would he divorce her and move in with you?"

"I don't know."

"Why don't you ask him, or are you afraid to?"

"Why should you care?"

"I don't really, but you are my friend and I care about you. I don't want you to get hurt. I would make sure if I was you."

For a while Rose was quiet and then she said, "I know you're right, but I know how I feel about him. I couldn't bear it if I lost him again."

"But you still might. Find out now, before it goes any further. You know I'll be there for you."

"OK, I know you're right."

That night when Rose met Dougie she asked him how things were at home.

"Just the same, she spends most of the time round at her mother's and just complains when she's home with me."

"Why don't you move in with me then?"

Dougie put down his drink. "Because I can't afford to keep two homes going."

"You won't have to. The house is mine, just pay towards your food."

"Are you serious?"

"Yes I am."

"We love each other, why not be together? If you have nothing to keep you at home, what have you got to lose?"

"Nothing. Nothing at all, OK. I'll move in this weekend. I better go and tell her."

Rose was so happy. Tina was wrong. He was going to make the commitment.

She could not wait to tell Tina the news the following day.

She said she would go home too and he said he would walk her to the corner of the road. He would have gone all the way home with her, but he had to go tell his wife he was leaving her.

When they got to the end of the road, they kissed before going their separate ways. As Rose turned the corner, someone stepped back into the shadows, lit a cigarette and walked the other way.

Rose wondered who it was. It was the third time this week she had noticed him, and he had always done the same thing. Still, she was too happy to worry about someone lighting up a cigarette; she thought nothing more about it. She climbed the steps to her front door and let herself in.

Next day, Rose told Tina that Dougie would be moving in with her at the weekend.

"I'm pleased for you, Rose, you deserve some happiness."

"Are you OK, Tina?"

"Yes, why?"

"You have dark shadows under your eyes." As she walked away she said, "I'd get more sleep if I was you."

Tina laughed to herself and went about her day.

Tina didn't see Rose again that day. She finished her work and went home. Solly was already there.

"'I'm so tired; it was hard going today."

"Why don't I take you out to dinner?" he said. "Have a glass of wine while you're changing."

"It sounds good to me."

When she was ready, they went out to a little restaurant just down the road. They had a simple meal and returned home.

"Did you see Rose today?" he asked her.

"Yes, this morning. She's been seeing Dougie and he's moving in with her this weekend."

"Is that the one she was supposed to marry and he went and married someone else?"

"Yes. But she's never stopped loving him and his marriage isn't working out."

78

"I hope she knows what she's doing. Are you ready to go to bed, love?"

She nodded her head. "Yes, I have a lot on tomorrow."

"I have to go to Doncaster for a meeting. I may not be back until late," he told her.

Next morning, Solly left before Tina. "I'll see you tonight; take care of yourself. I love you."

"I love you too. Please drive carefully and remember to have some lunch."

"I will."

When he had gone, she called Rose but there was no answer. *Maybe she left for the office early*, Tina thought to herself. *Never mind, I'll call her later in the day.*

That never happened. Tina had arranged to see the doctor. He told her she was expecting a baby. Then she was kept going all day and before she knew, it was six o' clock.

I'll call her when I get home, she told herself.

Tina had been home for about fifteen minutes and the doorbell rang. When she opened the door, two police officers stood there.

"Are you Mrs Ableson?" one asked her.

She nodded her head. "Yes." She was sick with fear.

"Can we come in?"

She let them into the living room.

"Would you like to sit down? Mrs. Ableson, I'm afraid we have some bad news."

"Oh God, not Solly."

"No." said the policeman. "Do you know a Miss Rose Hirst?"

"Yes, she's my friend, why?"

"I'm afraid she was found dead at her home this morning. A young man called Douglas found her. He gave us your name."

"She was my friend and she worked for us. How did it happen?"

"Can't say for sure yet, but we are treating it as suspicious."

Tina felt the room start to spin. The next thing she knew, she was on the couch and Lilly was at her side.

"Are you feeling better, dear?" she asked.

Tina nodded. "The police called the office before they came to see you. I knew Solly was away, so I came straight over."

Tina started to cry. "Why Rose?"

Lilly told the police that Tina and Rose had been friends for most of their lives.

"So you would know most of her friends?" he asked Tina.

"Yes, though we didn't have many. We knew the same people."

"What about the young man, Douglas?"

"She's known him years. He married someone else a couple of years ago. But they have been seeing each other for a while now."

"Do you think she was making demands on him?" he asked.

"I don't know. She did ask him to move in with her."

"Well, maybe he liked having the best of both worlds. A wife and mistress, until she started making him choose."

"No, I don't believe that. What about her mum, has she been told?"

"A police woman is round there now."

"I have to go see her," she told Lilly.

"Tina, you don't look well yourself. You have been overworking lately. Maybe you should leave it until tomorrow."

Just at that moment, Solly walked in. Tina threw herself into his arms and sobbed. Lilly told him what had happened.

"Òy, what is the world coming to? Rose was a good girl, she wouldn't harm to anyone."

"But she was seeing a married man," the policeman said.

Solly looked at him. "Young man, that girl was decent and hardworking. She had loved that man for years. When he married someone else, she never went with any other man. It was always him she wanted. Does that make her bad? Instead of standing there making your assumptions that are not true, you should be out there finding out why she's dead."

The policeman nodded. "Thank you for your time, I may need to speak to you both again."

"We're not going anywhere."

The policeman left. Tina was still crying; Solly took her in arms.

"Tina, don't cry, you'll make yourself ill."

"I have to go see Rose's mum."

"OK, I'll take you. Lilly, cancel all appointments for tomorrow, will you?"

"Yes, don't worry, just go do what you have to do."

When Mrs. Hirst opened the door Tina could see how upset she was. On seeing Tina, she started crying again.

"Oh lass, who could have done such a thing? She never hurt anyone."

"I know," replied Tina.

Gordon was there and he held Tina's hand. "Don't worry, I'll look after her."

Solly said, "If there is anything we can do, anything at all, just let me know. I was very fond of Rose. She was a good girl."

"Aye," said Gordon, "but someone had a grudge against her."

He looked at Tina. "Go home, you don't look too good yourself."

He shook hands with Solly and they left.

Lilly came to the house later, and all they could talk about was Rose. When Lilly left a couple of hours later Solly made Tina a hot drink and they went to bed. It seemed an eternity from when they got up that morning.

He kissed her and said goodnight. She was thinking of all that had happened that day, and remembered she had not told him about the baby.

"Solly," she said, but there was no answer; he was sound asleep. He must have been tired. He had looked under the weather himself lately.

The sound of the telephone ringing woke Tina. She still felt very tired. She had lain awake until the early hours of the morning thinking about poor Rose.

She got out of bed and answered the phone.

"Hello."

"It's him, Tina, he killed my Rose." Mrs. Hirst was shouting down the phone.

"Calm down. Who are you talking about?"

"That Dougie. The police have him locked up. They say he killed our Rose 'cos she asked him to move in with her."

Mrs. Hirst still had not gotten used to the idea that you didn't need to shout down the phone, and Tina held the receiver away from her ear.

"Look, I'll come round and see you. Thanks for letting me know."

She put down the phone. Dougie, she could not believe it, she was sure they must have got it wrong.

Solly came through from the bedroom. "Who was that?"

"Rose's mum. She says the police have arrested Dougie. They are saying he killed her because she was asking him to move in with her. I don't believe it."

"How well did you know him, Tina?"

"Not as well as Rose obviously. But if he hadn't been alright, she wouldn't have stuck to him."

"But he did desert her at one time."

"Yes, because he had a fling and got the girl pregnant. Her parents insisted they got married, that does not make him a murderer. Rose was a bit shrewder than I was. If there had been anything bad about him, he wouldn't have lasted. I want to go see him."

"Is that a good idea?"

"Please, for Rose. I need to be sure."

"OK, we'll go round to the police station and see if they will let us."

They dressed and Solly had breakfast. Tina could not face anything except some tea.

They got to the police station and asked the desk sergeant if they could see Dougie. He said he would have to ask. A little while later, he returned and told them they could have five minutes.

He led them through a door and down a corridor to the cells. They went into the room where Dougie sat at a table.

He was unshaven and his eyes were red through crying and lack of sleep. As they entered the room, he stood up and the officer with them immediately told him to sit down.

"I didn't do it, Tina," he said desperately. "Why would I have called the police if I had killed her? I was going to move in with her this weekend. When I left her, she was fine. I called round yesterday morning to tell her it was all arranged, and she was already lying on the floor, dead."

"Then why do the police think it was you?" she asked him.

"Because when I left her the night before, I went home and told Doreen I was leaving. We had a row and I walked out and spent the night walking the streets just thinking. I don't have an alibi. I went to Rose's to ask her if I could stay instead of waiting until the weekend. They think I killed her because she made me choose between her and Doreen."

"Have the police spoken to Doreen?" asked Tina.

"Yes, she told them that I intended to move out, that I hadn't been home all night. But I swear, I never killed her. I wouldn't hurt her. I could have said no to her when she asked me to move in with her. I wouldn't have killed her, honest."

"It's OK. I believe you," Tina said.

"We'll do what we can to help you," said Solly.

The policeman told them it was time for them to leave.

Over the next week, there was something happening every day. The inquest into Rose's death took place and they said she had been strangled. Mrs. Hirst and Gordon moved into Rose's house and, with Solly's help, they packed up Rose's things. He arranged for the funeral and paid the expenses. At first her mum refused. She said Rose had left plenty of money, but Solly insisted, and arranged for a solicitor to sort out her affairs so everything she had would go to her mother.

OUT OF THE GUTTER

Throughout all this, Tina had still not found the right time to tell him about the baby.

Dougie appeared in court and was charged with murdering Rose. The case was adjourned, until the police made further enquiries.

The day of Rose's funeral arrived. Tina felt dreadful. She had caught a cold and she felt weak. She hadn't been eating regularly since the day they had found Rose.

Solly and Lilly had done their best to persuade her to stay at home, but she insisted on going. She wasn't going to miss saying goodbye to the best friend she had ever had.

The funeral service was simple. Tina saw Gordon and Mrs Hirst at the front of the church, she was sobbing uncontrollably. She felt numb and so lost in her own misery that she vaguely remembered what the vicar said.

"Oh Rose," she said, "I'm going to miss you so much. We've been through some rough times together. I don't believe Dougie was the one who killed you, but I'll find out who did if it takes me the rest of my life."

She realised that people were standing up and Solly took her arm. Her head was thumping and her throat ached. Tina was not sure if it was due to her cold or because she was so upset.

Outside the wind was howling and it was bitter cold. By the time they reached the cemetery she was chilled to the bone. She let her eyes roam over the crowd who stood at the grave side and then beyond to the trees and she saw someone watching. She assumed it was either the police or a photographer. The murder had attracted a lot of publicity. Tina blinked, looked again, and whoever had been there was gone and she wondered if she had actually seen anyone at all.

When it was all over, they made their way back to Rose's house. Mrs Hirst and Gordon came over to them.

Gordon shook Solly's hand. "Thank you for all you have done; we won't forget it."

"We wanted to do it; she was my friend," Tina answered.

Mrs. Hirst looked at her,. "Tina tell me ta mind me own business, but you look all in, lass. Why don't yer go home and get some rest?"

Tina shook her head. "I'll be fine."

"No one's gonna mind if yer leave early."

"Go on," said Gordon. "I'll ring you later, that's if you don't mind, Solly?"

Solly looked at him and saw the concern in his eyes. "No, I don't mind."

He knew the look, even if Tina didn't. Gordon was in love with her.

When they got home, Tina went straight to bed. Solly made her a hot drink, but when he took it in to her, she was already in a feverish sleep. Even though her cheeks were flaming, she was cold and clammy to touch and there were dark circles under her eyes. Rose's death had taken its toll on her and he was concerned.

He left the room, went downstairs and called the doctor. It was the same doctor Tina had seen three weeks earlier when he told her she was pregnant.

The doctor came and looked at her and then he ushered Solly out of the room.

"I'll give you a mild medicine for her. Make sure she gets plenty of rest. Her friend's death has hit her badly. But in her condition, she must take care of herself now."

"What condition?"

"Do you mean she hasn't told you? Your wife is pregnant."

"How far on is she?"

"Four months."

He nodded his head. "Don't you worry, Doctor. She's going to rest whether she likes it or not."

When the doctor had gone, Solly sat thinking. Why, why had she not told him? Is it because she didn't want the baby? Was she going to keep it? He knew he was a much older than her but he did love her.

In the beginning, he had just wanted her company, and to make sure she got away from home. But as time passed he fell in love with her, and now they were having a baby.

A couple of hours later, he went in to the bedroom to see her and she was awake. He sat on the edge of the bed and took her hand.

"How do you feel?"

"Not too bad. I think I just got really cold, and I was so tired."

"Tina, why didn't you tell me about the baby?"

"I'm sorry. I had been to the doctor's on the morning they found Rose. With one thing and another, the time never seemed to be right."

"The time is always right when it's something like this, Tina."

His manner was a bit sharp and it was so unlike him. She realised he was hurt at not being told.

"I'm sorry, I should have told you. Are you pleased?"

"Pleased, of course I'm pleased, maybe a little old to be a first time father, but yes, I'm overwhelmed. I'll take care of you Tina; our baby will want for nothing. It will have every chance possible.

"More than poor Rose had," she said, her voice breaking.

"Tina, I understand how you feel but you have to take care of yourself and the baby now. We will see justice done, don't worry. Now, you have to be strong. Rest today, and we will see how you feel tomorrow."

It took a further three days before she felt well enough to get up and start moving around.

When she did, she looked pale, and was so thin; she had eaten so little she had lost weight. As she dressed, she caught sight of herself in the mirror. Her belly was starting to swell with the baby growing inside. Her breasts were filling out and her nipples turning brown the way they do when your body is preparing for a new life.

She ran her hands over her stomach. *At all costs, I'll make sure he or she has a better childhood than I ever had.*

She finished dressing and went downstairs. She drank a cup of tea, and they went to the office together.

Lilly smiled at her when they when they walked in.

"You look a lot better than when I last saw you."

Tina smiled. "I feel better, thank you."

Solly looked at Lilly. "What do you think about me being a dad, Lilly?"

Lilly jumped up, screamed and hugged Tina. "Well done, you have to take care of yourself now."

"What about me?"

Lilly laughed. "Well congratulations to you too. But you're just the father, it's Tina that has to do all the hard work."

He laughed. "Yes, I suppose you have a point there."

Tina continued to work. Solly told her not to, but she insisted. With her body changing shape, she could no longer model clothes and had to be content with working in the office, but she did not mind. It kept her occupied and she was learning more about the business.

The day arrived for the start of the trial. The police had questioned Doreen further, and made as many enquiries as they could. But no matter what anyone said, Dougie could not provide an alibi. The case the police presented suggested that he had changed his mind about moving in with Rose and they had rowed. He had lost his temper and strangled her. He, of course, denied it all. As they sat in the court, Tina glanced over to where he sat. He had lost weight and his face looked so drawn.

The jury found him guilty and sent him to prison for life. Tina and Solly asked if they could see him before they took him away.

"I didn't do it, Tina, you have to believe me."

Tina took his hand in hers. "I believe you. I can't imagine what it's like to be locked up for something you have not done. I promise you, we will keep looking for the truth and we will visit you when we are allowed."

"Please find out anything you can. I loved Rose, I would not have harmed her."

As they left, they said they would keep in touch.

Another two months passed and Tina stopped working all together. She paid regular visits to Mrs Hirst who was always pleased to see her and always fussed over her. She told her that she looked on her as another daughter. Gordon was always pleased to see her too.

She spent her time looking after Solly, and shopping so that she had all she would need for when the baby came.

Lilly was a regular visitor and Tina suspected she was lonely. After all, she had always had Solly to keep her company. Things had changed when Tina came on the scene, but Lilly was not the jealous type and now regarded them as her extended family.

She had about a week to go before the baby was due and Solly asked her not to go too far from home. If she needed to go anywhere, she was to ring the office and either he or Lilly would take her.

Tina was stubborn and she was tired of sitting around, so she decided to go to town for some last minute things.

She had finished her shopping and was just walking past a pub called The Grapes, when a figure lurched out of the door, nearly knocking her off her feet.

She came face to face with her father. He was unshaven and stank of sweat and stale tobacco. He grabbed a hold of her arm.

"Well look who we have here. Miss high an' mighty, an' it looks like you bin givin' Jew boy his rights."

"You're disgusting. He's my husband and it's nothing to do with you."

"Yer me daughter an' yer should look after yer old man."

"You've taken from me all you're going to get."

He snarled, "We'll see, yer a slut like yer mother. Yer need bringin' down a peg er two. Next time, there won't be any mistakes."

"What do you mean?" she asked.

"Never mind, yer'll find out." He leered at her and then let his eyes fall to her swollen stomach. "Yer ripe now," he said as he licked his lips.

86

"You're disgusting. I'll have my day with you."

"Not if I have mine first." He turned and lurched off.

Tina was shaking and all she wanted to do was to be in the safety of her home. A nagging pain had started in her back, so she stopped a taxi and, within ten minutes, she was walking through her front door.

She put her shopping away and was about to make some tea when she was gripped by pain, causing her to bend and gasp for breath.

When she could move again, she picked up the phone and dialled a number. Lilly answered and she asked if Solly was there.

"No, he's out, Tina, but he won't be long. What's wrong?"

"I think the baby's coming."

"Get your case ready and stay put. I'll leave a note and be there in ten minutes."

"Thanks, Lilly." She hung up, carried her case from the bedroom, and waited for Lilly.

True to her word, Lilly was knocking at the door just ten minutes after the call.

"Come on, I'll drive you to the hospital. Solly will meet us there."

As they drove into the hospital, the pain was almost unbearable. By the time they arrived, Tina could barely stand. The nurses took her straight through to the delivery room to get her ready.

Lilly waited outside to meet Solly. He arrived and was allowed into where Tina was.

"Are you OK?"

"I will be when this is all over," she answered.

For the next fifteen hours, Tina lay in labour. Sweating, tired and in agony, and still the baby not born. Solly was getting worried. He saw how tired she was and the pain taking its toll on her.

He held her hand as yet another wave of pain took hold.

"Solly, I've had enough. I can't take any more."

He left the room and returned with a doctor. After an examination, he decided that she had had enough.

"I think we have to help her along."

"What are you going to do?"

"We will do a caesarean section; otherwise, we could lose one or both of them. Wait outside; we will come for you when we have finished."

Solly went outside and waited with Lilly.

"Don't worry," she told him. "She's a strong girl; they'll look after her.

He was tired, so only God knew how Tina was feeling.

An hour later, a nurse came from the room. She smiled at him.

"Mr Ableson, would you like to see your wife and son?"

He beamed. "A son, I have a son?"

"Yes, your wife is very tired, but you can see her for a moment."

He walked into the room and Tina already had the baby at her breast. The baby had a mass of dark curly hair.

"How are you?"

She smiled. "No wonder he didn't want to be born, he weighs nine pounds."

He kissed her. "Thank you."

The nurse came back into the room. She said they would have to leave as they wanted to take mother and baby to the ward, and she needed to rest.

"We'll be back later."

When they had gone, the nurse took Tina to the ward. She got her into bed and made sure she was comfortable. She was sore and tired, but so pleased it was all over.

Later that evening, Solly arrived carrying the biggest bouquet of flowers she had ever seen.

"They're beautiful."

"What are we going to call him?"

"Why don't we call him Maurice after your father?"

The look in his eyes told her she had made the right decision. "Are you sure?"

"Yes, I'm sure."

He stayed until the end of visiting time and, before he left, he kissed her and again, told her how proud she had made him.

The following day, her door opened slowly. Mrs Hirst and Gordon walked in.

"There yer are, luv, how yer feelin?"

"Fine, thanks, Mrs Hirst."

"Tina, don't yer think we've known each other long enough fer yer to call me Annie?"

"Yes, if you're sure."

"Course I am. Ah look," she said, looking at the baby. "He's grand, just like the grandson I would have had from our Rose."

She sniffed and her eyes filled with tears.

"You can pretend," Tina said. "Treat him as your grandson, I won't stop you."

"Yer mean it, luv, can I?"

Tina nodded.

Gordon, who had been quiet up to now, looked at Tina and smiled.

"He's a fine baby, Tina. Congratulations."

"Thanks, Gordon."

They stayed until Solly arrived, then Annie said, "We'll go now, luv. You rest an' I'll pop and see yer again."

As she left, she patted Solly's arm. "He's a big lad, he'll tek some feedin', but he's lovely. Ta'ra, luv."

Solly laughed. "She doesn't change much, does she?"

"She cares though and she'll love Maurice."

"So will I."

Solly felt uneasy when Gordon was around. He could find no fault with him and he always behaved properly towards Tina, who still couldn't see how he felt about her. Solly thought it was a man's thing. One man could tell what another man was thinking.

It took Tina another month to recover and regain her strength. Meanwhile, Solly made sure she rested and did all he could to help. Maurice was such a good baby. They only had a couple of sleepless nights and then he started sleeping straight through.

Tina and Solly had already agreed to bring him up in the Jewish faith and she was going to convert as soon as she felt strong enough.

She liked what she knew about the Jewish faith and her own religion had done nothing to protect her. Little Maurice had already had the traditional circumcision done two weeks after he had been born, and seemed to have suffered no ill effects.

The first day she took the baby out was warm and sunny. She took the short walk to Annie's house, pushing the big Silver Cross pram with pride.

She spent two hours there, and Maurice was thoroughly spoiled.

"Just look at him, Tina, he's the best bairn I've ever seen. Apart from me own, that is," and she laughed.

"You spoil him, Annie."

"Yer said I could."

"Well I had better make tracks home. I'll get him settled before Solly comes home and then we can have a bit of time together."

"You tek care, lass, come again soon."

"I will, give my love to Gordon," she said, giving her a kiss on the cheek.

She walked along the path through the park. Just as she got to the entrance, a figure stepped out in front of her. She had seen him before.

"Yer dad said you owe him."

"I owe him nothing."

"He said to give me fifty quid."

"I'll give him nothing; he's had everything he's going to get from me."

"This the Jew boy's brat?" he asked, nodding towards the pram.

"He's my son."

"Yer dad said you'd got high and mighty. Said yer needed bringin' down a peg or two."

"You can tell him, if anything happens, I'll go straight to the police."

"Yer word agin his."

Tina knew she should have gone to the police before. She couldn't prove anything now, but she wasn't going to give in to him.

"I don't owe him anything. In fact, I don't even recognise him as my father. Just tell him to leave me alone to get on with my life."

"Kids should look after their parents."

"Why, he never looked after me, and why are you delivering his message? Is he too cowardly or too drunk to deliver it himself? What's in it for you?"

"He owes me."

"You and the rest of this town. Well, it looks as if he's going to continue owing you."

"I want what I'm owed." he snarled. "If you don't pay up, then I'll have to tek it. Yer dad said yer'd oblige."

"Did he now? Well you can tell him he better not try anything, and neither had you. I know people just as you do, and they will take care of anyone who harms me."

It was all bravado, but she wasn't going to be threatened. He stomped off making threats, leaving her shaken. She managed to get home, and as soon as she was inside, she locked the door. Only then did she feel safe.

After she had been to the bathroom and washed, she made a cup of tea and then lifted the baby from his pram. She carried him to the nursery, sat and undid her dress to feed him. As he snuggled into her and suckled contentedly, she reflected on her encounter with the man in the park.

Would he ever leave her alone? Would she never be free of him? He was too idle to go out and earn a living, and he thought that she owed him something, just because he had sired her.

I suppose I could go to the police for him harassing me, she thought. *I won't tell Solly; he has looked tired lately and I don't want him to worry.*

She had told Lilly that she thought he could do with a break. Lilly agreed with her, but Solly did as he pleased.

A few days later, he came home from the office early, and he looked grey.

"What's the matter, are you ill?"

"No, don't fuss, I just have a headache. I thought that I would come home early and spend some time with my son. Is that such a bad thing?"

"No, it's good as long as you feel OK."

"You should not worry your pretty head. Get me something, a drink maybe, yes?"

"Would you like some tea?"

"Some tea and maybe a little schnapps."

"Schnapps! Solly, is everything alright?"

He smiled. "Yes, everything is fine. Today I have had a meeting with my solicitor. I have made sure you and little Maurice will be secure for the rest of your lives. So maybe I am feeling a little content, mmm? Now do I get my drink?"

She kissed him on the cheek. "Of course you do. I love you; you are a good man."

"You know Dougie is still saying he's innocent."

"I know. Is there nothing we can do? He's been in prison almost a year now."

Solly shook his head. "Not really. There is no new evidence. Nothing that points to him being innocent."

"I don't believe he killed Rose."

"Neither do I, but what can we do?"

She shook her head. "I don't know."

She went to get him another drink and they spent a quiet evening just chatting.

At nine thirty, she said, "The baby will be ready for a feed, then I'm going to bed."

"I'll go now if you don't mind, I have a little indigestion."

"Was it the meal?"

"No, I had lunch with Hilda. Every time I eat there, I get it. I keep telling her not to make the horseradish so strong with the fish, but she does."

Tina laughed. "Why have it at all then?"

"Óy! With Hilda, you cannot refuse."

He kissed her on the cheek. "I'll see you in a while."

He went upstairs and she went into the nursery to feed and change the baby. She put him in his cot, kissed him goodnight, turned down the light and went to their bedroom. Solly was already in bed. She slipped in beside him.

"How are you feeling?"

"Much better." He took her into his arms. They had not made love since the baby had been born. Now Tina felt the time was right.

When making love, what seems erotic to some people, may not appeal to others. Solly was always gentle with Tina and considerate of all her needs. He had never done anything that may offend her and made sure she got full pleasure too.

Now, he cupped her breasts. "You are still feeding Maurice, maybe you have a little to spare for me also, mmm?"

"Oh, Solly, I do love you."

He gently ran his hands over her swollen breasts, down over her now rounded belly, and she held his head like a baby's while he sucked at her nipples, tasting her milk.

This excited her beyond belief. She could not wait until he entered her, and when he did, the passion was so strong and fierce, not once did she feel threatened or afraid. Together they reached a climax then lay in each other's arms.

"Solly, I love you more than I ever thought possible."

"I love you also. You have brought me so much pleasure and I thank you."

"You have done more for me than I for you."

"You deserve it."

They slept with arms around each other and woke at seven the next morning. Tina thought it was strange that Maurice was sleeping late; he usually woke early for his feed.

She walked into the nursery and screamed.

Solly ran through; in the cot lay the baby. He was cold and blue, no sign of life. Solly touched him and guided the hysterical Tina from the room. The tears streamed down his face as he looked at his son.

He phoned the doctor and Lilly; they both arrived at the same time. After the doctor had looked at the baby, he said he had been sick during the night and it had choked him.

The doctor gave Tina a sedative, and Lilly stayed on to answer any phone calls that came.

When the doctor had gone, Solly sat in the chair opposite Lilly.

"How am I going to get through this, Lilly? How is she going to get through this?"

"You have each other and you must support one another, never blame. I don't know what else to say. Sorry is not enough. I can only offer to be here for you both."

"Thank you."

Very soon, the undertaker arrived with the rabbi. They removed the baby and the rabbi said he would see Solly later in the day. The doctor came back to check on Tina who was still asleep; he left another two tablets.

"Try to get her to take these; they will dry up her milk, if the shock hasn't done it already. She doesn't need to be reminded of the baby right now. After the funeral today, I suggest you get her away from the house, and remove all reminders of your son."

He had to do all this, yet he was grieving also. He still had to go through the funeral today. Jewish custom was they buried their dead the same day whenever possible. Tina would not be going, as the women usually stayed home.

When the doctor left, Solly said to Lilly, "I have to tell Mrs Hirst."

"Shall I do it for you?"

He shook his head. "No, she was like an adopted mother to Tina. I have to do it. I won't be long, will you stay, Lilly?"

"Of course I will."

He left the house, and as Lilly watched his dejected figure walk down the path, she thought, *Why do these things always happen to good people? Yet people like Tina's father, get away with it.*

He arrived at Annie's door and knocked.

She opened it. "Solly, come in. Are yer on yer own?"

"Yes, Annie. Tina's at home, in bed."

"Is she ill? Solly, what's wrong, yer look all in."

"Maurice is dead."

"Oh God luv us, what can I say? What can I do?" She stood with her pinny up to her face, sobbing.

"Tina fed him and put him in his cot. When she got up this morning, he was dead. Doctor thinks he was sick and choked. I need to get her out of the house, Annie. The funeral will be this afternoon, then we have to remove his things."

"So soon, Solly?"

"Yes, it has to be done today."

93

"Bring her here, I'll look after her. Poor lamb, she's suffered enough, an' you, what about you?"

"I have to be strong for her. Lilly is at the house just now. When can I bring her?"

"As soon as yer like, lad."

"I think she will sleep for the rest of the day; she won't know the funeral has taken place. I'll bring her tomorrow."

"Eh lad, don't yer think she'd want ter go ter her own babby's funeral?"

"Women don't usually go to Jewish burials."

"Well that's a strange how ter do. Still, it's now't ter do with me. Termorrow will be alright, lad, you just bring her here."

"If it's not too much trouble can I leave her here a couple of days? Then when I have things sorted, I'll take her away for a few days."

"She'll need it. She can stay here as long as she wants."

"Fine, I'll bring her in the morning."

"Tek care, lad, and I'm right sorry."

After Solly had gone, Annie sat and bawled as if it was one of her own, and that's how Gordon found her when he came in.

"Ma, what's wrong?"

"That babby, he's dead, poor mite."

She explained what Solly had told her. "He's bringin' her here termorrow."

"Can you cope, Ma?"

"Someone 'as to, she's no one else. There's that now't of a father of hers, an' he's made her life hell, an' she has all the trouble. Life's not bloody fair, our Gordon."

"No, Ma, it's not," he answered.

Solly returned home. Lilly told him Tina had woken up and had a drink, but she was still in bed. He went to the bedroom and he was just staring at the ceiling.

"Tina, my love, speak to me."

She looked at him and a tear ran down her face. He took her into his arms and they both cried together.

"Why, Solly? Why our baby?"

"I don't know, but we have to get through these next few hours. I'm taking you to Annie's tomorrow."

"No, I have to be here."

"It's better if you're not. Annie loves you and she'll take care of you."

"What are you going to do?"

"I have things to do. Tina, the funeral has to be in a few hours, and women don't usually go.

"But he's my baby, I have to go. I have a right to be there."

Solly sighed. "If you insist, then I suppose it will be acceptable."

Tina got out of bed to dress. The black dress she wore made her appear even more fragile than she was. She went downstairs and Lilly gave her a hug. They left the house and drove to the synagogue. It was full of people Tina had never seen before. She did recognise Hilda. Gordon and Annie had also come. She went upstairs with the other women, and Solly went downstairs to where the men sat.

The rabbi started the prayers and, from her seat, she could see the tiny coffin. She never took her eyes from it throughout the service.

The tiny coffin started to slide back as red curtains parted, and the coffin slid behind. Tina felt numb. She was aware of people around her, crying. Blackness surrounded her, and she sensed she was falling. A strip of light shining and fresh air pushed through the darkness. Tina realised she was outside with Solly, Lilly, Gordon and Annie.

"Come on, lass, terday's one of the worst days of yer life, and it's over with now."

"It will never be over with, Annie," she replied.

They arrived home and Solly took Tina upstairs.

"Together we have to be strong. Tomorrow, I will sort things out, and then we'll go away for a few days. I'll be here for you, Tina, I love you."

"I love you too, but I want my baby back."

He held her in his arms and she cried once again. As she sobbed, his tears fell silently into her hair. He lay beside her and they both fell asleep. When Lilly opened the door a little while later, that's how she found them. She crept to the side of the bed and touched his arm. He woke and she put her finger to her lips.

He silently got up and made his way downstairs.

"I thought I had better wake you, Solly. You have to be at the synagogue in a little while." He was going to pick up the ashes of Little Maurice.

"Yes, yes thank you, Lilly."

He drank the tea she had made him before leaving the house.

Darkness fell and he still had not returned. She took a blanket from a cupboard and covered herself, and fell asleep.

The smell of coffee brewing woke her next morning. She got up and went into the kitchen and was surprised to see Tina, not Solly.

"I can do that, Tina, you should be resting."

"No, it's fine. I can do it. In fact I need to do it."

Lilly nodded, understanding what she meant.

"Have you packed a bag to go to Annie's?"

Tina nodded. Her eyes were vacant as if all life had gone from her body. They were on their second cup of coffee before Solly came into the kitchen.

"Would you like some coffee?" she asked him.

He shook his head. "No thank you, I'll make some tea."

He made the tea and they all sat in silence. No one asked what time he got home the night before, and no one mentioned the funeral of little Maurice. It was as if it had never happened. He sighed and stood up. "I'll take you to Annie's if you're ready?"

She nodded her head and Lilly cleared away the cups. As they were ready to leave, Lilly hugged her and said, "I'll see you later, Tina. Take care."

Solly took her case and they got into the car. She looked so small and frail. Her colour was ashen, and she looked like a panda with the black circles under her eyes. Her clothes hung from her and looked as if they would fit a woman three sizes bigger. Solly realised how thin she had become.

He wasn't looking all that great; he looked old and haggard, but he must remain strong for her.

They pulled up in front of Annie's, and before they had opened the car door, her front door swung open. Tina got out of the car and walked up the path. As she walked up to her, Annie put her big ample arms around her and guided her into the house.

"Come on, luv, I'll tek care of yer."

Gordon spoke to Solly. "Do you need any help with clearing out?"

Solly shook his head. "No, I can manage, thank you. Lilly is there to help me, but I really appreciate you asking. Look after her," he said, nodding towards Tina.

Solly followed them into the house, kissed Tina, and told her he would be back the next day.

When he had gone, Annie asked Tina if she wanted anything. She said she just wanted to rest so Annie took her upstairs and showed her the room that she could use.

As the door closed, she sat on the bed. This was the room she had shared with Rose the first night she had stayed. She lay down on the bed and sobbed.

She cried for Rose, she cried for herself, but most of all, she cried for her baby.

What had she done to deserve so much misery? She fell asleep, and when she woke again, she had a cover over her.

She washed her face and went downstairs. Annie and Gordon sat in the kitchen.

The kitchen was warm. There was a clean cloth on the table and the kettle was boiling on the range over the fire.

As she sat at the table, she said, "I don't think I was meant to be happy. I think that every time I find happiness, something will come along and spoil it."

"Nay, lass, don't say that. Yer will be happy, won't she, Gordon? We all have to have the bad times to appreciate the good ones."

"I wish I could believe you, Annie."

Gordon cleared his throat. "If there is anything I can do to help, I will. We care very much for you and we grieve with you."

"Thanks, Gordon. I hope you don't mind, but I think I'll go back to bed."

"You go along, duck, we'll see yer in the mornin'."

Tina went upstairs. She loved Annie, but she just wanted to be on her own. Tina slept fitfully and woke early next morning. When she looked at the clock she saw it was only five o' clock.

She didn't rush to get up and the time passed in a blur. The next thing she heard was Gordon knocking on her door, telling her it was eight o'clock and Solly would be here for her soon.

"Thanks, Gordon."

She dressed and went downstairs. Annie had made breakfast, but all Tina could manage was a cup of tea. She felt so distant from everything and everyone. The world seemed out of focus like a TV without an aerial.

Suddenly she was aware that Solly was asking her if she was ready to go.

Tina nodded her head. "Bye, Annie. Thanks for letting me stay. I'll contact you in a few days' time when we come back."

"You tek care now; go, get some rest. I'll see yer when yer get back."

Gordon drove them to the station, because Solly did not want to leave the car there, and he asked Gordon to bring it back for him.

Solly no longer had reservations regarding Gordon; he realised that, like Annie, he was a good friend. He also knew that he would never make advances towards Tina, while they were married.

They arrived at the station and Gordon took their bags out of the car.

"Have a rest if you can, Solly. Just let me know when you're coming back and I'll pick you up."

"Thanks very much, and thank Annie for all she has done. We'll see you in a couple of days." They shook hands and Solly and Tina walked into the station.

"Where are we going?" Tina asked.

"Whitby."

"Why Whitby?"

"It has a nice quiet country hotel. We can be on our own for a few days. We can rest before we have to go back and face the world. I love you, Tina. If I could do anything to stop the pain, I would, but I'm hurting too. I loved my son. We need this time together."

When they arrived in Whitby, they took a taxi to the hotel. The hotel was warm and welcoming and the maid showed them to their room. It was large and comfortable and had a four-poster bed.

Tina said how nice it was, and even though she was still feeling numb, she realised that life must go on. Outside her grief, the world kept turning, and she had to pull herself together.

Over the next few days, they talked, slept and cried. They walked round the historic seaside town and spent time healing. On the day they returned to Leeds, they both felt strong enough to face everyone again. Tina still looked pale, but that was to be expected.

They had contacted Gordon before they left Whitby and he was waiting at the station for them.

"Welcome back," he said as he shook Solly's hand. "Mum's made tea and she insisted that I take you back home."

"How is Annie?" asked Tina.

"Same as ever. She's had too many knocks in her life to stay down very long."

As they pulled up in front of Annie's, the door swung open and she ran out to meet them. First she hugged Tina, and then Solly. "There yer are. Come in both of yer, tea's ready."

As usual, the fire was burning and she had made a homely, hearty meal.

"You've gone to a lot of trouble, Annie. This is lovely," said Tina.

"Ta, luv, but it was no trouble. I expect yer ready for some plain cookin'. Saves yer the trouble when yer get home."

"Thanks."

"I think your Lilly 'as been lookin' out fer things at home."

Solly said, "You have all been so kind, and I can tell you, we really appreciate it."

"You were there fer me when we had that trouble, with our poor Rose. I don't ferget things like that."

They stayed another hour or so after the meal and then Solly said he thought it was time to get home. They thanked Gordon and Annie again, got into the car and drove home.

Lilly met them at the door.

"Have you been to Annie's?"

They both nodded.

"Good, everything's sorted here. There's a meal in the oven, but if you have already eaten, it will save until tomorrow."

"Thank you very much, Lilly. It was good of you."

"It's no trouble. I'll go and let you get unpacked. Get a good night's sleep and I'll see you later." She hugged them both and left.

"Would you like something to drink, Tina?"

She shook her head. "No thank you. I think I will have a shower before we go to bed."

As she went along the landing to the bathroom, she had to pass what had been Maurice's room. She could not resist opening the door.

The room was empty. It was as if it had never been a nursery.

"Oh Maurice," she cried.

She closed the door and went into the bathroom. As Tina stood under the shower, she reflected on her life so far. She'd had some good times and some bad times, and she'd had some unbearable times, and she vowed that no one ever would hurt her again. She would protect herself by never allowing anyone to get too close.

Routine returned to her life. She couldn't say it was normal, because she felt that life would never be normal again.

Solly returned to the office and she started doing the promotions. Over the next six months, she worked nonstop, but still managed to call Annie regularly.

Annie told Tina she had been to see Dougie in prison, and having spoken to him, she believed he was innocent.

"No way could that lad have killed my girl."

Tina was pleased she thought that, because initially, Annie had been so bitter towards him.

One afternoon, Tina told Solly and Lilly that she was having a quiet afternoon at home.

"You go, maybe we will go out for a little while later on, mmm?"

"That would be good. I'll see you when you get home." She left the office and went home.

She unlocked the door and she was pushed violently forward. She looked round and saw the leering face of her father.

He had been drinking, but he wasn't drunk His eyes were bloodshot and his clothes dirty.

"Well, miss high and bloody mighty. Too good fer us now are yer?"

"What do you want?"

He laughed. "Fer all yer stuck up ways, yer can't keep kids can yer?"

"What do you mean by that?"

"Well yer get rid o' one an' the other dies."

Tina felt as if someone had kicked her in the stomach.

"I'll tell yer this fer now't, if yer don't come up with some cash, it'll be more than yer friend wot dies."

"What do you know about her death?"

"More than yer think," he leered at her.

"I'm not giving you anything. I'm going to the police."

"I wouldn't do that if I were you."

"You disgust me."

He laughed. "Keep looking over yer shoulder. By the way, yer mam's gone."

"She wasn't my mother."

"No, I know that, yer real mam was a stuck up tart."

"Well, she did the right thing in leaving you didn't she? Otherwise you would have dragged her down to your level."

"Yer should have some respect fer me, miss, I'm yer father."

"Respect! What happened to my respect? The only thing I feel for you is contempt and disgust. I wish I had never known you. All my life I have wanted to please you. All I ever wanted was for you to say you were proud of me, but what I am today is of no thanks to you. You have made my life a misery. No, I don't owe you anything. Now leave, and if you so much as come near me or try to contact me again, I shall go to the police."

"Bitch," he spat. "One day, I say, one day, yer'll be sorry."

He lurched forward and went out of the door.

More than ever, Tina was sure that he had something to do with the death of Rose. She just couldn't prove it. She wished she could trace her mother and find out what really happened and why she left.

She was not going to tell Solly about her father; he would only worry and he'd had enough of that lately.

A week later, she was walking in the town when she bumped into Gordon.

"Hi, Tina, how are you?"

"I'm OK. How's Annie? I'm sorry we haven't had time to come and see her recently, especially when she's been so good to me."

"She's not been too good. You know, Tina, since our Rose has gone, some of the light's gone out of her."

"I will make time to go see her."

"That'll do her good. Have you got time for a drink?"

She nodded. "Just a quick one."

He led her into a pub and sat her down at one of the tables, then went to the bar for drinks. When he sat down again he said, "How have you really been, Tina? You look tired and a bit thin."

"You know how it is, it takes some time getting over things. You know, Gordon, I can't help feeling that my father had something to do with Rose's death, but it's being able to prove it. Meanwhile, poor Dougie is in prison, and I know he would have never hurt her."

He nodded. "I don't know why I didn't think of it before, but I may know someone who might be able to help."

"Who, is it a friend?"

"Not exactly, but he knows some very unsavoury characters and usually hears what's happening on the grapevine."

"Would you ask him, Gordon? You know there are so many people who would be grateful. Me, your mum, and poor Dougie."

"What if your dad was involved, how would you feel?"

"I would feel nothing. I never thought I could hate anyone the way I hate him. If he is involved, then the police will take care of him and he will have got what he deserves."

"Right then, I'll see what I can do."

"I must go, Gordon. Tell Annie I'll see her tomorrow."

"I will, you take care. How are you getting home?"

"I'll get a taxi."

"I'll walk you there."

Tina sat in the taxi and wondered about Annie. Knowing how it felt to lose a child, she knew how Annie must feel. At present, there was no motivation for Tina to carry on. There seemed no purpose to her getting out of bed in the mornings. All her life had been a struggle and now she was tired. She didn't want to fight any longer. She didn't have to work; she had a nice home and clothes. By most women's standards in the 70s, she was quite wealthy.

There was no meaning to her life anymore. She had been robbed of her childhood, her best friend and her baby. She had a husband who loved her, and she supposed she should be thankful, but, in her present frame of mind, she found it difficult to appreciate what she did have.

She arrived home and let herself in. Solly would not be home for another two hours.

Tina prepared tea and poured herself a glass of wine. She wasn't very hungry, but the wine would help numb the hurt.

When Solly arrived home he kissed her. "How was your day?" he asked.

"I was in town and I met Gordon. He told me Annie isn't very good and I said I would visit her tomorrow. He also told me that he knew someone who could ask around to see if there was anything that could help Dougie."

"I don't want you getting involved in anything, dear. If these people are capable of killing, then they don't care what else they have to do, do you understand my meaning, Tina? I don't want anything to happen to you."

"Don't worry, I won't get involved in anything. Are you ready to eat now?"

"Yes," then noticing only one place set he asked, "are you not eating again?"

"I'm not very hungry."

"Tina, you should eat more and maybe drink a little less?"

"I'm not very hungry these days and the wine helps. I can stop anytime I like though."

"Just look at yourself, you're all skin and bones."

"I look after you well enough don't I?" she retorted.

Solly let out a long sigh and took her into his arms. "Yes you do, very well, but can't you see how worried I am about you? I love you and I care."

"Then don't worry. I'll be fine."

The following day Tina visited Annie. She knocked at the door and Annie opened it.

"Come in, lass," she wheezed. "God luv yer, just look at yerself, all skin and bone. Are yer not feedin' yerself?"

"I'm not very hungry these days, Annie. Anyway, how are you?"

She was wheezing and she could not talk without coughing, but she said she was OK.

"I'll tell yer something, lass, that husband o' yours luvs yer, and our Gordon really cares about yer as do a lot of folk round here. Yer might not think it, but there is, an' if yer don't tek care, then yer just bein' selfish. Solly has enough ter worry 'bout without all this."

"What do you mean, Annie?"

"Oh God, yer don't know? I saw him at the clinic the other day. 'is heart's playin' up. Said he didn't want ter worry yer."

"But he could have told me. Why didn't he?"

"Why do yer think, Tina, have yer looked in the mirror lately? Tek a good look."

"Oh Annie, I've been so miserable I've ignored everyone and everything around me. I've been so wrapped up in myself. I've been so selfish."

"Nay, lass, it's normal, but yer have ter start livin' again. Life 'as ter go on."

Tina nodded. They sat by the fire drinking tea and catching up with all the gossip. Tina looked at the clock and said she must go. She wanted to be home when Solly arrived from work.

When Tina got home, she had a bath, and before she dressed, she looked at herself in the mirror. She had dark circles under her eyes; she was thin and her skin looked sallow. No wonder Solly hadn't told her that he'd been to the clinic.

Solly arrived home looking tired and drawn. Over these past months, he had looked after her and cared for her, and now it was her turn to do the same for him. She fussed over him, made him his favourite drink and gave him his meal on a tray in front of the fire.

In the following weeks, Tina did her best to try to get things back into some kind of order. She started to gain a little weight and the dark circles faded under her eyes. It took the pressure from Solly, and she looked after him and they seemed happy once more.

One evening when they were relaxing in front of the fire, someone started pounding on the door.

Solly opened it and Gordon stood in the pouring rain. "It's Mum, she's in the hospital and she's asking for Tina."

Solly nodded. "Come in out of the rain. Which hospital is she in?"

"The infirmary."

"I'll get my coat and drive you both down there."

Tina threw on her coat and Solly grabbed the car keys. It took twenty minutes to get to the hospital. When they arrived, they went to the ward where Annie was. Tina looked at the figure lying on the bed. To her, Annie had always seemed larger than life, now she looked so small.

"Tina, lass."

Tina bent down to hear what she was saying. "Let Gordon help yer when it's needed."

Tina didn't understand what she meant, but nodded her head.

The nurse came into the room and said they had to leave. They said goodbye, and Solly drove Gordon home.

As he got out of the car Solly said, "I'll collect you tomorrow and take you to the hospital, but if you need us before, call us."

"I will, thank you."

Annie died during the early hours of the following morning. Gordon called before eight o' clock to tell them.

Tina wrapped her arms around him. "I'm so sorry."

"I've been expecting it for a while. She was worn out."

Solly took him through to the kitchen. "Come and have some tea, lad. I'll help you sort things out in any way I can."

"You've done enough, Solly. You were good to us when our Rose died."

"Tina would have been in a sorry state if it hadn't been for your family. It's the least I can do."

"Thanks. Mum has been paying the Co-op each week, only sixpence, but it helps."

Solly nodded. "I'll still help."

The funeral took place three days later. The coffin came out of the house first, followed by Gordon and other members of the family, then Tina and Solly.

As a sign of respect, all the houses in the street had closed their curtains. People in the street removed hats and bowed their heads as the hearse drove by.

Annie was well known and loved in the neighbourhood. She had always been ready to help, with a cup of sugar or lending a sympathetic ear or giving a bit of advice.

She had done the odd delivery or two when the local midwife was late; yes, she would be sadly be missed.

It seemed that in no time at all, they were back at the house. The remainder of Annie's kids went to live with various aunts and uncles. Gordon still had to work, so would continue to live in the house; it was his now anyway.

He coped with the wake very well. People came to pay their respects. Eventually, only Tina and Solly remained.

"Gordon, can I do anything to help?" asked Tina.

"No, you've both done so much already. I'm very grateful. Thank you."

"I did love her, she was like a mum to me."

"You and half the neighbourhood."

If you need anything you will let me know won't you, Gordon?"

"Yes, I will, thanks."

Solly and Tina said goodbye and drove home in silence.

Once they were home Tina said, "I'm exhausted."

"So am I. Would you like a drink?"

"Yes that would be nice. I'm going to miss Annie. I will keep in touch with Gordon though."

"He's a nice lad. He should be married."

"It would be good for him, but he's shy."

They finished their drinks, and he said he was going up to bed. She noticed how tired he looked.

Solly continued going into the office each day. Tina didn't work; she had no need to, although she still needed something to occupy her mind.

One day she went to shopping in the market; she loved the atmosphere. The architecture was amazing, It was said to be one of the finest in the country.

A few years previously there had been a serious fire. They had managed to save most of the market, and the damaged section was rebuilt.

She loved to wander down the rows, the smell of fish alley and the noise on butcher's row. The outside market was full of fruit and vegetables. It had everything you needed, and if you couldn't buy it in the market, you couldn't get it anywhere.

She had just been to fish alley, and as she walked round the corner, she bumped, literally, into her younger sister, Susan.

"Well look who it is? Lady muck."

Tina looked at her sister. She was a mess. Her makeup was plastered on her face, but not thick enough to hide the dark circles and bags under her eyes. Her bleached blonde hair was straggly, and there were two inches of black roots growing through. She wore the shortest skirt Tina had ever seen, and she teetered on heels that were so high, she was in danger of breaking her ankles.

"Fancy seeing you here. Don't tell me you are here to shop. I thought that was beneath you."

"Cheeky mare," said Susan. "Anyway what you doin' here? I thought you had a maid."

"No, Susan, I work for my living, and I do all my own work."

"Well I think it's disgustin', you with all that money and our dad struggling. You should look after him."

"Why?"

"Because you owe him."

"I owe him nothing. If you feel so loyal, you support his boozing and bingo and smoking."

"He gave yer life, but then yer always have been ungrateful. Think yer too good fer the likes of us."

"That's as maybe. How is Paul?"

Susan had been married a couple of years. Her husband, Paul, worked away from home quite often, and that suited Susan. He was also a successful power lifter and had won quite a few competitions.

He earned good money and Susan spent it. When he was away, she was never at home. Tina did not understand why Paul put up with her.

"Now't ter do with you," she replied.

"I have to go," said Tina.

"I'll give yer love at home, not that it would make any difference."

Tina just nodded her head and walked away. As she turned the corner, she saw Gordon walking in her direction.

"Gordon, it's nice to see you. How are you doing?"

"I'm fine, thank you. Listen, Tina, I saw an old mate yesterday. He heard some men talking in the pub a while back about how they had done a job for an old mate. They said they had made a mistake and got the wrong one, and now this mate won't pay them until it's done properly. I don't know if this has anything to do with our Rose, but I heard them saying they had to meet this other bloke."

"When?"

"Tonight. I'm going with a friend to the pub and see what I can find out."

"I'll meet you."

"No you won't. It will look suspicious. Anyway, decent women don't go into pubs like this one."

"Thanks, Gordon, please be careful."

"I will, but you don't have to thank me. It was my sister they killed."

He smiled. "I'll be in touch if I find anything out." He then walked away.

When she got home she told Solly about her meeting Gordon.

"I hope he does find something out. I feel sorry for Dougie being locked up for something he didn't do."

Tina agreed and then said, "Oh, and I bumped into Susan."

"Why don't you ask her here sometime?"

"Because if you saw the state of her when she goes out, you would cross to the other side of the street. You would think she was going to proposition you."

"Oh, it's like that is it?"

"Yes, I've told you about her before. I don't know why I'm so different. What a family I have. I don't know why you ever bothered with me in the first place."

"Because I liked what I saw and I saw the goodness in you."

"I am so ashamed of my family. They have done nothing for me."

Solly walked over to her and took her into his arms and nuzzled her neck.

"You know how much I love you and I think you're a good person. You know what they say about being the black sheep of the family. Well all your family are the black ones and you are the white one."

"I still can't understand why I'm so different."

"Well you are. Now let's go to bed, it's been a long time since I last showed you how much I love you."

They went to bed and made love; he was always kind and gentle with her. Later, they slept with arms around each other and Tina felt warm and safe.

Two days later Gordon called to see them.

"I hope I'm not disturbing you. I just thought you would like to know. I went to the pub to see what was going on, and these two fellows I told you about, they met someone all right. Tina, it was your dad."

Her face went white.

"From the conversation I heard, it seems they were meant to get rid of *you*. They didn't know it was our Rose who was there that night."

"Let's go to the police now," she said.

"I don't know if it will be enough—we have no evidence—only what I heard, and we can't prove it. It's only hearsay."

"But we have to do something. Your sister and my best friend is dead, and an innocent man is in jail."

Solly said, "Look, I have a good friend on the police force. Let me have a word with him and see what he suggests? Gordon, I'm forgetting my manners, would you like a drink?"

"Yes, please."

Over their drinks, they speculated as to what they could do. Then Gordon got up to leave.

"Thanks for the drink. I'm sorry I've taken up your time."

"No problem, I'll keep you informed."

Gordon shook Solly's hand and kissed Tina on the cheek. Not for the first time, did Solly see the love in Gordon's eyes when he looked at her. He knew Tina only thought of him as a friend and he admired Gordon for the way he kept his feelings in check. He only visited when it was necessary and he was never intrusive.

Next day Solly came home and told Tina he had invited someone for supper.

"Who?"

"My friend Dan. Remember last night I told you he was in the police force?"

"Have you mentioned anything to him yet?"

"Not yet, all I told him was that I wanted a bit of advice on something. He was at a loose end so I invited him round."

"Good, what time is he coming?"

"About six thirty."

Tina got busy making something for their guest to eat. Sometimes, she and Solly only had a sandwich, but she thought she had better make an effort. After all, she had never met this Dan.

At six thirty on the dot, the doorbell rang. Solly opened the door and brought his friend in.

Dan was a large man, but not overweight. He was about fifty-five years old, and his hair was greying at the temples. His eyes were steely blue and when he smiled, they twinkled. He shook hands with Tina, and she could feel the strength and the power of him.

"Nice to meet you," he told her. "Solly's talked about you a lot."

"I hope he's not told you everything?" She laughed nervously.

Solly took his coat and then took him into the lounge and poured drinks.

"How long will supper be?" he asked Tina.

"About twenty minutes."

"Would you like a drink also?"

"No thanks, you two catch up on old times. I'll be in the kitchen."

Tina went through to see how the food was doing. She liked Dan but felt uneasy. She didn't know why; she had done nothing wrong.

She served the food and called them to the table. While eating, there was only small talk between them. Then Dan said, "Solly has told me something of the problem you have. At this stage, there's not much I can say to you except that we are aware of certain activities going on. If the two men in question are the ones I think, then we are keeping an eye on them. There's all sorts going on at the moment, and we need as much proof as possible."

Tina nodded.

"What I will say is this, how will you feel if your father is involved? I have to remain detached. Solly is my friend and so are you I hope, but it could make things a little awkward."

"I don't care if my father is involved. I hope he gets the punishment he deserves. I don't regard him as my father anyway."

"OK, things will start happening very soon I think."

For the remainder of his visit, they had a few drinks and played cards, until Dan looked at his watch.

"Time I made tracks home. Goodnight, both of you. I'll be in touch."

Two weeks later, Solly thought it would be good for them to get away from it all and take a holiday.

"Where would you like to go?" he asked her.

"Portugal. Do you remember I went on that assignment just after I started working for you?"

"Vaguely."

"I would like to go back and see more of the place."

"OK. I'll book for us to go in two weeks' time. Can you be ready by then?"

"Just try and stop me. I can't wait. It seems so long since we had any real time together."

The next day he came home and told her he had arranged everything for two weeks' time.

"Why don't you go shopping and get some pretty holiday clothes?" he suggested.

"Thank you, I will."

The idea of the holiday filled her with excitement.

She was lonely; she was always on her own these days. She had no friends her own age to have coffee with or have a girlie day out shopping. She was constantly in the company of older people. The only person near her age was Gordon, and he worked and she was married. It would not be right to spend time alone with him. Even poor Annie had gone.

Over the following days, she shopped, packed and made sure she and Solly had everything they would need for their holiday.

The day before they went away, she met Gordon. He was just coming out of a shop that she was going into.

"Tina, you look good. How you doing?"

"Fine, how about you?"

"I'm OK."

"Have you got yourself a girlfriend yet?"

"I haven't met the right person."

"Gordon, will you come for a drink with me?"

"Yes, I'd love to. Where do you want to go?"

"I want wine not coffee, so I'll leave it up to you."

They walked down the road and stopped in front of Yates Wine Lodge.

"I think this will suit you," he said.

He bought the drinks, and when they had sat down, she said, "We're going to Portugal tomorrow."

"That's good, you deserve a break."

"Gordon, do you know I have no other friends my own age. Everyone I know apart from you is older than me. Sometimes I feel so lonely. I miss Rose."

"I miss her too. I only have my work mates. If Solly doesn't mind, maybe we can meet for a drink now and again."

"Thanks, Gordon, I'd like that. I'm sure he wouldn't mind."

They finished their drinks and then he said he had to go. "I hope you enjoy your holiday. Take care; give my regards to Solly."

"I will, and thank you again. We'll see you when we get back."

The following morning they were up early, and after breakfast, they loaded the car and left for the airport. They would leave the car there so that it would be easier for them to get home when they returned.

They checked in their luggage, and before they knew it, they were on the plane in the air. The flight was three hours long and it passed quickly. By the time they had their meal and things cleared away, it was almost time for them to land in Portugal. When they landed, they collected their luggage and boarded a bus outside that would take them to the car hire office.

They had booked to stay in Ferragudo, the same fishing village Tina and Rose had stayed in previously. They arrived and found the hotel. When they had unpacked, they went for a walk. Very little had changed and Tina pointed out certain places she had been with Rose. Jamie and his fish bar was still there, and Tina introduced Solly to him. He remembered her and asked if her friend had come with them. There was a solemn moment when she told them that Rose was dead.

Tina and Solly spent the days exploring. They visited Esteril and Lago, and travelled over the border and had two days in Gibraltar. The rest of the time they just relaxed on the beach.

For the first time in a long while, Tina felt rested and well. She felt that she could at last get her life back on the right track

She loved the time she had with Solly and it drew them closer than ever, and even though he seemed to be aging before her eyes, he was still as loving and as attentive as always.

They took long walks and each night he would make love to her. She loved these times, as she never imagined she would be like this with a man after what she had gone through.

All too soon, the holiday was at an end. They returned to England looking well and tanned. They decided to stay over in Manchester for the night and travel home the following day.

When they arrived home, Dan had left a message asking them to contact him.

Solly would call him the following day, when he was alone in the office.

"Hi, Dan, I got your message."

"Solly, it's nice to hear from you. Have you had a good holiday?"

"Yes, yes, it was good. I think the break was good for Tina. She was ready for it. What's new?"

"You remember I told you we had been watching a certain party. Well we have arrested two undesirables for burglary and selling stolen goods. We have enough evidence to put them away for a long time. When we told them, they said they had some information regarding a murder and asked for a deal."

"So what happens now?"

"Solly, I can't say any more just now and not on the phone. Give me a couple of days and I will get back to you. By the way, I don't have to tell you not to say anything to Tina, do I?"

"Óy, Óy Óy, Danny boy, you should know me better than that."

"Yes, but Tina is your wife, and these are different circumstances."

"Don't worry, I won't tell her anything, but she has a right to know."

"I know, but I do' want to worry her. When I find out all the facts, we will get together again. I must go now. Cheerio."

"Yes, you take care; see you soon."

As he sat thinking over what Dan had said, Lilly came in the office with a cup of coffee. She looked tired.

"Thanks, Lilly, when did you last have a holiday?"

"I can't remember. Anyway, why would I need a holiday?"

"Because you look tired, why don't you go stay with that friend of yours in Whitby? Tina will come into the office."

"That's a good idea, I'll give him a call. You know, I never think about taking a break, but now you mention it, it sounds nice."

He nodded his head. "Why not, you work hard."

A little later Lilly came back in the office.

"I called my friend, and I can go anytime."

"Good, go this weekend."

"Are you sure?"

He held up his hand. "Would I say to go, if I wasn't sure? Go, Lilly, shoo, enjoy yourself."

"Thank you very much. I'll leave everything done for Tina."

While Solly and Tina were having dinner he said, "Lilly is going to stay with a friend in Whitby this weekend. Would you mind covering the office for a few days? It's a long time since she took a break."

"I don't mind at all. It would make a nice change, and besides, I will be able to keep my eye on you."

"Why would you want to do that?"

"To make sure you eat properly and not smoke too much."

"Óy, Óy, women."

That weekend Lilly went away, and on Monday morning, Tina and Solly drove to the office together. By Wednesday, they had fallen into a nice routine. Solly took care of his usual business and Tina kept the office side going.

One afternoon she had gone out to the bank and the phone in the office rang. Solly answered and he heard Dan on the line.

"Solly, can you meet me for a drink somewhere? I have some news."
He said he could. They arranged a time and a place and then Solly hung up.
When Tina got back from the bank Solly already had his coat on.
"I have to go out for an appointment, Tina."
"Where? There's nothing in the diary."
"I forgot to put it in and I've just had a call to remind me."
"OK, see you soon." Tina knew it was unlike him or Lilly to forget to put things in the diary. They were both very meticulous when it came to noting appointments.

While he was out, Tina had her own lunch and then sorted out the wages. They had quite a few people working for them now, both in promotions and advertising.

Two hours later Solly returned.
"Everything OK?" he asked.
"Yes, I have done the wages."
"Good, good. Do we have anything else pressing today?"
"No, it's all up to date, why?"
"Let's lock up and take a half day off."
"We can't do that."
"Why not?"
"The boss won't like it."
"I am the boss. Come on, get your coat."
They gathered their things, locked the office and went home.

"Let's have a drink, and go out tonight," he said.
"That sounds good. Where shall we go?"
"I'll think of somewhere. Now come and talk to me while I take a bath."
Tina sat in the chair in the bathroom and looked at him. He was aging, he had put on a little weight, but he was still attractive in a way. He still looked distinguished, and he was still a very virile man. She loved him.

"I met Dan this afternoon. They have arrested two men for a string of crimes, house breaking, burglary and selling stolen goods. They have asked for lighter sentences in exchange for information. It seems they have named a man who killed someone for someone else."
"Who did they kill?"
"Rose."
Tina broke out in a cold sweat.
Solly carried on, "The thing is, they killed the wrong person."

"They should have killed me, shouldn't they?"

Solly nodded. "They think your dad's involved. So from now on, I don't want you to be alone until all this is cleared up. I don't want anything to happen to you. We must make sure someone is with you wherever you are. Yes?"

"Yes, Solly. I just can't take all this in."

Over the next week, they travelled to the office together and home. She stopped going to the bank and she was never left on her own.

One good thing came out of all this and that was, if it was proven that this man had killed Rose, Dougie would be released. He had served two years for something he had not done.

"You know, Solly, when Dougie is released, what's he going to do? Even though he's innocent, who is going to employ him?"

"I will."

"You, but what can he do?"

"I have been thinking of expanding into overseas promotions. I could train him and he could manage that side of things."

Over the next two weeks, the newspapers reported the crime and the trial. Solly went to the court every day, but insisted Tina stay with Lilly.

At the trial, the two men named the man who had killed Rose, but refused to name who had hired him.

They looked shocked when they both got life sentences. As they left from the court, they shouted that this was not the deal they had been promised.

Outside the court, Solly met Dan. "That was good, Solly."

"Yes it was. What about Dougie?"

"He's being released in the morning."

"Will he get compensation?"

"Certainly. You know we still think Albert was involved."

"Albert? You mean Tina's dad."

"Yes."

"But where would he get the money from?"

He knows a lot of shady characters. Has Tina given him any money?"

"I don't know. She may have given him some to keep him away from her. I really have no idea. I have to get back to the office, Dan. Keep in touch."

"I will. See you later. Give my regards to Tina."

Tina was waiting for him when he got back to the office.

"Dougie is being released from prison tomorrow. Do you want to come with me when I pick him up?"

"Yes I do. Where will he stay?"

"He could stay with us until he gets settled. Is that OK with you?"

"Yes, we have no choice. He has nowhere to go and no money."

The following morning Solly said he was going to the office, but he would come back at ten thirty to pick her up. He also told her to make sure she kept the door locked.

Tina made sure the spare room was ready for Dougie before she had a shower. It was a long time since she had last seen him, and she wondered if his spell in prison had changed him.

Being in prison was bad enough, but being there when you were innocent, she could only imagine what it was like.

At ten thirty sharp, Solly was back. "Are you ready?"

She nodded and they left to go to the prison.

They waited outside the prison gates for about twenty minutes. Then the gates opened, and Dougie walked out. His possessions were wrapped in a brown paper parcel tucked under his arm. He looked thin but otherwise well.

He looked around him and took a deep breath, taking in the fresh air.

Solly and Tina got out of the car and walked over to where he stood.

"Dougie, glad to see you," said Solly, holding out his hand.

He nodded his head. "Good to see you too."

"Have you anywhere to go?" asked Tina.

"No. I could try and get a room somewhere."

"Come and stay with us until you get sorted."

"Thank you both. All I want to do now is have a bath and to get out of these clothes. I can smell this place on them and I want to forget I was ever here."

They arrived home and Tina showed Dougie his room. "Is it all right with you if I have a bath now?"

"Do whatever you want. I'll make some tea and a bite to eat. Come down when you're ready." She went downstairs so he could have some privacy.

Tina and Solly were in the kitchen drinking tea when Dougie appeared.

"I feel better now. You have no idea what it's like having to shower in front of twenty blokes. You are never on your own."

"Sit down, I'll get you a drink. I'm glad you're out, Dougie."

"We have been told that you will get some compensation."

"Yes I know, and when it comes through, I'm leaving this place. I'm going as far away from here as I can get."

"Don't do that."

"Why? I have no ties here now. I've had enough."

"Dougie, I have a proposition to put to you that could benefit us both. The office is doing well, but things are changing in the modelling world. For us, it's slow. I think the big guns with the money are getting all the contracts. Promotions and advertising are on the way up and we are getting busy with that side of things.

"I am thinking of opening another office in Southampton and opening up links across the water. I need someone to manage it. How about you doing it, Dougie?"

"I don't want charity, and anyway, what do I know about the business?"

"This isn't charity. I can train you, and I am giving you the means to be able to leave Leeds with a paid job, and it saves me interviewing people I don't know."

"You don't know me all that well."

I think I know enough to trust you, and I also know you will be able to manage the office and do it well. Think about it, Dougie. Let me know what you have decided tomorrow."

"I'll think about it."

"If you decide to do this, you can come into the office with me and see how things work. What have you got to lose?"

"That's true. Thank you very much for your offer, Solly."

"Don't forget, I'm also helping myself. You will earn your wages, make no mistake about that, but running the office will take a lot of doing."

The rest of the day they spent taking Dougie to get things he needed. When they had all eaten, they were tired and decided to go to bed early.

Next morning at breakfast, Dougie told Solly he would take him up on his offer.

"I only hope I can do justice to the faith you have in me," he said.

Solly nodded. "You'll be fine."

Solly took Dougie under his wing, and for the next two weeks, took him into the office every day and trained him up in the basics he would need to know to get the new office off the ground.

"Don't forget, if you are unsure about anything, all you have to do is pick up the telephone and ask."

At the end of the two weeks, Solly gave Dougie an envelope.

"What's this?"

"Your pay for two weeks' work."

"I told you, I don't need charity."

"And you've not been given it. Wherever you go, even if you're training, you get paid. There's a little extra for clothes and personal things you will need. If you feel the need, you can pay me back once you get on your feet. Is that fair?"

"Thanks, I don't know what I would have done without you and Tina."

"Do it by showing me I have made the right decision. Now enjoy the weekend, because on Monday we will be going to Southampton for a couple of days to look at some offices. Then we'll come back here and get things rolling."

"OK," he said.

Over the weekend, Dougie shopped, looked up an old friend of his and spent time going over plans with Solly.

On Monday morning, Solly took Tina to the office. During the day, she would stay there with Lilly, and she would see Tina home and make sure she locked the door and was safe.

As he left her he said, "I'll see you Wednesday. Take care and look out for yourself. Make sure you are not on your own, and when you go home, make sure all the windows and doors are locked."

"I will. Don't worry, I have Lilly here."

Even though the office was busy, Tina and Lilly still managed to chatter throughout the morning.

"It's good of Solly to give Dougie this chance," Lilly said.

"Yes, but he's had it a bit rough hasn't he?"

"Yes, it must be a nightmare being locked up for something you didn't do. By the way, I'll be going to Whitby again this coming weekend."

"Oh, any special reason?"

Tina looked at Lilly and saw that she was blushing.

"Well, I have a friend there as you know. I met him when I was there on holiday and we got along very well. We like the same things. We both like reading books, and walking and the same kind of food. He asked if I would be going again. So I have decided to go again this weekend."

"Good for you, you deserve it."

"I don't know, Tina, I'm a bit long in the tooth for romance. But I do like his company, and I do get lonely sometimes."

"You are welcome to visit us anytime you feel like that, but why not have some male company. I hope it goes well for you, Lilly."

They worked on for the rest of the day. When they were closing up the office Lilly said, "Why don't you and I eat together seeing as we are both alone?"

"Great, let's go into town and take our pick."

They chose to have a Chinese meal. When they had finished Lilly said, "I'll make sure you get home safely."

Tina laughed. "Who's going to make sure you get home? Why don't we both walk to the taxi rank. That way, we'll both be safe."

At the taxi rank, they got into separate taxis. As Tina settled back in the car, she wondered how Solly and Dougie were getting on. No doubt he would ring her when she got home.

The car pulled up outside her house. She paid the driver and let herself in. She thought she heard a noise come from the kitchen, but when she looked, she could not see anything. She walked into the living room and switched on the light, and decided to have a glass of wine before she went to bed.

A movement caught her eye and she turned. She saw her father stood in the corner of the room.

"How did you get in?"

"You should lock yer windows better."

He had been drinking and his clothes were as filthy as the last time she had seen him.

"You better go, Solly will be home soon."

He laughed. "Don't lie. Jew boy's not home ternight, I checked."

"What do you want?"

"You fer a start."

"If you come near me, I'll start screaming."

He took a step nearer, but before Tina could scream, he clamped a dirty, smelly hand over her mouth. With his other hand, he landed a blow to the side of her face, and all she was aware of was pain and a blackness descending upon her.

Vaguely she felt the tugging at her clothes and a searing pain in her breast. She was unable to do anything other than moan. Then she blacked out completely.

Tina was semi-conscious and there was a pungent smell, but she didn't know what it was.

She felt gentle hands holding her and bright lights and voices.

"Can you hear me, Mrs Ableson?" someone was asking. She tried to open her eyes, but the pain was so intense.

She felt a sting in her arm and nothing more. When she woke again, she managed to focus her eyes. A doctor and nurse stood at the side of her.

"Tina, you're in hospital. Your husband is outside, do you feel up to seeing him?"

She nodded her head.

In seconds, Solly was at her side taking a hold of her hand.

"Tina, thank goodness you've come round. Who was it?"

"My father."

"How did he get in?"

"I don't know. He said the windows were open, but I know I closed them. How did I get here?" she asked.

"A passing neighbour saw the door wide open and she called the police and they found you on the floor."

"How come you're here?"

"I called home and didn't get an answer. I called Lilly and she told me you had been for a meal together and had gone home in separate cabs. I thought it strange and called the neighbour. She told me what had happened and I came straight home.

"Tina, the police are waiting outside. You don't have to speak to them now if you are not up to it. But they've been here ever since you were brought in."

"I'll speak to them. Oh Solly, I will never be free of him. For the longest time I've tried to be free. Every time I think I've escaped he finds me. He's like something out of the gutter, and he makes me feel that way too. So many times I have been dragged down and I wonder if it's all worth it."

"It is, Tina, believe me, it is. You are better than all your family put together. You have strived to make something of yourself. I saw that, that's why I employed you. I could see how hungry you were to make something of yourself. You had pride too. You have to tell the police everything. I suspect he's wanted for other things and this is your chance."

Her tears fell onto the pillow and Solly wiped them away. "I'll send them away if you want me to."

"No," she said. "It has to be done sometime, and you're right, I have to stop his evilness."

Solly left the room and returned with a policeman and woman. The policewoman took hold of her hand. "My name is Emily. If you want to talk to me on our own, it's OK. I'll help all I can."

Tina nodded. She noticed Emily was only a year or so older than she was. So young to have such a responsible job, she thought.

Emily started by asking Tina a few questions. Before long, Tina was telling her all that had happened and much more about her life. The only other person she had ever said anything to was Rose.

"I don't want everyone to know, only what happened last night."

Emily nodded. "Don't worry. Get some rest now and I'll come back tomorrow."

"I have nothing else to tell you."

"Maybe not, but can I come and see you as a friend?"

Tina nodded, feeling the pain in her head. "That would be nice."

After she had gone, Solly came back into the room. "The nurse said you have to rest. So I'll come back later to see you."

He kissed her and left.

Tina closed her eyes and was soon asleep. Solly did visit later on, but Tina was not aware of his visit as she slept through the night. The bright lights woke her and another day in the hospital had begun.

The first thing she focused on was the beautiful flowers in the room. The nurse came and asked her if she would like to try and get to the bathroom. Tina sat on the edge of the bed. Her head thumped and it was painful for her to move.

The nurse picked up her toilet things and change of nightwear brought in by Solly, and slowly they walked to the bathroom that was just a few feet away from her bed. Tina sat on a stool at the side of the bath.

"I can manage on my own, thank you."

"Are you sure?"

Tina smiled. "I'll call if I need you."

"Ring the bell when you are ready to go back to bed. Sooner if you feel ill."

Tina nodded and watched the water fill the bath. She stood up and removed her nightgown. She looked at herself in the mirror. One side of her face was an angry red turning slightly blue; one of her eyes was almost shut. On one of her breasts was an ugly bruise, caused by a bite. She could not see the other breast, because it had a dressing on. She would have to be careful she did not get it wet.

The water was hot, but she thought it might wash away the dirt she was feeling.

Tina sat in the bath and thought. She had never been a vindictive or violent person, but at this moment, she wished her father dead. Since she realised the abuse she suffered was not normal, she had tried to rid herself of him, but he kept coming back. What about her stepmother, she must have known what was happening, unless she didn't wanted to know.

Tina thought that she fell into the category of women who chose to ignore such things as long as she was left alone; she wouldn't have believed Tina if she had told her.

She let the water cover over her body and winced as it stung, but then it soothed. She did not know how long she sat in the bath, but was suddenly aware that the water had gone cold. She pulled the plug and watched the water drain away. As she eased herself out of the bath, her body felt heavy. She put on clean pyjamas and brushed her hair, careful not to catch the side of her face.

The nurse came back and helped her back to bed.

"Do you feel better? I'm sorry, of course you don't."

When Tina got back to her bed, the nurse asked if she would like some breakfast.

"No thanks, just tea I think."

As the nurse walked away Tina called, "Nurse?"

The nurse turned. "Yes?"

"Thank you."

She smiled. "I'll get your tea."

"What's your name?"

"Joanne, but everyone calls me Jo."

"Thanks, Jo."

"It's alright, Mrs Ableson."

"Call me Tina."

"We're not allowed to use first names."

"No one is around."

Jo smiled and Tina smiled back, the way two teenagers would when sharing a secret.

"I must go. I'll see you later."

Tina was drinking the tea when the door opened, and the doctor walked in.

"Good morning, just came to see how you are mending."

He looked at her face and the side of her head. "May I see your top?"

The nurse who was with him, helped her to pull down the top of her nightdress.

"The bite scar will heal. The breast with the dressing on has stitches round the nipple. The other bruising will fade in time. But I want you to rest as much as you can, and hope that all this hasn't affected your baby."

"Baby. What baby?"

"You're three months pregnant, Mrs Ableson. Didn't you know?"

Tina shook her head.

"Well you are. Congratulations."

The nurse helped her to cover up again. "I'll call and see you later," he said and left the room.

Tina wrapped her arms round her body. Another baby. She closed her eyes and prayed.

When this baby is born, she will make sure that this time, nothing would go wrong. She must have fallen for the baby while they were on holiday. She felt so excited. Now she had something to look forward to, and she couldn't wait to tell Solly. She wondered if he would be as pleased as she was.

He was getting on in age, maybe wouldn't want another baby around, but Tina didn't care. For as much as she loved Solly, now this baby was more important.

She lay back against the pillows and must have fallen asleep. When she woke, she could smell food. The door opened and Jo walked in.

"You've had a good sleep."

"What time is it?"

"Noon, would you like some lunch?"

Tina shook her head. "No thanks."

"You should eat, Tina. Have some soup."

"OK." She knew she would have to eat. She had to start feeding the life that was growing inside her.

She had the soup and realised that she had been hungry; after all, it was over forty-eight hours since last she had eaten anything.

Jo came back to take away her things. "I'm going off duty soon and going into town, is there anything you need?"

"No thanks, Jo, Solly will be in soon. He'll be bringing anything I need, but thank you."

"OK, I'll be back around four this afternoon."

Tina lay back, and again, her thoughts turned to the baby she was carrying. At least something good had come out of this mess, but she could have so easily lost it. If that had happened again, it would have been the fault of her father.

Solly arrived and kissed her. "How are you feeling?"

"I hurt," she told him.

"The police have arrested your father. Of course, he's denying it. He told them you were blaming him to get back at him."

"Solly, you know better than that. I have no reason to lie."

"I know that, love. I'll tell you one thing, if the police don't lock him up, I'll get him one way or another."

"You don't want to get into trouble on his account, he's not worth it. Solly, what would you say if we had another baby?"

"If having another baby will make you happy, then that's all I want for you. But I think you should wait until you are stronger."

"It's too late for that," she smiled, "I'm three months pregnant. It must have happened when we were in Portugal."

"Well, I must be fitter than I thought. Do you realise that you could have lost it?"

"Yes."

"I think we ought to tell the police. What he did was bad enough, but with you being pregnant, he must not be allowed to get away with it."

"You're right, Solly, but I'm so afraid of having to face him in court."

"He can't hurt you anymore, love, I'll see to that."

He spent the next two hours telling her about the office he had found in Southampton, and he thought Dougie would do very well.

"He's picked things up quickly. We have to go back down there next week and we have to find him somewhere to live. Would you like to come with us, I'm not happy leaving you on your own?"

"I'll think about it."

Shortly after he had gone, Emily, the young policewoman, turned up.

"How are you feeling?"

"A bit sore and bruised, but otherwise OK."

"I would feel like that if it had been me in your place."

"Emily, we are going to have a baby."

"You are."

"Yes, the doctor told me today. I'm three months pregnant."

"Can I put that in your statement? He won't get away with this, Tina, we have been after him for a long time."

They chatted a while longer and then she left so Tina could get some rest.

Over the next week, Tina grew stronger, and even though her bruises faded a little, they were still visible. The doctors had done a good job at repairing her torn nipple, but the mental scars would take a little longer to heal. The baby might help to heal the scars on the surface. The ones deep down may never heal.

She didn't get out of hospital in time to go to Southampton with Solly, but at least Solly knew she would be cared for.

Solly and Dougie set up the office and found somewhere for Dougie to live. When Solly was leaving, he told Dougie to remember that he was only a telephone call away.

On the day Tina was leaving the hospital, Jo asked if she could visit her as a friend from time to time.

Tin said she would be delighted to have her as a friend. Now she would have a friend who was nearer her own age.

Tina got stronger and her bruises faded. Jo had visited her a few times. Tina told her all about Rose, and how they had been closer than sisters.

"It must have been awful to lose her like that."

"It was. Why haven't you struck up a friendship with any of the girls you work with?" asked Tina.

"Because I feel different from them. They all come from good homes, have good educations; they don't really need to work but see nursing as something worthwhile to do. Me, I got in by taking the entrance exam. I don't visit home often, because when I do, and because I am the only one working, they expect me to give them money, and I don't get paid that much."

Tina nodded, understanding her more than she knew. Maybe that's why they had clicked so well.

It took six weeks for the case to come to court. The day the trial started, Tina felt very nervous about going.

Her father stood in the dock looking a bit cleaner than when she had last seen him, and of course, he was sober, but the sight of him still repulsed her. The usher read out the charges.

He pleaded not guilty and stood leering at her. Her stepmother must have gone back to him, because she was in court with Tina's sister. Upon seeing her, her stepmother walked over to her.

"Yer evil you are. Accusin' yer own father of doin' that ter yer, how could yer? Miss high an' mighty, that's you, yer was always stuck up. Well I'll tell yer this, if he goes down, watch yer back."

A policeman came over and led her back to her seat with a warning that she would have to leave the court if she did not behave herself.

At the end of that first day, Tina was exhausted.

On the second day, the police gave evidence. They said in addition to the present charges, they were also investigating that he may have had something to do with the murder of Rose. They had been told that it should have been Tina but someone had made a mistake and killed the wrong one.

The judge looked at her father. "What have you to say to the accusations?"

"Yer won't pin that on me, I wouldn't have made the mistake."

There was people shouting in the court and the judge called for order.

On the third day, Tina had to give evidence. She told the court about the time he used to come to her bedroom, and the times they had met since she had left home.

"Liar," shouted her stepmother, "yer a bloody liar."

The judge banged his gavel. "Quiet in court."

On day four, the jury had to decide his fate. They were out of court just two hours then came back.

The judge asked him to stand.

"How do you find the accused?" asked the judge.

The spokesman replied, "Guilty."

Her father stood in the dock, still leering at her.

"You have been found guilty of all charges brought before me. I have no doubt I will see you in this court again once the police have completed further investigations, but for the charges now, I sentence you to eight years in prison, and let me tell you this, if it was in my power to give you more I would do so. You are evil and depraved. To do what you have done to anyone is unthinkable, but what you have done to your own daughter, leaves me at a loss for words. Take him away."

Only then did the smile leave his face as the guard took him out of the court.

As Tina left the court, her stepmother stepped in front of her, blocking her way.

"I hope you an' that brat yer carryin' have the worst luck in the world. He looked after yer when that slut of a mother left, why I don't know, cos I never wanted yer."

As she walked away, her sister passed her. "Yer deserve all yer get," was all she said.

Tina and Solly travelled home in silence. When they got in, Lilly was there. She looked at Tina, who even now, pregnant, was pathetically thin, and her face ashen.

"I've made you a meal. It's in the oven for whenever you're ready."

Tina nodded. "Thank you, Lilly. I don't know what we'd do without you."

"It's what friends are for. Now you're home, I'll get off."

Solly walked her to the door. "Get her to rest," she told him.

"I will and thanks again."

When he walked back into the room, Tina was in a chair, just staring into the fire.

"Are you alright, Tina, love?"

She nodded. "Is it really over, Solly?"

"Yes it is. Now why don't you go and have a lie down before dinner?"

"What about you?"

"Oh, I have some paperwork to do. I'll call you in an hour. Go on, rest. Think of the baby."

Tina went upstairs. Here she was, twenty-three, and she felt like an old woman. She lay down on the bed and fell asleep.

She woke when Solly brought her some tea.

"What time is it?"

"Eight o' clock."

"I've been asleep for four hours. Why didn't you wake me up?"

"Because you needed to sleep. Now drink this tea, you will feel better."

"I love you. You have been so good to me."

"Of course I'm good to you. I have loved you from the first time I saw you."

"Not many would take me on with all the problems I have had."

"But I did, and before I took you on, I knew you had problems."

"I do love you."

Over the next two months, Jo became a regular visitor, and she and Tina struck up a great friendship.

They went out together shopping, for walks and even to the cinema when Solly didn't want to go. Tina realised just how lonely she had been. She had Lilly, but she was like a mother figure to Tina.

Lilly spent a lot of time in Whitby these days. She, too, had struck up a friendship with her friend's neighbour. Tina thought it was more than friendship, as Lilly was talking about taking early retirement and moving over there permanently.

Dougie was proving himself worthwhile. He was doing well with the office in Southampton. He made lots of overseas contacts and got some very lucrative contracts. The books were all in order and he had even hired a secretary. Everything was running as it should be and Solly was pleased his judgement had been right.

Dougie let nothing slide. Solly could go to the Southampton office without prior notice and he would find everything in order, and Dougie was always pleased to see him.

The police now had evidence that her father had indeed been behind the murder of Rose. It transpired that he had called in a favour from someone, and Tina was the target. The mistake was because this person had never seen Tina, and poor Rose had been in the wrong place at the wrong time.

Her father had been to court yet again, but this time Tina had not been required to attend.

Gordon would turn up from time to time. Tina was always pleased to see him and regarded him as her other true friend. Nothing was happening in his life. He still lived in Annie's house; he still worked at the same place he always had, and he seemed very set in his ways. When he met Jo, they seemed to get on very well, but she didn't know if anything would come of it.

After one visit when Jo was there, they'd had a good afternoon and some fun. Jo said she had to go as she was on duty early the next day.

"I'll come with you to make sure you get home safe," said Gordon. It became a regular thing from then on.

One evening when they had gone, Solly said, "Is there a romance in the making there?"

"I'm not sure," she replied. "I like Jo and it would be good for Gordon."

"Well he's not badly placed, he has money in the bank and his own house. Anyway, it's about time he got someone and settled down. By the way, Lilly wants to move to Whitby."

"When?"

"I don't know, but she has mentioned that I start looking for her replacement. She said she would stay until I found someone who could do the job well."

"I could do it."

He stood up and walked over to her. "Yes you could, love, but I don't want you to do anything except look after yourself and our baby. It won't take long to find someone. Lilly could work with her and get her trained up."

The following day Tina and Jo went shopping for baby things.

"How are you and Gordon getting along?" Tina asked her.

A slow blush crept over Jo's face. "Very well, I quite like him although he's very shy."

"Yes he is, but he is a good man, very caring and sincere."

"Yes he is. We have gone out a few times, but my shifts at the hospital make it a little awkward. I may look for another job, but it's not easy."

"What kind of work would you be looking for?"

"I don't know. Work in a shop I suppose."

"Would you consider office work?"

"Yes, I don't know if I will be any good. I mean, I can type and answer the phone and quite good at organising, but what let me down before was that I cannot do shorthand. All those squiggly bits, I thought I could remember what they meant, until I came to translate it back. I could never remember."

They both laughed. "If you are serious about finding work, I may know of something going. I'll speak to Solly."

"Oh would you, Tina? I like nursing, but the downside is that the pay isn't good. I feel I'm missing out on a lot of things because I never have time or money."

"Leave it with me, I'll see what I can do, Jo."

"Thanks very much."

They finished their shopping and returned home. Jo was staying for tea, and while they were in the kitchen, Solly came home and he had Gordon with him.

"Look who I've just bumped into?" he said.

Tina smiled. "Hello, Gordon, this is a coincidence."

"I thought I would just call and see how you were."

"I see, it wouldn't have anything to do with the fact that Jo was here would it?"

Jo and Gordon looked at each other and Jo blushed.

"Tina, don't tease them," Solly told her.

She laughed. "I'm only joking. Why don't you both stay for tea and then you can go off somewhere if you want to. Don't look surprised. If you two can't make up your own minds, then someone has to give you a push."

They smiled and Solly shook his head. "Óy, Óy, Óy. What must I do with you, Tina? I'm going to wash before the meal." Laughing to himself, he left the room.

Later when tea was over, Gordon and Jo left, saying they were going for a drink, leaving Solly and Tina to have a quiet night on their own.

"Have you found anyone to replace Lilly yet?"

"No, why?"

Jo is looking for something else. She says nursing is long hours and doesn't pay much. I think she wants to spend more time with Gordon."

128

"It could work, if she leaves the hospital and works with Lilly until she's sure she can do the job."

"Oh, she can do the filing and answer the phone. She can even type. The only thing she can't do, is those squiggly bits on paper."

"Eh?"

"Shorthand, her words, not mine. She said that's what let her down before."

"I don't think we have to be too worried about that. It could work out well. Lilly's been with me many years, and she's tired now. I will be sorry to lose her. But if she has a chance of long-term companionship in her later years, then I wish her luck."

"Yes, she deserves it. Shall I tell Jo tomorrow then?"

"Yes, tell her to come into the office when she can and we will see what we can do. Do you know something, Tina? I thank my lucky stars for the day when you first walked into my office. I wouldn't have you any other way. I love you, but I've never told you just how much."

"What's brought all this on?"

"Nothing, but I know I'm not getting any younger, and I want you to be sure how I feel. I need someone beside me forever and I am so glad it's you. I will never leave you or let you down."

"I know that, Solly."

"When the day comes that I am no longer around, remember my love will live on in our child."

"Solly, are you ill?"

"No, but as I said, I'm not getting any younger. When I am gone, if you should meet someone else, then marry him. You need someone to love and care for you. I just want you to know that my love grows stronger for you each day. Why you love someone like me I will never understand."

"Because you're kind and gentle. Most of the men I have known in my life all wanted something from me. All you wanted was my company. Most men would not have put up with what you have. That makes you special."

"You know at one time, I thought that Gordon carried a torch for you."

"Gordon's been like a brother to me and nothing else. I'm glad that he and Jo are getting on so well."

"I'm pleased you and Jo have become friends. Don't think I haven't noticed that you have no friends your own age; for that I feel guilty."

"It is nice to have someone nearer my age, but you don't have to feel guilty. It was of my own choosing to be with you."

129

"Good, let's call it a night, love. I'm tired."

When Tina looked at him, she saw that, indeed, he looked tired. The depth of their conversation that night concerned her. However, when they got into bed and he wrapped his arms around her, she felt loved and safe and soon forgot her worries.

The following day, Jo rang Tina, and Tina told her to ring Solly at the office. Jo was delighted. Tina spent the morning doing the few jobs that she had to do, and at lunchtime, Solly rang to ask her if she would like to meet him for lunch.

"Yes, I'll come to the office."

"Make it about one, I know I'll be free by then."

Tina bathed and changed her clothes, then made her way to office. She walked in and Lilly was telling Jo how some things worked.

"Hi, Tina, sorry, I'm just leaving. I'm going to the hospital to give in my notice."

"Great, Jo, I'll see you later. She sounds happy enough," Tina said to Lilly.

"Yes, she's a bright young woman. She will work out well here. I think she works harder at the hospital."

"Yes, and for less money."

At that moment, Solly walked out of his office. "Ah good, you're here. OK, let's go." He turned to Lilly. "We won't be long."

"Don't worry. After all, you are the boss."

They all laughed and Tina and Solly left the office.

They went to a little café not far away. When they had sat down, Solly pulled a little box from his pocket. "Tina, this is just to say I love you."

She opened the box to find a beautiful ring laying on red velvet.

"Solly, this is lovely."

"It was my mother's. I was waiting for the right time to give it to you. If it's too big, I can have it altered."

She tried the ring on and it fit her perfectly; there would be no need to have it altered.

"Thank you, Solly. I really don't know what else to say."

"Nothing, don't say anything, just be happy."

Over the next few weeks several things happened.

Jo finished at the hospital and started to work in the office. Lilly was pleased how quickly she picked things up, and she started making her own arrangements for the move to Whitby.

Dougie phoned at least three times a week to let Solly know how things were going in the Southampton office. Business was booming and he thought he would have to take on another person.

Gordon and Jo continued to see each other, which was much easier now she wasn't working shifts at the hospital, and Tina was blooming. Her body seemed to be expanding very quickly with this baby, but she felt better and fitter. She was actually enjoying the pregnancy.

Life was going on at a steady pace, and Tina loved buying things once again for their baby. Solly had kept nothing from Maurice; he and Lilly had gotten rid of everything. Tina had to buy a crib, bedding and pram all over again.

Her check-ups at the hospital all were good, although Tina continued to be concerned over Solly's health.

He was cheerful and continued to work as hard as ever, but he looked so tired, and in the evening, it was an effort to get him to do anything. All he wanted to do was sleep in his chair.

She asked him to have a check-up, but all he said was that he was fine and didn't need one.

In the early hours one Sunday morning, Tina woke with an excruciating backache. She eased herself out of bed and padded downstairs to make some tea. She walked round the kitchen drinking her tea because she could not sit down.

She went back upstairs, washed and dressed before she woke Solly.

"Solly, I think it's time to go to the hospital."

He was slow to respond, but once he realised what she had said, he got out of bed.

"Don't rush," she said, "we have plenty of time."

"Are you sure?" he asked. "Are you sure? If I had been younger and not so tired, I would have heard you get out of bed, I'm sorry."

"Why? There was no need for you to be up any earlier."

He laughed with her as he picked up her case and he took her arm and led her out to the car. By the time they arrived at the hospital, her contractions were coming at regular intervals. A nurse met her at the entrance with a wheelchair.

"I can walk," Tina told her.

"No you can't. We don't want you giving birth in the corridor, do we?"

Tina felt foolish as she sat in the chair, but then she was glad as a sudden contraction tore through her body, causing her to gasp and bend over double."

She was taken into the delivery room and put into a bed. It seemed as if she had been in pain for hours, but it was only just nine o' clock. Then she felt the urge to give a final push and pushed her baby out into the world, screaming.

"It's a girl, Tina," said the nurse. Tina was exhausted but still managed to smile. If they had another boy, they said they would have called him Soloman after Solly, but a girl, she decided to call her Sally, which was as near to Solly as she could think of.

When she was clean and things cleared away, Solly was allowed to see her and his baby daughter.

Tina held the baby in her arms and she was still screaming.

"She's got a good pair of lungs on her that's for sure," he said.

The nurse came in the room and removed the screaming infant. "She'll settle down. It's probably the shock of coming from someplace warm into the cold world." They all laughed.

When she had gone, Solly took hold of Tina's hand. "How are you feeling, love?"

"I'm tired, but otherwise fine. But you look just as tired, why don't you go home and get some rest?"

"Are you sure?"

She nodded her head. Tina would have liked him to stay, but he looked more exhausted than she did, and she had just had a baby.

"I'll come back later today."

"Get a good rest, Solly. Leave it until this evening." She wanted him to have a good rest, not just a couple of hours' sleep.

After he had gone, they moved her to another room. When they had made her comfortable she closed her eyes and slept.

The noise of trolleys and the bright lights woke her. Tina sat up as a nurse was bringing lunch. In the next bed to her was a big woman, all her hair piled high on top of her head.

"Wot hav yer had, luv?"

"Girl," replied Tina.

"Oh I'd luv another girl. This is me tenth, and only one a girl. All the rest have been bleedin' boys, but now that's it. I told my Albert I aint havin' no more. He can sleep in the spare room from now on."

She laughed and Tina smiled at her. "How many have yer got?" asked the woman.

132

"Just this one."

"Blimey yer got a long way ter go, lass. By the way, me name's May, what's yours?"

"Tina," she replied.

"Well, Tina, if yer want my advice, keep everything closed and together, and that way yer won't have a big brood like me." She laughed again.

May was loud and brash, but Tina had grown with women like her. They were the salt of the earth.

They had lunch and when the plates were clear, the nurses brought the babies in for feeding. Sally was still asleep, and she looked so angelic. Completely different from the screaming bundle she had seen earlier.

The nurse gave May her son, who was a big, lusty boy.

"How big was she?" May asked, nodding towards Sally.

"Just over six pounds."

"Bloody hell, all mine have bin over ten pounds, even my girl. Still, yer only a bit of a scrap yerself," she boomed out.

Tina could just imagine her home. All the kids, big ones, May and her husband, shouting over each other to make themselves heard.

In the afternoon at visiting time, Jo and Lilly came through the door. They were all smiles and made a big fuss of the baby.

"How's Solly?" Tina asked Lilly.

"He rang to tell me you'd had the baby. I told him to stay home and get some rest. We could manage in the office without him; he'll be in to see you tonight."

"He looked so tired this morning, that's why I told him to rest all day."

The three of them talked until the end of visiting time. When it was time for them to leave, they said goodbye, leaving her with magazines, flowers and a teddy bear for the baby. When all visitors had gone, the ward was quiet, and the babies were sleeping.

"Posh friends," said May.

Tina knew she was being nosy, but she answered anyway.

"They work in the same office as my husband." Tina didn't want to say that they worked for Solly.

She did not want to give May the impression that she thought she was better than her.

Tina fell asleep, and when she woke again, she went along to the bathroom. She had a bath, brushed her teeth and combed her hair; she went back to bed feeling much better. The babies were brought from the nursery for another feed, and Sally was awake and screaming. Tina picked her up to feed her.

May looked at her and said, "She might be a little 'un but she can't half yell."

They laughed. "I hope she quiets down," said Tina.

After the feeds, the babies were taken back to the nursery. The mothers had another hour to rest before the evening visiting time.

Solly came in and kissed her. "How do you feel?" he asked.

"I'm fine, how are you? Did you get some rest today?"

"Yes I did. When I went home I went to bed and slept until four this afternoon. I couldn't believe it."

"You must have been really tired, Solly. Jo and Lilly came this afternoon and they said they could manage in the office without you. Why not take some time away and rest while we are in here? You'll feel all rested when we come home."

"I'll think about it."

Tina gave him the run down on all the other mothers in the ward, and then the bell rang signalling the end of visiting time.

He kissed her and said, "I love you. I'll see you tomorrow."

"I love you too. Remember, get some rest."

When all the visitors had gone, May said to her, "Yer dad seems nice, luv."

Tina smiled. "He's my husband, not my dad."

"Oh, sorry. I thought…"

"It's OK. I know he's older than me, but he's so good."

"Well suppose that's all that matters then."

They settled down for the night and Tina slept well. Which was not surprising, as she'd had so little sleep the night before.

The few days she spent in hospital were restful, but all Tina wanted to do was to get home so she and Solly could settle down with Sally to family life once again.

The day came when Tina and Sally left the hospital. May had left the hospital two days earlier, with a promise to keep in touch.

Sally was not the perfect baby; she was always screaming. After her feed, she was quiet for a while, and then she would start up again. Newborn babies had a little cry, not Sally. Hers was a piercing scream that hurt your ears.

Solly came to take them home; there was a delicious smell of cooking when she entered the house.

She looked at Solly and simultaneously they both said, "Lilly."

"I don't know what I'm going to do without her. I shall miss her," said Tina.

"So will I, but she will come and visit."

The baby was crying again. "I'll go and feed her." Tina took her upstairs into the room they had prepared for her. She sat and thought about the last time she had sat here and she felt a pang of sadness.. After all this time she still missed her lovely baby Maurice.

Still, she had Sally now, who, judging by her performance, was not going to be an easy baby. When Tina had finished feeding her, she lay her down in the cot. She went back downstairs to Solly, who had made her a cup of tea.

"I'm so glad to be home."

"I'm glad you're home too."

"When you hear Sally, you may wish we were back in the hospital. She's not quiet like Maurice was."

"Yes, but she's not Maurice, and I think my daughter will have a mind of her own from a very early age," he said with pride.

Tina could see that he would be putty in her hands; he was lost to her already.

Over the next few months, Sally blossomed into a bonny baby, but she had a temper on her, and when she started, everyone knew about it.

Solly went to the Southampton office a few times. Dougie was making the office really pay and Solly was proud of him.

Jo and Gordon announced that they were getting married in the summer, and the beloved Lilly left to go live in Whitby to be with the man she had met. They were all sorry to see her go. She had been with Solly twenty-five years, and she had been a sort of mother figure to Tina.

Sally's first birthday was approaching. Tina decided that she would make a little tea for her and have the few friends to share it. Sally had taken her first steps a month before.

During the tea, Sally snatched a toy from one of the other toddlers. Tina took it from her and gave it back, telling Sally not to be mean. Sally promptly sat down and screamed.

"My God," said one of the women, "she's a right pair of lungs on her for one so little."

Sally, who thought she was being ignored, just screamed louder. Tina felt so embarrassed that it was her daughter causing the scene.

"I don't know who she takes after. Solly is so placid, and I certainly don't have a temper."

A few minutes later, Sally toddled over to Tina. She picked her up and sat her on her knee. Sally promptly fell asleep.

One of the women nodded and said, "That's good, you can hear yourself speak now. Anyway, got to go, thanks fer havin' us, luv."

"Thank you for coming."

The woman left and it was a cue for the other women to follow suit. There was only one left, and that was May, the woman who had been in hospital at the same time, and Tina had kept in touch with her.

Theirs was a strange friendship and she reminded Tina of Annie. She was loud and brash, but she was good hearted, and she would give you her last penny if she could.

Her boy was fast asleep on the rug.

"Well, luv, I've seen some tempers in me time, but she teks the biscuit."

"Solly ruins her, she's his little girl. But when she starts, there's no pacifying her, she's hard work."

"Blimey, girl, is she like that often?"

Tina nodded.

"Well I don't old with smackin', but I reckon a bit of a slap now and then would bring her up sharp."

"Oh, I don't know, May. Solly would go mad."

"Solly doesn't have ter listen to her, and I'll tell yer somat, yer going ter have yer hands full with that 'un. It's not fer me to say, but I can see it comin'."

"Perhaps you're right, May, but she seems so little. Sometimes I can't believe that she's capable of such a temper."

"Well, luv, I have ter go. Me old man will want his tea. Yer know where I am if yer need me."

"I do. Thanks, May, I'll call you later."

She nodded to the sleeping Sally. "Don't get up, let 'er sleep. At least she's quiet like that."

When May had gone, Tina thought about Sally, and wondered if maybe she was ill, or was it just pure temper that made her act like she did."

Neither she nor Solly had a temper. The only one who was capable of a temper like that was her sister Susan. *God if she turns out like her, I'll disown her myself.*

Tina carried Sally to her cot and laid her down; she would sleep until Solly got home. Then, she would be all sweetness and light, sitting on his knee and laughing with him. Tina had just finished preparing the meal and put it in the oven, when Solly walked through the door.

"Hello, have you had a busy day?" she asked him.

"Yes, how did this afternoon go?"

"Fine, until Sally decided to have one of her tantrums. Then everyone left."

"Oh, where is she now?"

"She's asleep, but she won't be for long. Come and have your tea before she wakes."

They sat in the kitchen together and drank their tea, enjoying the rare peace and quiet.

"Tina, do you think Sally's ill?"

"No I don't, I think it is pure temper, my sister was just the same. I'll tell you, if she turns out like her, I'll kill her."

He just laughed.

For once, when Sally woke, she was good. She had her tea, Tina bathed her, then Solly played with her and she was back in bed by nine o' clock.

Tina and Solly thought they would take the opportunity of having an early night. She snuggled up to him and he made love to her. As always he was gentle and patient, but tonight there was an urgency to his lovemaking that she had not known before.

For some reason, Tina found it difficult to sleep even though she was tired. Solly was snoring gently beside her. She must have dropped off at some time because the next thing she knew was Sally shouting for her.

Tina got out of bed and went along to her room. She took her along to the bathroom, washed and dressed her, then took her downstairs for her breakfast. Solly must have been tired because he had not stirred.

When Sally was in her playpen, Tina made some tea and took a cup upstairs.

"Morning, Solly, I've brought you some tea."

He still did not wake and there was an eerie stillness in the room. She bent over him and took a hold of his hand. It was only then that she realised her precious Solly was dead.

"Oh God, no," she cried. She cradled his head and sobbed. He had been her friend, her protector, her husband and lover, and now he was no more.

She gently laid his head back on the pillow and went downstairs. She picked up the phone and called Jo.

"Hello?"

"Jo, can you come?" Tina sobbed. "It's Solly, he's gone."

"Gone where?" asked Jo sleepily. It was obvious that Tina had woken her.

"He's dead." She put down the phone unable to say anything more. She went through into the room, picked up Sally and held her close, her tears streaming down her face. "It's just the two of us now, baby," she said.

She put Sally back in the playpen, sat on the floor beside her and sobbed. She was aware of the doorbell ringing constantly, so she dragged herself up off the floor and answered the door. Jo and Gordon stood on the doorstep. Jo stepped forward and put her arms around Tina.

"What happened?" she asked.

Tina shrugged her shoulders. "I took him some tea and he was dead."

Jo turned to Gordon. "Take her into the room. I'll go and look at him."

While she was gone, Gordon took Tina into the room.

Jo came back downstairs. "I think it was his heart."

"What do we need to do?" Gordon asked.

"We have to inform the rabbi and the undertaker; he has to be buried before sunset."

"I'll go take care of things. You take care of her and Sally," he said to Jo.

Gordon informed everyone he could think of. First was the rabbi and the undertakers, then Solly's sister. Gordon then rang Southampton to tell Dougie.

Meanwhile, Jo told Tina to pack a few things and she and Sally could go back to her house.

"No, I want to stay here."

"Let me take Sally home then until you get things sorted?"

Like a robot, Tina got a bag and put Sally's things in. Gordon returned and said he would stay with Tina until the rabbi and undertakers had been.

Tina was unable to do anything other than sit and stare into space, thinking of all the good times she and Solly had had. He had always tried to make sure she was safe. The times she had been in danger were beyond his control. She had been his first priority. Now, she would have to do the same for Sally, alone.

Jo left with Sally and Gordon made Tina a cup of tea. An hour later, it was still on the table, cold.

The undertaker arrived and went upstairs. When they left the house, he gave all the details to Gordon. Tina was still unable to handle things. To her it seemed she was in a fog and nothing was clear.

What would she do now? She still had Sally, but an important part of her life had gone. It was hard to believe that only last night, he had held her in his arms and made love to her.

The chiming of the clock brought her back to reality and Tina was surprised to see that it was noon. Where had the morning gone? She heard Gordon on the phone in the other room. She walked through and he put his arms around her.

"Tina, we have known each other many years and we have known a lot of sadness. I have tried to do everything I can think of, but if you think of anything else, let me know."

"You have done more than enough already. I have to get through this."

"You can leave Sally with us for a few days, if it helps."

"Thanks, Gordon, she's not easy at times you know."

"I'm sure Jo can manage. If we find we can't handle her, then we'll bring her back."

"Its good of you. The rabbi said the funeral is to be this evening after six."

"That's quick."

"The Jewish bury the dead more or less straight away," she said. "I suppose I had better inform his family."

"I've already done that for you."

"Thank you. I have to inform his solicitor. You go home and get some rest. You have done more than enough and Jo will need you."

"Under the circumstances, I think she will understand. Are you sure you'll be alright?"

She nodded her head. "I need some time on my own. Thank you for all you have done, and will you thank Jo for me?"

"I will. If you need anything else just let me know. When you feel you can take care of Sally again, we will bring her back."

After he had gone, Tina walked through to the study and slowly sorted through all Solly's papers. She just wanted to go to bed and stay there but this had to be done.

After a while, she went through to the kitchen and made a cup of tea. She would drink it this time, as she had not had anything all day.

Tina sat at the kitchen table drinking the scalding hot tea. *I have to get through this*, she told herself. The doorbell was ringing, and she got up to answer it. She opened the door to find May there.

May looked at her face and said, "Eh lass, what's up, yer looking like a proper wet weekend. Are yer poorly?"

"May, Solly died."

"Bloody hell, when?"

"Sometime during the night. It was his heart."

"Eh lass, I am sorry. Where's the bairn?"

"Jo and Gordon have her."

"Would yer like me to tek her?"

"No, it's OK. You have enough to do, but thank you."

"One more mouth ter feed won't make any odds. She might be better with me, cos she can play with mine. Jo might find it hard, because she 'as no kids of her own."

"I didn't think of that, May. I'll ring and let her know."

"Is there anything else, lass?"

Tina shook her head. "Gordon came this morning and he has done everything."

"I'll tell my Albert to pick the bairn up, she'll be OK. I'll keep her until after the funeral. They don't waste no time buryin' them, do they?"

"No, they don't."

"Why don't yer go lay down, luv, yer look all in."

"I'll try." She was tired, but she knew she would not sleep.

When May had gone, Tina rang Jo and explained that May had offered to look after Sally.

"She's fine at the moment, Tina, you don't have to worry about her."

"Yes I know, but May has other children she can play with. I know she's not easy, Jo, I think it's best."

"Well if you're sure." Secretly Jo was relieved. She had found Sally very demanding and didn't know how Tina put up with her tantrums. She would have never told Tina though; she would have looked after Sally as long as it was necessary.

"Albert will call and collect her later today, thank you so much."

"Fine, Tina, Gordon and I will be over to go to the funeral with you."

"Thank you, both of you. Gordon has been such a help in sorting this out this morning."

She hung up the phone and walked into the sitting room. She sat in a chair and closed her eyes. Her days had revolved around Solly, and later Sally. She had waited for him to come home every day. Now was the time when Solly would have been coming through the door, and she knew that it would never be the same again.

She must have slept because the ringing of the doorbell woke her, and the house was dark. She switched on the light and opened the door.

"Are you ready, Tina?" Gordon and Jo were at the door, waiting to take her to the funeral.

"No, I fell asleep. I can be ready in ten minutes. Come in."

Tina went upstairs, closed the curtains and changed into a black dress. When she was ready, she went downstairs and they all left the house.

"May collected Sally early this afternoon," Jo told her.

"Was she good?"

"Yes, she was excited because one of the other children was there. I think she was pleased to have some company other than mine."

"Thank you for taking her, Jo."

They arrived at the synagogue. Again, the women had to go upstairs and the men downstairs. The rabbi said the prayers, and other men spoke about Solly. All of this was a blur to Tina, and before she knew, it was all over.

Gordon and Jo took her home. Unlike other funerals, Tina had not asked anyone back to the house.

"Would you like us to stay with you for a while, Tina?" asked Gordon.

She shook her head. "No thank you, I just want to go to bed."

They said they understood and to ring them if she needed anything. When they had gone, she poured herself a drink and sat in Solly's favourite chair.

"Well this is it, just me and Sally." The doorbell rang.

She opened the door to see Lilly and a man with her. Lilly looked well and tanned. She stepped into the house and wrapped her arms around Tina.

"We came as soon as we could. What happened?"

Tina told her how she had found Solly and that the doctor had said it was his heart.

Lilly nodded her head. "I bet you haven't had anything to eat have you?"

Tina shook her head. "I'm not very hungry."

"Well you're going to need your strength now, you have Sally to care for, and it will be hard for a while, but you'll get through this, Tina."

Tina went upstairs. She had a bath and changed. When she came downstairs, there was the smell of fresh coffee and toast.

"Where is Sally?" Lilly asked.

"At May's, you know, the woman who was in hospital at the same time as I had Sally."

"That loud, brash baggage?"

"She may be loud, Lilly, but she has a heart of gold. I know Sally will be cared for."

"Well, you know best, I suppose."

Lilly's friend, who she had introduced as David, had said little up to now.

"Have you got everything in order, Tina?"

"Yes, thank you. Gordon has been so good at getting me through everything."

Tina drank her coffee and ate the toast that Lilly had made. She was surprised to find that she had been hungry after all.

"As long as Sally is well cared for, it's all that matters."

"I'm sure you won't have any worries, Tina. Solly would have made sure of that."

Then David said, "Tina, I don't know you, only what Lilly has told me. If there is anything you need or I can do, just let me know."

"Thanks, David."

Lilly said, "We came to see if you needed help, but you have done it. If you need me for support for a few days, I'll stay."

"No thanks, I'll be fine, I have to get used to managing on my own, and the sooner I get on with it the better."

"If you're sure, we will be leaving tomorrow. You will come and visit us won't you? Bring little Sally and have a holiday."

"The solicitor will be here to read the will in the morning, will you come for that?"

"If you want us here, yes," Lilly answered.

"Good, I'll see you both in the morning, ten-thirty."

As they left, the telephone was ringing in the hall, and when Tina answered it, May was on the other end of the line.

"Tina," she boomed down the phone. "Just thought I'd let yer know the bairn's alright."

"Thank you, May, will you be bringing her back tonight?"

"No, don't you worry, we'll keep her 'til tomorrow."

"Thanks again. I don't know what I would have done without you."

"That's OK, chuck, just thought I'd ring. Bye."

Tina had to smile. May was loud, but she was a character. It was good of her to take Sally."

The following morning, the solicitor arrived. He offered his condolences to Tina and said he was here to do the reading of the will. David and Lilly were already there.

When they sat down, he started to read the last will and testament of Solly.

"To Lilly I leave the sum of one thousand pounds for her loyalty and service. To Dougie, I leave the sum of three hundred pounds for running the office so efficiently in the short time he has worked for me. To my wife Tina,

I leave the house, the antiques and the business, which amounts to one hundred thousand pounds, plus the business in Southampton."

There was about seventy five thousand pounds in the bank, five thousand was to go into a trust fund for Sally until she was twenty-five and Tina was to get the rest. Upon Tina's death, it would all go to Sally.

She could not take it in. She had no idea that Solly had been so wealthy, and now she realised that she too was a very rich woman.

Everyone left, apart from the solicitor. He took her aside and said, "Tina, I knew Solly from when he was a small boy. He trusted me and I hope you can feel the same way. I will help you all I can. Serve you the way I did Solly. I will help you look after the businesses and invest this money for you so that it will be safe and you will never be without."

Tina nodded. "Thank you, Mr Bergman."

"Call me Hyme."

"I want to learn about the business. Solly taught me a little, but I have to know more to run it efficiently."

The solicitor nodded. "Don't worry, I'll teach you. I will contact you in a few days' time."

After he had gone, Gordon came back. "I was just passing and called to see if you needed anything."

"No, the solicitor has just gone. I have to know about running the business. I want to keep it going like Solly would want it."

"Shall I make some tea?"

"No, but I will have a glass of wine. Get yourself a drink if you want one."

"Thanks, I will."

He got her wine and he had a tot of whisky.

"How are things going between you and Jo, are you going to get engaged?"

He shuffled his feet uncomfortably. "Jo wants to get engaged soon."

"And you?" she asked.

"I don't know, Tina. I have always had feelings for someone else and when they became unavailable, Jo was fun to be with. I am hardly a man of the world. I just don't feel it's the real thing with Jo."

"What about this other person, do they know how you feel?"

"No, it wouldn't be right."

"You have to tell Jo, Gordon, it's not fair to her."

"I know, but she has done nothing wrong, except be the wrong person."

"You have to do the right thing."

"Yes, I know, and you are right. I should go. Maybe this is the right time to tell her."

"There's never a right time, Gordon. It's just not fair to let it go on."

He nodded. "Yes, I'll call tomorrow to see how you are."

As she let him out, he gave her a brotherly peck on the cheek and was gone.

The next day May rang and asked her to go for dinner and then she could bring Sally home.

Tina noticed that May's home was not the tidiest of homes, but it was clean, warm and filled with love.

Tina sat at the table and May made some tea.

"Ah, there yer are, luv. How are yer?"

"She will keep me going," she said, nodding to Sally, who sat on the floor playing. She had hardly noticed Tina.

"What are yer goin' ter do now?"

"I'm going to look after her and run the office, May. The office in Southampton is running well. Dougie's doing a good job. I'm going to ask Gordon if he wants to learn how to run the Leeds' office for me and then I won't need to be there all the time."

"Aye well, mebbe it's for the best. I'll have little mite if yer want?"

"Thanks, May," replied Tina, "but you have enough on."

"One more's no different. Any road, she keeps mine happy."

"Is she good for you, May?"

"Aye, she has her tantrums, but I just ignore them. She soon gets tired."

"The little monkey. She really plays up for me."

"Well you should try ignorin' her. She'll soon give up."

"Thanks, May. I might take you up on your offer sometimes. Well, I better make tracks and get her home."

Sally wasn't very happy about being taken away, and decided to let them all know just how loud she could scream.

"Well she can still make a noise."

"Aye mebbe because she's occupied here. She has no one ter play with at home."

"Maybe, but she will have to learn that life is not going to revolve round her and she can't always have her own way."

She dressed Sally and they left. By the time Tina reached home, Sally was fast asleep, sucking her thumb and looking angelic.

Over the next week, Tina was busy organising the office. Jo continued working, but was very quiet. Tina presumed that Gordon had talked to her and she did not want to pry by asking.

During the week, Tina told Jo that she would be taking Sally to Whitby for a break.

"That's great, it will do you good."

"Yes, Lilly and David said I could stay there. I was thinking of asking Gordon to help you."

"There's no need, I can manage. Anyway, Gordon and me have split up."

"I'm sorry, Jo," Tina said.

"It's OK. I think I have known for some time that he doesn't feel the same for me as I do for him. I have not been fair either. I knew this, and I pushed him. I was going to wait a bit before I told you, but if you could find someone else to do this, I think I may go back to nursing. There again, I might move away all together."

"I'll be sorry to lose you, Jo. Will you wait until I get back? Then if you want to go, I'll take over until I find someone."

"Are you sure, Tina? I don't want you to think I'm abandoning you."

"I understand. Have you anything lined up?"

"Yes I have. But as I said, I didn't want to leave you in the lurch."

"Go make your plans, Jo, I wish you all the best. You can leave as soon as I get back."

"Thanks, Tina, I appreciate it."

Tina went to Whitby. Lilly and David took a delight in taking Sally down to the beach. Of course, Sally loved all the attention and not once did she have a temper tantrum.

This gave Tina some time to herself. She could relax, walk on the beach and watch the fishing boats come into the harbour. The weather was warm and sunny, and within a few days, she started to look better.

At night, she put Sally to bed and sometimes would eat with her friends. Other times, she would walk down to the harbour and sit in one of the little cafes, have some wine and think of Solly. Then she would go to bed feeling very lonely and cry herself to sleep.

By the second week, Tina felt much better and was glad that Lilly had asked her to come. She had needed this time away to grieve. Lilly and David gave her the space she needed, taking Sally with them whenever they went out.

The night before Tina was due to leave for home, Lilly thought it was warm enough to eat on the patio.

"I want to thank you both for having me and Sally here. It's been lovely and I feel so much better."

"We have loved having you, Tina, but do you have to go back?" asked Lilly.

She nodded. "Yes. Jo has decided to go back to nursing, and she's taking a job away from Leeds."

"I thought she and Gordon were an item. Is he going with her?"

"No. When I last saw him, he said that Jo was not the person he wanted to share the rest of his life with. Jo said she had pushed him a little. Gordon said he loved someone else, but she was unavailable to him."

"I see. Do you know who this other person is?" Lilly asked.

Tina shook her head. "Gordon has always kept things close to his chest."

"So now you have to find someone else to run the office."

"Yes, I can do it for a while and May said she would look after Sally. I was thinking of asking Gordon if he wanted the job. He said he was fed up with his job."

Lilly nodded and filled their glasses with wine. "I suppose you could. It would help you."

For the rest of the evening, they talked about various things, until Tina said she was going for one last walk before she went to bed.

"Will you be OK on your own?" asked David.

"Don't worry, I won't be long."

Tina took the path that led to the harbour. The tide was out; the boats were tied up and were leaning slightly to one side. The moon was shining on the little puddles of water that surrounded the boats, and everything was so still even the seagulls were quiet.

Tina leant against the wall and looked across the harbour. The lights on the other side gave a continental look to the place. She could see people walking over the bridge and the castle that stood on top of the cliff was all lit up.

She loved the smell of the sea, and the peace she felt here. Tina sighed. Tomorrow she would be going back to the hustle and bustle of Leeds. At the moment, it seemed like a million miles away. She could understand Jo wanting to move away, and Tina wondered if she would stay there herself.

She wanted to live away from the city, so Sally could grow up surrounded by fields and animals, not motors and pollution.

Tina walked back to the house. Lilly and David had cleared up and gone to bed. She let herself in and quietly went upstairs, but she lay a long time before finally drifting off to sleep.

The following morning was a bit hectic. Lilly looked after Sally while

Tina packed their things. They had lunch and then, all too soon, it was time to leave.

"Come back and visit soon," Lilly said.

"Thank you, it's been lovely. I really needed this time. Now, it's back to reality."

Lilly and David took them to the station and waited until the train arrived. As the train pulled out of the station, they waved until it was out of sight.

When she arrived in Leeds, she was just getting off the train and looked up to see Gordon waiting for her.

"Hello, you're looking well. Did you enjoy the rest?"

"Yes I did. But what are you doing here?"

"I thought you would need some help getting home."

"I do, and it's nice to see you. Thank you for coming."

On the journey home, they talked about the office, the weather and other things.

He carried the cases in the house and said, "Well, I'll be going, I'll see you later."

"Wait, Gordon, I need to talk to you. Do you feel like popping back later when I've put Sally to bed?"

"If you're sure, yes."

She nodded and he was gone.

Tina bathed Sally and gave her some food. When she had put her to bed, she rang the office and spoke to Jo. She assured her everything was running like clockwork and there was no need for her to worry. She called Lilly to let them know she had arrived back safe.

After unpacking, she phoned May. "Hello, luv, I'm glad yer back, we missed yer."

"I'm glad to be back too, May. It feels as if I have been away for ages."

"Well that lad Gordon'll be glad as well. He's bin moochin' round her with a face like a wet weekend," she said.

"Gordon came to meet me at the station. I forgot to ask him how he knew which train we would be on."

"It were me, lass. I hope yer don't mind, I think he has the hots fer yer. If yer ask me, I think his candle has bin burnin' a long time."

"Oh May, how do you know? He's been going out with Jo for ages."

"Aye maybe, but it's you he's sweet on. It stands out a mile."

"Does it?"

"Well just wait and see."

"I don't think so, May. Gordon has known me years and he's never said anything."

"Aye, well mebbe I'm being daft. Will I see yer termorrow?" she asked.

"Yes, it's Saturday and I have some things to do, and I have to see Jo, but I'll pop in."

"Right, lass, see yer then. You tek care."

Tina put the phone down. May always made her smile. She also had an over-imaginative mind. Fancy her thinking that Gordon had a thing for her. She was sure she would have known if he had.

Tina went upstairs and had a bath. When she was dressed again, she poured a drink and sat down to read all the mail that had piled up whilst she had been gone.

The business was doing well. There was a letter and bank statements from Dougie in Southampton. He told her all the news, and that he had a girlfriend. It sounded as if it was serious.

She picked up the phone and called him.

Dougie answered. "Hello."

"Dougie, it's Tina."

"Hello, did you enjoy your holiday?"

"Yes I did, I got your letter. Everything seems to be going well down there."

"It is, all running very smoothly. Have you got the copy of accounts?"

"Yes, I must say I am very impressed. What's this about you having a girlfriend?"

"Yes, her name is Pauline. I'm thinking of asking her to marry me."

"Well why not, you deserve some happiness, Dougie. Listen, I have a business proposition to put to you. Can you close the office and come up for a couple of days?"

"Yes I think so. But not until next week, Tina."

"That's fine. Bring Pauline with you, I would like to meet her. You can both stay here if you want."

"Great, I'll look forward to it. I'll ring you over the weekend once I have spoken to her."

"OK, Dougie, see you then. Goodbye."

As she put the phone down, the doorbell rang. She opened the door and Gordon stood on the doorstep.

"Hi, come on in," she said. "Would you like a drink?"

"Yes please, wine would be fine."

She poured the drinks and they sat making small talk for a while. Tina saw no outward signs to indicate anything was true that May had said, and she felt sure she must have been mistaken.

"Gordon, do you know that Jo is leaving?"

He nodded. "Yes, she said she wants to go back to nursing."

"Well I think she's going to go this weekend."

"Oh, who is going to run the office for you?"

"I am, until I can find someone else. That brings me to what I wanted to ask you. You said that you were fed up doing your job. Would you consider running the office for me? I have Sally to take care of, and I can't give the office the time it needs to be run efficiently."

"I don't know, Tina."

"I'll match what you're earning and more, plus the hours are better."

"It's not that, it's just that I don't know anything about running an office."

"I'll work with you for a month. But I know you'll be OK. Look at Dougie, he's worked out very well."

"Can I think about it? When would you want me to start?"

"As soon as you can, but I know you will have to work your notice. Dougie is coming up next week. As I've already said, he's doing very well with the office down there. He's bringing his new girlfriend with him. I think he will get married soon. I'm going to give him a chance to buy the business down South."

"Are you sure about that?" he asked.

"Yes, Solly only started it down there because Dougie wanted to get away from here, and to give him a start after he came out of prison. He's built it up into a thriving business, and anyway, I have enough coping at this end."

"Will he be able to raise the money?"

"I'll make it easy for him. I'm sure he will jump at the chance. It will give him some independence."

"Yes, I would say so. It's a golden opportunity for him."

"I think he's earned it, Gordon. He spent time in prison for something he did not do. He has been as honest as they come within the business. It will be one less worry for me."

"Well as long as you make sure you do it properly, it should be alright."

By this time, they had finished all the wine and Tina was feeling very light headed. Gordon stood up. "I have to go."

"Yes, and I have a lot to do tomorrow, so I should go to bed. I have to see Jo and I promised to call and see May."

Gordon went to the front door. "I'll think about your offer, Tina."

"Please do, I would rather have someone I know in the office. Give me a ring when you have made up your mind."

He kissed her on the cheek as a brother would, and then left. Tina cleared the glasses away, turned off the lights and went to bed. She was asleep in five minutes and woke next morning to bright sunshine.

When she and Sally were dressed and had breakfast, she made her way to the office to see Jo, who was clearing her things from her desk. They spent two hours going over details.

"Are you sure this is what you want, Jo?"

"Yes, I'm staying with friends for a few days and then I have a job at Bath United hospital. I have to get away, and nursing is what I do best."

"You've done a good job here," Tina said as she handed her a cheque. "Here are the wages I owe you."

"But, Tina, this is far more than you owe me."

"I know, call it breathing space money. That way, you will be able to take a little time without having to worry."

"Thank you. As I already said, I am starting work in a week or so. Still, it will come in handy, thank you."

"I'm going to miss you, Jo. I'm grateful for all you have done for me, and I'm really sorry to lose you both as a friend and someone I can trust here. But you will keep in touch, won't you?"

"I will, you don't get rid of me that easily." They hugged each other and Jo left the office.

Tina felt a pang of loneliness. Jo had been her one friend nearest her age and now she was gone. She did not have Solly to rely on anymore. She stayed in the office a little while longer and then left to visit May.

At May's house, everything was the same as it always was. Kiddies all over the place, toys in the garden. She could hear the noise coming from inside the house as she walked up the garden path. Still it was a house full of love, and even though in chaos, it was warm and friendly.

Sally ran to get inside when she realised where they were. She loved May and her children, and for some reason she never played up or had a tantrum when she was there. When she was with Tina, it was a different story. May opened the door.

"Eh lass, it's good ter see yer."

Sally held out her little arms for May to take her. "Eh, I've missed this little mite yer know. How are yer, luv?" she asked Tina.

"Fine, May, how's everything here?"

"Middlin', luv, just middlin'. Now't alters round here, lass, yer should know that. I'll make us a brew. Have yer seen Jo?"

"Yes, she's going to stay with friends for a few days before she starts her new job."

"Well I think she suits nursing best. Yer've either got it or yer don't."

"Yes, but she was good in the office too."

By now, Sally had toddled off with one of May's children. They all seemed to look after each other and they always included Sally.

"Did yer see Gordon?" asked May.

"Yes, and I asked him about working in the office. He said he would think about it."

"He will do it."

"How do you know?"

"Because I know. I told yer before, he's sweet on yer that's why."

Tina laughed. "You're imagining things, May. When he came round last night, there was no indication that he felt like that."

"Bidin' his time I say."

Tina laughed again and they spent a pleasant day until May's husband Albert arrived home from work.

"Hello, lass, how are yer?"

"Fine, Albert, but you look tired."

"Aye I am. But I have ter work ter keep her in the style she lives in." He nodded towards May and winked.

May laughed, and Tina could not help but notice the look that passed between them.

They hadn't got much, but they loved each other in their own way. They loved their family and would look after their friends to the end.

"Well I'll make tracks home."

"Yer could stay an have a bit of tea, luv, there's plenty."

"No, May, thank you, you have enough to do."

"Nay, lass, with a family like this, two more isn't goin' ter mek much difference."

"Stay, lass," said Albert. "I'll run yer home later. Little 'un is enjoyin' herself. She'll be more than ready fer bed later."

"OK, thanks, it's good of you."

May talked as she made the tea, and then she called them all to the table. They were rowdy at times, but manners were strictly in order when they were having a meal. When the meal was over, each of them had a little job to do. Even the youngest helped to carry dishes to the sink.

One would wash, one would dry and one would put away. They knew the quicker they had done, the quicker they could go outside to play again.

"You have them well trained, May."

"Aye. I do me own cookin' and cleanin'. My bairns are not slaves, but havin' a job ter do meks them aware that meals don't turn up by thee selves. So they have to side the table and help wash up. They do it good an' all."

Another hour went by and then Tina said she would take Sally home who, by this time, was showing that she was tired.

"I'll tek thee home, lass," said Albert.

"You don't have to really, you've been working hard today."

"Nay, lass, it'll give me some peace while our May gets this lot to bed. I might stop fer a jar on the way back."

May smiled at him. "Aye, thought yer might. Get yerself off then, an' don't be too late back."

"Thanks, May, I really have enjoyed today, and I think Sally has too."

"So have I, lass, so have I. Go on, I'll see yer later, tek care."

May stood at the door until they were out of sight. Albert drove her home. When they arrived she said, "Thank you, Albert, that saved me travelling by bus."

"I don't mind. Gis' me a chance ter be on me own fer a while. Not that I don't love our May, but the noise gets a bit much sometimes, know what I mean?"

"Yes, I know what you mean. Thanks again, Albert. Drive carefully and I'll see you soon."

"Aye, yer will tek care." She got out of the car and watched him drive away.

She took Sally inside, bathed her and put her to bed. Before she had finished cleaning up the bathroom, Sally was fast asleep.

She went downstairs and poured a glass of wine. Just as she was about to sit down, the doorbell rang. When she opened it, Gordon was on the doorstep.

"Hello, Tina, I hope you don't mind me coming round. I wanted to have a chat."

"That's OK, come in. Sally and I have been out at May's for most of the day. Would you like a drink?"

"Yes please."

She poured his drink and they sat down. "Well what did you want to chat about?"

"I've been thinking about your offer. I'll give it a go, but I don't know if I'll be any good."

"Neither did Dougie, but he soon picked it up; so did Jo."

"OK, I'll give it a go."

"When will you be able to start?" she asked.

"If I give my notice tomorrow, it will be next week."

"Good, that'll give me a week to get things sorted, then I'll work with you until you're confident you can do it. But I'll only be a phone call away."

They discussed the salary she would pay him, and after some more small talk, he said she looked tired and it was time for him to leave.

"I'll speak to you soon. I hope you won't regret your decision."

"I'll do my best for you, Tina, you know that."

She nodded. He kissed her on the cheek as he had done before and then he was gone. Tina locked the door, turned off the lights and went to bed.

The next week was a little hectic for Tina. May looked after Sally and gave her tea, so when Tina got her home all she had to do was put her to bed.

One day she was at May's having a cup of tea, and May said, "Yer look tired, lass. When's Gordon startin'?"

"Next week."

"Not before time I say. Yer can't run that office all the time on yer own."

"I'll still have to work with him for a while to show him how things are done."

"Aye, but it'll still be a help ter yer."

"Yes and I hope he gets to grips with it all quickly. I can't keep this pace up all the time."

"Well, lass, I'll tell yer what I would do. Yer don't need the money, why don't yer sell out all tergether?"

"It's an investment for mine and Sally's future, May."

"Mebbe yer right. If yer need any help with Sally, all yer need ter do is ask."

"Thanks, May, you've been more help than you know."

She left May's with Sally and looked forward to the fact that tomorrow was Saturday and she would not be going to the office.

Next morning Tina caught up with all the jobs that she had neglected to do during the week. In the afternoon, she went shopping and then took Sally into the park for half an hour before taking her home, feeding her and putting her to bed.

The telephone rang.

She picked it up. "Hello."

"Hello, it's me," Gordon said. "I just wondered if you wanted some company. I can bring a bottle of wine."

"That would be nice, yes, come on over."

As she replaced the receiver, Tina realised that she was looking forward to his company. It was times like this, when Sally was in bed, she felt lonely.

Soon after his call, Gordon arrived.

"Hi, how has your week been?"

"Quite tiring. This is the first time I have been able to relax all week."

They drank the wine and talked about everything, Rose and Annie especially. The work in the office, and what he would have to do.

"I'll try not to let you down, Tina."

"I know. Now, I don't want it to seem as if I am being rude. The wine and company was lovely, but I have to go to bed. I am so tired."

"That's OK, I understand. I'll see you in the office Monday morning."

"Fine. Don't forget Dougie and his girlfriend are coming up, so you'll have a taste of working on your own on Wednesday. But you can always phone me if you need anything."

"Yes I know. I'll see you Monday. Goodnight, Tina."

After he had gone, she locked the door and went to bed.

Sunday she spent relaxing and playing with Sally. She was fine all day, and then spoilt herself by having a tantrum in the afternoon.

When Sally had gone to bed, Tina had a bath. She went to bed early, and woke up on Monday morning ready to face another week.

When she arrived at the office, Gordon was already waiting for her. She worked with him all day and when they were closing the office, she said, "Well, what do you think?"

"If every day is like today, I can't see any problems. I have been thinking, will it help if I took you to May's to pick up Sally? Then I can drop you at home."

"I can't ask you to do that, Gordon."

"Why not? I have nothing else to do. It will save you an hour's travelling time."

"I can't say it won't be helpful, I just don't want to put you out."

"You won't. Get your coat."

They collected Sally and he drove them home. "Goodnight, Tina, I'll see you in the morning."

"Goodnight, Gordon, and thank you."

He nodded and drove away.

The next day went well. Gordon was learning fast. At the end of the day she said, "Don't forget, I won't be in the office tomorrow, Dougie will be here. They are staying until Friday and then going away for the weekend before going back to Southampton. If you need me, just call. But I think you will be fine."

Just before dinner time the next day, Dougie arrived. There were greetings and he introduced Pauline. She was nice and Tina liked her straight away. After dinner, Pauline said, "Why don't I take Sally for a walk while two talk business?"

"That would be nice," said Tina. "Are you sure?"

"Yes I would enjoy it."

When she had gone Tina said, "I like her, Dougie, she's nice."

"Yes she is."

"Will you marry her?"

"I think so, if she'll have me."

"Well I hope so, and of course she'll have you. Dougie, I wanted to talk to you about the business. You have built it up down there and I am so pleased at what you have done. But I have enough running things here, how would you like to buy me out?"

"Buy you out, Tina, where would I get that kind of money? I've been in prison don't forget. I wouldn't get a bank loan."

"I know, and don't think I haven't thought about that."

"And?"

"You could take over the business and pay me a percentage of the profits now, and pay me what I ask over a period of time. When you have paid me in full, then I would cease to take any of the profits."

"You would do that for me?"

"Yes I would, because you're honest and you work hard. This could set you up for life, especially if you are going to get married. You can discuss it with Pauline and let me know before you leave on Friday."

"I will. I can't find the words to thank you."

"Don't thank me until the day it's all yours, Dougie. It may be hard for you and sometimes you may regret it."

"I don't think so, Tina. This is just what I needed. I don't think anyone else anywhere would have given me the chance you have."

"Just make it work for you, that's all I ask."

"I will."

Pauline returned with Sally and they all spent the rest of the day catching up with news and discussing the business.

"What have you two got planned for tomorrow?" she asked. "Unfortunately I have to go into the office."

"I think we'll visit some of the old places I used to go to. Show Pauline where I grew up. Later we are going up to the lake district for the weekend."

"Good. Well, I am going to bed. Stay up as long as you want, make yourselves comfortable. I'll see you both in the morning."

The following morning Tina went to the office. Gordon was already there and he had managed very well on his own. He had not called her for anything.

"You did well, I told you it would be easy."

"Yes, there was nothing I couldn't handle."

They worked steadily throughout the day and Tina was amazed at how well he had picked things up.

They closed the office, and he drove her May's to collect Sally. When they got to Tina's she said, "Dougie and Pauline have gone, why don't you come in and have some supper with us?"

They had a pleasant evening until Gordon said he had to go.

"I mustn't be late for work, the boss is very strict."

Tina laughed as he said goodnight. When he had gone, Tina realised that it was a long time since she had enjoyed herself so much.

The following day Dougie rang her and told her that he would take her up on the business offer.

"Good, I'll get my solicitor to draw up the necessary papers and get them to you. Have a nice weekend, Dougie, it was nice seeing you again. I'll speak to you soon."

"Yes, goodbye, Tina. Speak to you soon."

Over the next few weeks, Tina got the papers sorted for Dougie. Gordon worked well and he took her for Sally at the end of the day. He would stay at least twice a week for supper. He had proved to be invaluable in the office and she started to leave him on his own more.

Since her father went to prison Tina heard very little about her family. One day, she was shopping in town and she bumped into her sister Susan. Her hair was bleached white, the roots showing through, and her skirt shorter than ever. She was with a man older than her father, and they were clinging onto each other. Neither of them was very sober.

"Well look who's here. Wher've you bin hidin' yerself?" she slurred.

Tina looked at this woman and was ashamed that she was related to her.

"Oh I've been around," she replied.

"This is Charlie," she slurred. "He lives in the flat above me."

Tina looked at him. Not only was he a lot older than Susan, he wasn't very clean either. When he smiled, she could see the gaps where his teeth were missing and the ones he had left were rotten.

Tina could only imagine what he was doing with her sister, and she would make it easy for him.

"Have yer bin ter see Dad?" asked Susan.

Tina shook her head. "I hardly think so."

"Mam's getting older yer know."

"She's not my mother."

"Well she's all yer've got."

"I think she'll survive without seeing me."

"Oh yeh, I forgot, we're not good enough. Oh by the way, Dad's coming home soon."

"But he got eight year," cried Tina. "He's only been in there three."

"Good be'aviour."

"When is he coming out?"

"Dunno, yer'll have ter ask him."

Susan smiled vehemently, knowing Tina would never do that.

"Well see yer, kid, got things ter do."

She shrieked with laughter as she tottered away on her high heels, clinging onto the arm of Charlie.

Tina slowly made her way over to May's. She had told Gordon not to take her tonight because she was staying for her tea.

Tina knocked at the door. May opened it. "Hello, luv, where've yer bin?"

"Oh, I went into town."

"Did yer get anything nice?"

"Well no, I didn't buy anything."

"You OK, lass, yer look a bit peaky."

"I'm fine. I bumped into my sister."

"Oh aye?"

"She told me my father's being released from prison. But she wouldn't say when."

"The little cow."

"I won't feel safe, May."

"Why don't yer ask the police? They'll know."

"I might do that."

"Come an have a cuppa?"

That was May's answer to everything, and just now, Tina thought it sounded like a good idea.

Tina spent three hours there. As usual, May had made a mountain of a meal, and insisted Tina have some. She stayed until it was time for her to take Sally home.

"I don't know where my Albert has got to, lass. He could have teken yer home."

"It's OK, May. The weather is mild, and the journey will tire her out." She nodded towards Sally, who had decided to throw one of her tantrums because she had to leave.

"Now you stop that, young un," said May. "By ek, you lead yer mother a dance. She don't do it with me, Tina. She knows she'd get a crack."

"I know, Solly spoiled her and she can be so stubborn at times."

Sally stopped screaming and let Tina put her coat on.

"Well I'll see you tomorrow, May, and thank you for tea."

"That's OK, ducks, see yer later, ta ra."

By the time Tina got Sally home, she was tired and well ready for her bath and bed. When Tina had finished clearing up, she had a bath herself and went to bed.

Next day, in the office, she opened her mail and there was a letter from Jo. She said she had met a doctor and that they were going to Africa to do some relief work. The letter was short but she said she would send her a postcard and to let her know how she was.

Tina showed the letter to Gordon.

"Do you mind?" she asked him.

He shook his head. "No, Jo wanted more than I could give her. I'm happy for her."

"Good, so am I. I have to ring the police."

"Why?"

"My sister informed me yesterday that my father was being released."

"What! But he's only done three years."

"Good behaviour she said."

"Good behaviour my arse. Sorry, Tina, somehow it doesn't sound right to me."

"I know and now I have to find out. I won't feel safe knowing he's back on the streets again. If he comes out, I'll move from here."

"Where will you go?"

"Whitby."

She made the call to the police who told her it was true. Her father would be out of prison in six weeks' time. The police had tried to stop it, but said there was little they could do, except to keep an eye on him.

"It's true," she told Gordon. "He's coming out."

"What are you going to do?"

"I have to think, Gordon, but one thing's for sure, I can't stay in Leeds. He knows where I am, and he blames me for going to prison. I will not put Sally at risk. If I go, will you be able to manage the business now?"

"Yes, you know I can."

"Good, I'm going to see May. She's sensible, maybe she'll have an idea."

"Why don't you ring Lilly as well, see what she has to say?"

"Yes, you're right, I'll do that, Gordon. Would you like to come to supper tonight? I might be able to think a little more clearly by then."

"I'll be there, Tina. Don't worry, we'll sort something out."

When Tina arrived at May's, she was hanging out the washing. Sally was playing with the rest of her brood in the garden.

"Hello, duck, what brings you here so early? Yer just in time, I've just put kettle on ter brew up."

"May, I need to talk to you."

"What's up, lass?"

"My father will be out of jail in six weeks' time."

"Bloody hell."

"He will find me, and I can't put Sally at risk. I know he'll come looking."

"Aye, he will. I don't know what ter say, lass. Yer right though, yer have ter think of her." She nodded toward Sally.

"I have asked Gordon to manage the office full time. I'll sell the house and move."

"By ek, that's a bit drastic in' it, but it might be fer the best. Eh, I wish we could flit, it fair does me head in. Our Albert's getting on and these lads are runnin' wild. They need to be away from here, still that's my worry."

"You wouldn't move would you, May?"

"Aye, I bloody well would. I've had enough of round here."

"Well, I'll take Sally home with me now. I'll let you know what I decide to do."

"Right, you do that. But think on, if there's owt I can do ter help, just let me know."

159

"I will, and thanks."

Tina took Sally to the park where she let her feed the ducks. She then took her home to feed her before she went to bed. Tina poured herself a drink before she sat down to call Lilly.

"Hi, Lilly, how are you?"

"I'm fine, Tina. It's always nice to hear from you. How are things?"

Tina brought her up to date with all the gossip and news, told her about Jo going to Africa.

"Well as long as she's happy."

"She is. Lilly, I've just heard that my father is coming out of jail in six weeks' time."

"Surely that's not right, Tina. They can't let him out."

"They are. The police are not happy, but they say they can't do anything about it."

"What are you going to do?"

"I've asked Gordon to run the business for me. I'm going to sell the house and move."

"Where to?"

"Anywhere, I can't stay here. He will come looking for me and I have to think of Sally."

"Would you move here, Tina?"

"I would if I could find the right place."

"Why don't you come over for a week, bring Sally? Leave her with us during the day and have a look round the Estate Agents. If you find something, you could stay with us until you get things sorted out."

"Could I? That would be great. I'll give you a ring when I've arranged things at this end."

"You do that, Tina, and take care."

"I will, thank you."

Tina hung up and went to the kitchen to prepare supper. She was not hungry, but she had invited Gordon, so she had to make something.

Gordon arrived a little after eight. " I thought you could do with this," he said, handing her a bottle of wine.

"Thank you. Supper's nearly done, why don't you pour it?"

"Did you see May?" he asked.

"Yes, she said she was fed up of where she was living, and if she could move, she would."

"Pity you couldn't move in together. Sally wouldn't have far to go to be looked after."

"You're right, but as much as I love May, I couldn't live in the same house with all her lot. I need peace and my own space. It's always noisy in May's house."

He laughed. "Maybe you're right."

Then she said, "Look, Gordon, I want to go to Lilly's at the weekend, can you manage on your own next week?"

"Of course I can. I can drive you over there at the weekend and then drive over next weekend and bring you back."

"You don't have to do that."

"I want to. I've nothing else on."

"Well I can't pretend it won't be a help. It saves me struggling with cases and Sally, especially if she decided to throw a paddy."

"Good, ring Lilly and tell her. I'll clear away these dishes while you're doing it."

Gordon cleared away and she rang Lilly and said she would be there at the weekend.

"Good, I look forward to seeing you and Sally again."

"She's grown, but she's still demanding."

"She'll love it by the sea, Tina. David will pick you up from the station."

"No, it's fine. Gordon has offered to drive me over. He said he would get a room somewhere and drive back the next day."

"It'll save you struggling with Sally and suitcases."

"Yes, that's what he said."

"He can stay here."

"Are you sure?"

"Yes, we have plenty of room."

" Thank you. We'll be there Friday teatime, is that OK with you?"

"Yes, drive carefully. We'll see you then. Goodbye, dear."

As she hung up Gordon came back into the room. "All arranged?" he asked.

"Yes, and Lilly said that you can stay there with them."

"That's good of her." They sat and had another drink then he said, "You know if I can help in anyway I will."

"Yes I know, but you do more than enough for us as it is. You've not mentioned your lady friend lately. How is it going?"

Gordon shook his head. "Tina, don't you know yet?"

"Know what?" she asked.

"You're the one I love."

161

"Me?"

"Yes, ever since I first saw you, I have loved you."

He walked over to her and took hold of her hand. "I only got involved with Jo because you married Solly. Don't get me wrong, I liked him and he was good to you and I was very fond of Jo. I just could not commit to her the way she wanted. It wouldn't have been fair."

"I'm very fond of you, Gordon, but to be honest, I haven't thought about getting involved with anyone else."

"Don't worry, I'll wait. Do you like me a little bit, Tina?"

"Yes, yes I do."

"Good, at least that's a start." He kissed her gently, but this time on her mouth instead of her cheek.

Up to that moment, Tina had not thought about having another relationship; she had been too busy. When he kissed her, it aroused a stirring deep inside her. This was a feeling that she thought she would never feel again after Solly. Tina found herself responding to his kiss.

He took hold of her hand. "Let me love you, Tina?"

"It's been a long time, Gordon."

"I'll take things slow. If you tell me to stop, I will."

He led her upstairs, and he slowly undressed her and let her clothes fall to the floor. He kissed her lips and then her neck. She had forgotten how good it felt. What she was feeling now, she had never experienced, even with Solly, and even though she had loved him, this was completely different.

He laid her gently on the bed and undressed. He lay beside her and cupped her breast in his hand. She moaned and kissed him harder. His hands moved over her belly and down to the soft crevice at the top of her legs.

"Oh, Tina, I've waited so long for this." His lips moved down to her nipples and it felt like an electric shock going through her body. He rose above her and gently entered her, and he slowly, ever so slowly made love to her.

When it was over, he held her in his arms and they slept. Next morning after breakfast, Gordon said he would go home and pack an overnight bag for the weekend.

"What time do you want to leave?" he asked her.

"I think about eleven. We will be at Lilly's just after lunch. Is that alright with you?"

"Yes, I'll be ready; pick you up then."

As he kissed her he said, "Have you any regrets, Tina?"

"No, none at all."

When he had gone, she bathed and dressed before she woke Sally. She packed their stuff and Gordon was back for eleven.

"Are you ready?" he asked.

"Yes, I think I have everything we need."

They packed the car and they were on their way. The journey would take them around two hours.

"Do you know what kind of house you'll be looking for?" he asked her.

"Yes, I'd like a cottage near the sea with plenty of room for Sally."

"Would it be alright if I came over to see you at the weekends?"

"Yes, you do understand why I have to move don't you?"

"Yes, I would do the same if I was in your shoes."

You have to promise me that you won't tell anyone where I have gone."

"Are you going to tell May?"

"Oh yes, but she won' tell anyone. If anyone says they have to contact me, for whatever reason, take their details and tell them I will contact them. I'll set up an office when I move and then I can deal with things."

"Sounds as if you have it all worked out," he said.

"I've given it a lot of thought."

They arrived at Lilly's around lunchtime, and for a while, things were a little hectic, then Lilly said she had made some lunch. Everyone sat down and Lilly told Tina that she and David would take Sally out each day so that she would be free to scout around and look for a house. Lilly had already been to some property agents and picked up some details for her.

"Thank you, that will save me some time. I may as well start looking this afternoon. Do you want to come with me, Gordon?"

"Yes, I have nothing else to do."

"We'll take Sally with us," said David.

Lilly and David put an excited Sally in the car. Lilly said, "If you want to go out tonight feel free. We won't be back until late."

"What about her?" asked Tina, nodding towards Sally.

"We'll stop and eat somewhere. Don't worry, go on, leave her with us."

"That's great, Lilly, but she can be demanding."

"We'll cope."

"If she doesn't tire you out first."

Lilly and David drove off with Sally waving from the car window. Gordon took Tina in his arms and kissed her.

"I love you so much and I'm glad that we have a little time together. I would never hurt you, I hope you know that?"

"I do, Gordon."

"Now where shall we go?"

"I think we should start looking at this list of properties."

They started to look through the leaflets that Lilly had collected for them, and discarded two of them.

Of the two remaining, one was a fisherman's cottage and the other a terraced house.

They decided to look at the house first. The price was right, but when they saw it, Tina said it was unsuitable for Sally. The house was near the road, and there was no garden for her to play in.

They went and found the fisherman's cottage. It was lovely but very tiny and was barely big enough for one person, never mind a lively toddler.

Tina thanked the man who owned the cottage and explained that she had a little girl and that it was just too small.

"What size was you lookin' for?" asked the old man.

"Something that has a good bit of room and a garden or yard is a must."

"Well, my old mate at other end of town is sellin' his farm'ouse like. He's movin' in with 'is daughter, over in sandbanks it is."

"I don't know if I could afford a farmhouse," Tina said.

"It ain't much dearer than this. You go see it, then make your mind up."

"He gave her the address and directions on how to find it. They drove past the harbour and round the coastline before they found the farmhouse. At first, the directions he had given them looked as if it was quite a distance away, but it only took them fifteen minutes, so it wasn't as far as it had first seemed.

"It's so lovely here. It seems a million miles away from Leeds, Gordon."

"Yes it does. It would certainly be better for Sally. Tina, before you decide on this, are you certain this is what you want to do?"

"I'll always have a soft spot for Leeds. After all, I was born there, it's my home, but I can't afford to take any chances with Sally's safety now my father is coming out of jail."

"Maybe you're right."

"The other thing is, that I'm not moving too far away from everyone. They will be able to come and visit us, it will be a cheap holiday for them."

"Well yes, there is that to it."

They found the farmhouse and drove through the old white gates. Tina wondered why it was called a farmhouse. There was no farmland attached that she could see.

Lying in front of the door in the sun was an old dog, and in a rocking chair sat an equally old man smoking his pipe.

"You must be the young couple what's lookin' ter buy some place."

Tina looked surprised. "Yes, that's right."

"Old Sam jest let me know. Got one of them old message machines, handy like. Well, ye best 'ave a look round, see what ye think."

As they stepped through the door, Tina looked around, impressed. The place was spotless, and everything in its place.

"Me daughter looks after me."

All the rooms were the same. The walls were all painted white and each room neat and tidy.

"Don't like mess, can't abide a mucky hole."

They laughed. "Tek the'selves round, look at what you need to. I'm too old ter bother. I'll be outside with Bess when thee's finished."

"Nice old man," remarked Tina.

"Nice old place," Gordon said.

In the main room was an old fireplace made from Yorkshire stone. The room itself was large, and one wall had a large window that let in all the light. Old brass lamps hung round the walls, and Tina thought that her old furniture would fit well into this room. A door led from this room into the kitchen.

Looking at the kitchen, she saw now how the cottage earned the description of farmhouse. The room was a typically big farmhouse kitchen. A long rectory table occupied the middle of the floor. There were pots and pans, all gleaming, hanging from a rack suspended from the ceiling. The Aga cooker stood in the corner, and enough cupboards to be able to open a store.

The door led out to a large back yard.

"We'll look at that in a minute," Tina said.

Upstairs was a double bedroom and two smaller bedrooms. They were the same as the downstairs rooms. All white washed and stone floors. There were wooden beams that ran the length of the ceiling. The view from the windows was breathtaking. She could see the sea and the boats from one of the windows and the fenland from the others.

They went downstairs and out into the yard. A shed stood in the corner that housed gardening tools, and another shed used for storage. At the end of the yard was a gate; this led out onto the cliff top, high above sea level, and you could look out over Whitby and see Scarborough and Filey.

Tina exhaled in and smelled the saltiness of the sea air. "I could sit here for hours," she said.

They walked to the front of the house, and the old man was still sat in his rocking chair, his dog at his feet.

Around the courtyard there were a couple of other outbuildings, all empty, but clean. In the far corner was another building that looked like another small cottage. Tina tried the door but it was locked.

She walked back across the yard to the man. "What is that building over there?" she asked.

Another house with four bedrooms. Was gonna let it out ter mek a bit of money. I couldn't bide the thought of other people in me yard. Here's the keys, go have a look see."

They walked back across the yard and let themselves into the house. It was in the same condition as the main house, white walls, stone floors and spotless. A door led out the back into a large garden. The house was far enough away from the main house, but close enough to have good neighbours, if you wanted them, that is.

"This is great."

"The whole complex is too big for you, Tina," said Gordon.

"Yes, but I have an idea. I could live in the main house with Sally, and make one of the rooms into an office. There is enough room for us to have a dog and a cat, and I think that this is big enough for May and her brood."

"May, what makes you think she would be willing to move here?"

"She would, I know. Albert wants to finish work. Some of her kids will soon leave home. She would look after Sally and do a bit of cleaning."

"But you don't know how much he's asking for this place."

"How much do you think I would be able to sell my home in Leeds for, Gordon?"

"Well, taking into consideration the size and the location, fifty thousand maybe."

"I bet he wants less than that for this place," she said.

"Whatever he asks is worth it. You still have the business and all the savings that Solly left you. I don't know how much that was, but it will see you through comfortably."

If I came here, would you run the business for me and sell the house? I would pay you as my manager, Gordon."

"I can do that, but I wouldn't mix business and pleasure. I would keep both separate. So whatever goes on between us, will not make any difference to how I run the business."

"OK," she said.

"Do you think you should find out how much he's asking for the place, before you make any more plans?"

"I hope I can afford to buy it. I love this place so much already."

"Of course you will be able to afford it, just ask him."

They walked back over to the old man, who in their absence had brought some glasses and a jug of beer outside.

"Sit the'selves down and have a drink," he said.

For the next few minutes, they made small talk, and he asked Tina about herself and where she was staying.

Tina told him she lived in Leeds, but she was staying with friends on the other side of Whitby. She told him she wanted to live here, but not the reason why.

"What are you asking for the farmhouse?" she said.

"Well now, I don't need to mek a big profit. Just cover me costs, though it has a lot goin fer it. I want fifteen thousand pounds, that's me final price. Tek it or leave it. I'm too old to haggle."

"I'll take it," Tina told him. "I'll get my solicitor to draw up the papers and send them to yours and get things moving."

"Don't have no solic…well whatever fancy name they call the'selves. Don't see why they should mek a livin' from me, always done me own business."

"But I have to know where to put your money," she said.

"Pay me one of them cheques, and me daughter will see to it. This was handed down to me, bin in the family a long time, so the only paper I have will be one sayin' I've sold it ter yer. Will that do?"

"Well yes, I suppose it will. When can I move in?"

"End of the month do yer, me daughter will help ter clear me things."

"That will be great." She gave him her details, shook hands and left.

"Well," said Gordon, "you don't mess around do you? I didn't think you'd find a place so quickly."

"Neither did I. It's perfect and such a bargain. It won't even need decorating. I don't want to change anything anyway."

"I hope you're doing the right thing, Tina."

"Oh I think so. I will have to go back to Leeds with you tomorrow now, there are arrangements I have to make."

"Knowing you, that won't take you very long."

When they arrived back at Lilly's, they found that Lilly, David and Sally had been back a little while.

"Hi, I thought we would come back early. The weather is so nice, we could have a bar-b-cue."

"That would be nice," Tina said.

Then Lilly said, "Let's leave the men to do the cooking. You and I can go inside and throw a salad together."

"OK. I could feed Sally at the same time and then she can go to bed. She's had a long day."

"Good idea. Are you OK with that?" she asked David and Gordon.

"I think we'll survive," David said.

"Get a beer in your hand, Gordon, that's the way to handle this cooking."

"Thanks, I think I will."

Once inside, Tina started to feed Sally. "Did you see anything you liked today, Tina?"

"Yes, and I have so much to tell you. Let me get Sally settled first and then I can tell you and David together. Can I take her upstairs for a bath?"

"Of course you can, you don't have to ask, you know that. I bet she's tired, she's run herself ragged this afternoon."

"Maybe that's why she is so demanding at home. She has so little space to run around."

"She's been fine today."

"What, are you telling me she hasn't had a tantrum?"

"No, not at all."

"She behaves herself for May too. With me, she's a little monster at times."

"She'll grow out of it, Tina."

Over the next hour, the men got the cooking under way. Tina heard them laughing outside. They seemed to be getting on well and she was pleased. She finished feeding Sally, then took her for her bath and brought her downstairs to say goodnight. Lilly was preparing salad and potatoes.

"Don't wanna go to bed," cried Sally.

Lilly took hold of her. "Listen, Sally, you go to bed and we'll take you to see the boats tomorrow."

"And the fishes?"

"And fishes."

Sally's face broke out into a grin. She said goodnight to everyone and went to bed without another sound.

"She gets too much of her own way. May can handle her, but I find her hard work at times."

"She's still young; give her time. Here, take this wine. Let's go and sit with the boys and you can tell me all about your day."

Once outside, Lilly said. "David, Tina has seen somewhere today."

"Oh good. Where is it?"

"Over at Sandbanks."

"Sandbanks. But they're all big properties on the hill."

"Do you know the farmhouse on the right side?"

"Yes."

"That's the one." Tina and Gordon told them all about it, even about the house that would be good for May.

"Are you sure she would move?" asked Lilly.

"Yes, once she sees it. It's better than where they live now."

"But she has all those kids."

"May can be rough and ready and her kids rowdy, but she controls them better than I can control Sally."

"How much is he asking for this house?" David asked.

"Fifteen thousand," Tina replied.

"That is a bargain, you should snap it up, Tina."

"I have, and that's why I'm going back with Gordon tomorrow. I can put my house on the market and if it hasn't sold by the end of the month, Gordon said he would take care of it."

"You don't mess around do you? When are you hoping to move in?" David asked her.

"At the end of the month. The old man said his daughter would help him to move out."

"Is that long enough for you to organise things?" asked Lilly.

"Yes, don't worry, I can manage."

The meal was cooked and they had a pleasant couple of hours eating and drinking and telling jokes. Tina realised that it was a long time since she had enjoyed something like this.

Lilly made to get up and clear the dishes away and Tina stood to help her.

"No it's OK, Tina, why don't you and Gordon go for a walk. Relax. You have had a busy day. David and I will clear up."

"You've been busy too, are you sure about it?"

"Yes, go on, it won't take us long."

"Thank you, we won't be too long."

Tina and Gordon walked down to the harbour where the moonlight was shining over the boats and across the water. They stood a while and Gordon put his arm around her shoulders.

"It's nice and peaceful here. Do you know, Tina, this is the first time I have been to Whitby."

"Is it? The surrounding areas are lovely. I love the smell of the sea."

He gently turned her to face him and kissed her, and she responded. Then she said, "Do you know, Solly was the only man I would trust, and when he died, I thought I would never trust or love another man again. But I think I could love you, Gordon."

"Good, because I have loved you for years."

They walked back to the house hand in hand. David and Lilly were just coming onto the porch again.

"Oh good, you're here. I've just made a pot of coffee if you would like some?" Lilly asked.

"Yes, please," they both said simultaneously.

"David and I have been discussing things and we think you would be able to get things sorted out better if you didn't have to worry about Sally. Why don't you leave her with us?"

"I couldn't ask you to do that."

"Why, we love having her. You could get the house packed up and put on the market, get the other things, and then come back here next week. I'm sure you'll get more done not having to worry about her."

"I can't say it won't help."

"It makes sense. If you're going to move in at the end of the month, why take her back and forth?"

"It's very good of you both, but I want you to promise me that if she gets too much for you, you'll phone me, and I'll come and collect her."

"We will, but I think we'll manage. Well I don't know about the rest of you, but I'm ready for bed."

They said goodnight and David and Lilly went inside to bed. They sat on the porch talking a little longer.

"You know, Gordon, the more I think about that farmhouse, the more I love it and I feel quite excited at the thought of moving in; and I know Sally will be happy, she has so much space to run around."

"I'm pleased for you, Tina. As long as you feel safe and happy, that's all I want for you."

"What time are we setting off tomorrow?" she asked.

"We don't have to leave until after lunch. We'll still be home by tea-time."

"Good, I think I'll go to bed now. I'm tired."

"Very well. Goodnight, Tina, sleep well."

He kissed her and they went to their rooms. Tina slept soundly until the sun, shining on her face, woke her the next morning.

When they sat down for breakfast Lilly said. "What time are you two heading home?"

"We thought that after lunch would be soon enough," said Tina.

"David and I thought we would go off for the day and take Sally. But if you want us to hang around or you want to keep Sally here, that's what we will do."

Tina shook her head. "Don't change your plans. We will leave early, and we can stop on the way back and have lunch. Are you sure having Sally won't be too much for you?"

"No, don't worry. When you leave, lock the door and put the key through the letterbox. We have a spare one with us."

"I'll ring you during the week to make sure Sally is behaving herself. I hope you don't regret it, and please don't spoil her."

Lilly laughed. "We won't."

When they had cleared the breakfast things, David, Lilly and Sally said goodbye and left for the day.

"It won't take me very long to get ready," she told David. "Most of my things are still in the suitcase. I only unpacked Sally's things. I was going to unpack mine later. I thought I was staying all week."

"I won't be too long before I'm ready either." He put his arms around her and kissed her. "Are you happy, Tina?"

"Yes I am, but I'll feel more settled once the farmhouse is mine and I've moved in."

His kisses became more urgent and she responded as his hands caressed her body. They lay on the bed and he gently made love to her.

Later she had a shower, and when she was ready, he carried their cases down to the car.

She looked around to make sure everything was tidy. She scribbled a note for Lilly, thanking her again for taking Sally. Then she locked up the house and left the keys.

They drove through Whitby and took a detour through Filey, then onto Malton and finally into Scarborough. They parked the car and walked hand in hand along the sand.

She loved Scarborough. It had an atmosphere of its own. The amusement arcades, the funfair, children laughing, running in an out of the water. The fishing boats bobbing up and down where they were tethered until their owners took them out at night, and the seagulls swooping down on anything that looked like a meal.

"I've always loved it here," she told him.

"I've only ever been once before, when I came on a school trip. I remember we stopped at the transport café for a drink."

"I know the place you mean. My granddad would stop there every time we came."

"Did you come here a lot then?"

"Yes, my granddad owned a caravan; he used to have it in a field just outside Scarborough. It must have been there over twenty years. The family who owned the field used to train racehorses. Granddad and the owner were old friends. Grandma would make breakfast for everyone and then we would spend the day here."

They spent the next two hours in Scarborough and had a meal before continuing their journey back to Leeds.

The traffic was light and they made good time. When they pulled up in front of her home, Tina said, "Why don't you stay here tonight, Gordon? In the morning, you can go to the office while I see my solicitor and May. In the afternoon, I can contact the Estate Agent and start packing."

"That's a good idea if you're sure."

She nodded. They took the cases inside and Tina said it was pointless unpacking them, only to re-pack them. Instead, they had a couple of drinks and discussed all that had to be done.

When they went to bed, they were so tired they just fell asleep in each other's arms.

Next morning, they both felt much better. Gordon drove to the office, dropping Tina off in town on the way.

"If you go to May's, give me a ring and I'll pick you up and take you home."

"Thanks, ring me if you have any problems at the office."

"I will," he said before driving away.

Tina went to her solicitor's office and gave him all the details of the farmhouse. She told him that the old man did not use a solicitor, and that he just wanted cash paying into his bank and he would hand her all the paperwork.

The solicitor told her that he would have everything completed within two weeks, and if all went according to plan, there would be no reason why she could not move in at the end of the month as she had planned.

Tina left his office and made her way to May's house. So much had happened since she had last seen her that she could not wait to tell her all the news.

May answered the door. "Hello, chuck, come in."

"Hello, May, how are you?"

"Oh not so bad. My Albert's been feelin' a bit off though. I think it's all the hours he works, never lets up. Just going ter mash tea. Sit down and then you can tell me all yer news. E' I 'ave missed yer."

When May had made the tea, they sat down at the kitchen table.

"Now, lass, what's new? Where's little 'un?"

"She's still at Lilly's. As you know, we were going to stay the week, but I came back with Gordon. Lilly said to leave Sally with them until I went back this weekend."

"That'll be a nice break fer yer."

"Well, yes it will. But, May, I'm packing up to leave Leeds."

"Yer what?"

"Yes, I have found this lovely old farmhouse in Whitby. The old man who owns it wants to move in with his daughter." Tina continued to tell her all about the house and the outbuildings.

"Eh lass, yer don't do things by halves, do yer?"

"That's why I had to come back today, May."

"When are yer movin' in then?"

"Hopefully by the end of the month."

"What about the business?"

"Gordon is going to run it for me full time. I'm going to make an office in the new house and work from there."

"Aye well, mebbe yer right, but I'm goin' ter miss yer, lass, and the bairn."

"May, that brings me to another part."

Tina told her about the cottage at the end of the yard, with its own little garden and the field surrounding it.

"If Albert is thinking about retiring, and you want it, it's yours, May."

"What?" May yelled. "I can't afford 'owt like that."

"Listen, I am buying the place, and whether you move in or not, I will still have the cottage, It comes as part of the package. I would much rather have you living there than some stranger. If it makes you feel better, you can pay me rent, but only a token amount. All I ask in return is that you take care of Sally when I need it, and maybe do a bit of cleaning, but only when I am busy. I will do my own cleaning and have Sally when I'm not working."

"Eh lass, it sounds grand. I'll have ter talk ter Albert of course."

"Of course. All I ask is that you give me a month after moving in and then I will have the place ready for you. It will be better for the kiddies. The cottage is ten minutes' walk from the beach. I have to go back at the weekend. I'll ring the old man and ask if you can go look at the place before you make up your mind."

"Eh lass, how can I thank yer?"

"You've been good to me, May, and I am glad I can repay you."

Gordon arrived to take her home, and she left a very excited May, who could not wait to tell Albert.

"I won't come in tonight, Tina. I have a lot to do at home."

"That's fine. I want to get on with some packing, and see if I can ring the farmhouse."

"OK. Let me know if you need help."

"I will. Goodnight."

The first thing she did when she went in, was to call the farmhouse and ask if it was all right to bring her friend to see the cottage. She also said that she had been to her solicitor and she was putting her house up for sale.

The old man was more than happy to get things sorted as soon as possible. He just wanted rid of the place and to move in with his daughter.

Tina then rang Lilly and spoke to Sally who was having the time of her life. Lilly said she had been fine; they had been taking her out and she had been good.

May and Albert went to see the cottage in the farmhouse. They fell in love with it, and now May, too, was busy packing up her house.

Within two weeks, Tina had an offer for the house. She had finished packing and completed all the paperwork for the farmhouse. The couple who were buying her house, wanted to move in as soon as possible, which coincided with the time Tina wanted to move to Whitby.

The weekend Tina moved was a little hectic, but the removal men were good and made everything run smoothly. She and Gordon worked throughout the day putting things in their places, and by Sunday night, everything was finished.

Tina had a bath, sat in the living room and looked around.

She was so pleased with how everything looked; it was warm and cosy and she loved it. She walked round the rooms again, taking in the newness of it all. The old man had taken most of his things, but the few bits he had left her added character to the place.

This week she would go across the yard to the other cottage and make it clean and warm, ready for May.

Over the next few days, she got busy with the room that would become her office.

She called Lilly to go collect Sally.

"Why don't you come on Friday and we will drive you back so we can see the farmhouse," said Lilly.

"That would be lovely."

On Friday, she went to Lilly and David's; they had lunch and all drove back to the farmhouse.

"You've got yourself a bargain here," said David.

"Yes, I know. I am so happy with it."

Sally was running all over the place. She loved all the space, and Tina knew she would be safe.

Lilly and David did not stay long. They were meeting friends in the town. They said goodbye and said they would visit the following week.

Within a few days, Tina had settled in. Gordon rang her every day and visited them at the weekend.

A month later, a removal van turned up with all May's furniture. She, Albert and the kids had followed on in the car. Within minutes, kids were racing round the yard. May was shouting for them to help move things inside and Albert just carried things backwards and forwards in his own quiet way.

Tina left them to it. There were enough of them to help without her getting involved.

The following day May came over to the cottage.

"Eh lass, I can't thank you enough. Me an' my Albert have never lived in a place as posh as this."

"No need to thank me, May. As I told you before, it all came together."

"No matter, it's a chuffin palace, compared to what we had. Thanks again, lass."

"You're welcome, May, you deserve it."

Over the following months, life improved and had never seemed better for Tina. She was happy, healthy and safe. Sally was happy and had not had a temper tantrum since they had moved, and May was proving to be a godsend.

She saw Lilly and David every two weeks, and Gordon visited most weekends. Tina was growing more than fond of him.

May would babysit Sally while Gordon took Tina out. They would come back and Gordon would tell her how much he loved her.

One day Gordon rang Tina and told her he needed her in the office. There was a problem he could not deal with. May said she would look after Sally, and Tina caught the train to Leeds. When she arrived, Gordon picked her up from the station.

"What's wrong, Gordon?"

"He knows."

"Who knows what?"

"Your father. He's out of jail, and he paid a visit to your old house. The couple that live there told him you had moved to Whitby, but they didn't have your address."

Tina felt sick. "I'll get in touch with Dan," she said.

"Who's Dan?"

"An old friend of Solly's, he'll know what to do."

Gordon took her to the office. She phoned Dan and told him of the problem.

"He's out on parole, Tina, and if he comes near you, he will go straight back inside."

Tina was worried, but there was nothing more she could do.

She got Gordon to take her back to the station and she took the train back to Whitby, where Albert met her at the station. By the time they arrived home, May had fed Sally and put her to bed.

May handed her a cup of tea. "Here you are, lass, get this down yer. I expect yer all in. What problem have yer got at the office that Gordon can't handle?"

"He knows, May."

"Yer what?"

"My dad. He knows that I'm in Whitby."

"Does he know exactly where?"

"It shouldn't be too difficult to find us. Someone will talk about the new people who have moved into the farmhouse."

"Mebbe it won't come to that. You shouldn't worry, lass, otherwise it could tek over yer life. Me an' Albert will look out fer yer."

"Thanks, May."

"Eat up, lass, yer look done in."

Tina ate the meal that May had put in front of her. She was not very hungry, but she did not want to upset May who had been so good to her.

When she had finished, she said goodnight and went back to her own cottage. The telephone was ringing before she got through the door.

It was Lilly asking her how things were. Tina told her about her trip to Leeds and the problem she had.

"I think you'll be safe here. Try and get a good night's sleep; we'll see you during the week."

"Thanks, Lilly. Goodnight."

Tina was going through to the kitchen and the phone rang again. This time it was Gordon ringing to make sure she got back safely.

"Yes, everything's fine. May had fed Sally and put her to bed; she also had a meal waiting for me."

"That explains things. I rang earlier and couldn't get an answer. I was worried. Well as long as you got home safe, now go to bed, and if you need me, you know where I am."

"Thank you, Gordon, I'll speak to you soon. Goodnight."

"Tina, are you still there?"

"Yes, why?"

"Tina, you know I love you. Why don't we get married. I will look after you."

"I'm sorry, Gordon, I'm not ready for that yet. Not when there is so much going on. I need to think clearly and have things sorted out."

"OK, you know where I am. Call me if you need me. Goodnight."

"Goodnight, and thank you."

Tina went to bed thinking about Gordon's proposal.

The next few months were very quiet. Tina managed to run some of the business from her office and look after Sally. Gordon would come over at the weekends and they would take Sally down to the beach.

She loved riding on the donkeys. She was easier to handle these days, and had not had a tantrum in months. Maybe because there was so much for her to do and so many people to keep her occupied. She was always running around with May's brood, and she was in and out of May's house; it was her second home.

May cleaned for Tina once a week and looked after Sally a couple of hours each day. Even though they were close, Tina and May still respected each other's privacy.

May looked upon Tina as an elder daughter. She would always be grateful to her for making it possible for them to move to this place.

Sometimes early in the morning, Tina would take a cup of tea and walk through the back gate to sit on the bench. She would look down to the town below. She could see the cliffs and all the seagulls flying round the fishing boats that were coming in after their night out.

It was her hour of peace before the rest of the world woke up. She noticed over the last month, a man walking his mongrel dog. He would pass each morning, say "good morning" and walk on.

She thought he must live further up the lane in one of the other houses, as they were the only other people who had access to this path.

On this particular morning he walked past her. "Morning, it's going to be grand today."

"Yes it is," she replied.

"Not many more now afore the winter sets in."

"Do you live round here?" she asked him.

He nodded towards the houses up the road. "Aye, up yonder. Me and my dog walk for miles we do."

Tina wondered at his accent. He wasn't from around these parts, she was sure of that.

"Where do you come from?"

"Used to live in Cornwall, wife got homesick so we moved back. When she died, I kind of got used to the place, so here we are, my dog and me."

Tina smiled. "Well you're always welcome to come for tea or coffee."

"Thank you kindly, might take you up on that sometime. Must get on, good day to you."

"Bye," she said.

She told May about her meeting the man and what he said.

"Yer want ter be careful, lass, he could be anyone."

"Oh I think he's OK, May. I see him every morning walking his dog, and he always says hello. He said he lives in the houses up the road."

"I've never seen him round here."

"No, he only comes this far down in the mornings to walk his dog."

"Well, be a bit wary, lass."

Tina thought she had no need to worry too much. She had not been in his company for more than five minutes, and she hadn't told him anything about herself; she thought no more about it.

The last weekend in October was Tina's birthday and Gordon was coming to take her out to celebrate.

"Will you take Sally for the night?" she asked May.

"What a question," May retorted. "Why do you have ter ask any road?"

"Because it's polite to do so. I don't want to take you for granted."

"You don't, and of course I'll have her. Get yerself out, and have some fun. Young lass like you, spends too much time on yer own yer do. When's he coming up?"

"Friday."

"Well I would like yer to do me a favour?" said May.

"Of course, what?"

"Would yer take me eldest into Whitby, into one of them shops and advise her on a dress? I'll give yer the money."

"Of course, but why me?"

"Well I haven't much idea, an' you have. Besides, I can't walk round all them shops. I'll have little 'un, an' give her tea. It would be a big favour ter me."

"Of course I will. In fact, I might treat myself to a new dress at the same time. I could do with something new to wear when Gordon takes me out on Saturday. Would it be alright if we spent the afternoon there?"

"Of course it is, luv. That's settled then."

On Friday afternoon after lunch, Tina and May's eldest daughter, Linda, set off for the shops in the town.

"Thanks, Tina," said May and then she turned to her daughter. "Mind what I told you, our Linda."

"Yes, Mum."

As they left the yard, Tina asked her what had May had meant.

Linda just shrugged her shoulders. "Oh not much, just to be polite to you and take your advice."

"But you're always polite to me."

"Yes, but you know Ma."

As they went off down the road, May picked up the telephone. "Coast is clear. See you in a while."

She went into the yard, and within a few minutes David, Lilly and Gordon drove through the gates. They carried boxes and baskets and they all got to work.

Within two hours, the yard had been transformed with coloured lights all strung up, balloons, there were several tables with food and drink, they had even set up some music so they could dance.

"We'll show her how ter have some fun," said May, to no one in particular.

"It was a good idea of yours," Lilly said.

"Least I could do after all that girl's done fer me and mine, and I managed ter get her a lovely present."

When everything was ready Gordon said, "Shall I drive down the town and see if I can find them? I could always say I came up early, but didn't say anything before in case I could get away."

"That's a good idea," replied Lilly. "Drive up the back lane and come in that way if you can. Bring her through the kitchen door and out into the yard and we'll be waiting."

"Fine. I have to pick up my gift for her anyway, but I'm not giving it to her until tomorrow."

Gordon drove into the town to see if he could see them. Whitby was only small place, so there wasn't too many places he could look for them.

As he drove down the hill, he saw them walking by the harbour wall. He parked the car and walked over to them.

"Now why are you two dawdling?" he asked.

Tina looked surprised. "Gordon, what are you doing here? I thought you were coming tomorrow. But it's nice to see you anyway."

"I didn't say anything before because I wasn't sure that I could get away today. Hello, Linda, have you had fun?"

"Yes thanks, I got a dress and so did Tina."

"Yes," replied Tina, "we must have been to every dress shop here before she decided on one. No wonder May wanted to stay at home."

Gordon smiled. "Come on, I'll give you a lift home. Go sit in the car, I need to pick something up. I won't be long."

Gordon opened the car door for them to get in. Then he walked back over the bridge out of sight. When he returned he said, "Right, I've booked us a table for your birthday meal tomorrow night, Tina."

"Oh good, I'm so looking forward to it. I haven't been out in ages."

They drove up the hill towards home. As they reached the top, he blew his horn.

"What was that for?" she asked.

"Just in case someone is coming round the corner down the hill. You know how steep it is."

"I've never noticed before."

"By the way, the gate to your yard is stuck. I will have to park at the other side. I'll have a look at it and then bring the car round."

"OK, I can't say I've noticed it. It's quiet isn't it?"

"Maybe May is feeding the kids."

"Oh yes, I didn't realise the time."

They walked through the back of the farmhouse into the front yard. As they walked in, someone switched on the lights and everyone shouted, "Surprise!"

Tina was unable to say anything, and May walked over to her.

"Happy birthday, luv."

Tina looked round and saw Lilly and David. She walked over to them.

"This is lovely, when did you plan all this? You crafty lot."

May laughed. "We wanted to say thank you an' we did all this after you had gone out with our Linda. Even the kids helped."

"This was why Linda kept me going from shop to shop."

Linda smiled. "Sorry, Tina, I only did as I was told."

"That's OK. Now I know why."

Tina turned to Gordon. "And you, did you know about this too?"

He smiled. "Sorry, couldn't spoil it."

"Well in that case, there's only one thing to do."

"What's that?" asked May.

"Let's have a party," she cried.

"And they did. The kids ran around; they danced and had a great time. The adults danced and talked. Someone had invited the neighbours, who were pleased to join in and get to know the people who had moved into the farmhouse.

At nine o' clock, May took time out to put the youngest to bed, including Sally, and then she went back to the party.

By midnight, everyone was tired and a little drunk, but very happy. When everyone had gone Tina said, "We had better get this lot put away."

"No we won't," said May. "Lilly and David are stayin' in me spare room. We will have it done in no time in the morning. Don't you worry, get yerself ter bed an' leave it."

Tina was too tired to argue, but she was very happy. She and Gordon went to bed together that night. As he gently made love to her, she thought, *It's been a long time since I felt like this, and it's wonderful.*

When she woke next morning, Gordon was still asleep. As she looked at him, she realised that she loved him. He was so different from Solly. She never realised that all the time she had known him he had wanted her.

As she gently kissed him, he stirred and took her into his arms. She snuggled into him and he kissed her lips. She felt the stirring of passion deep in her belly. She moaned and ran her hands over his back. He lowered his lips and took her nipple into his mouth. She pushed herself up to him and he rose above her and slowly entered her, and she pushed herself into him further. They made love with urgency, as if this was the last time.

Later as they relaxed he said, "Happy birthday, Tina, I love you very much."

"I think I love you too."

They showered and went downstairs, and when she opened the door, she saw all the tables from the party had been put away, and someone had even washed the yard.

Sally was playing in May's garden with the others and May sat scraping potatoes for dinner.

"Hello, you two, did yer sleep well?" she asked.

"Yes, thank you, May, and thank you for yesterday and having Sally."

"No matter. Happy birthday, lass. Here, it's now't much, but I hope you like it?"

Tina took the package. "Thank you." She opened it to find a lovely long red scarf. More like a shawl really.

"Oh May, it's lovely. It will go perfect with the black dress I bought yesterday. I'll wear it tonight."

"I didn't buy it. It was me grandmother's, bin in family years."

"But how could you give it away?"

"Because my lot won't appreciate it and you will."

"It's beautiful, May, I will take care of it."

"I know, lass, I know. What time do yer want me ter have bairn?"

"Are you sure you won't mind?"

"No, yer know I don't."

"Thank you. I don't know what I'd do without you," she said, kissing her on the cheek.

"Same as I would wi' out you. Get away with you, yer daft ape'orth. Go on, Gordon, get her out fer the day."

"But what about Sally."

"Is she cryin', is she neglected? Go on, it's yer birthday, enjoy it."

"Oh, May, you are lovely."

"Don't go getting soppy with me, or I'll change me mind."

May looked at Gordon and winked. "Well best do as she says," he said to Tina. "Come on."

They had a lovely day. They explored the outskirts of Whitby, taking in all the surrounding villages. After lunch in a little café, they visited Robin Hood's Bay.

Gordon had booked a table at one of the old pubs in Whitby. When they arrived at the pub, they sat at a table in the corner. The waiter seemed to know

182

Gordon and was very chatty. He came back with their drinks and took their order for their meal.

Gordon took a hold of her hand. "You know, I have really enjoyed spending today with you."

"Thank you."

Their meal came, and while eating, they talked about the party the night before. When they had finished, he took her hand again and said, "I haven't given you your birthday present yet."

"I didn't expect one, you have given me a lovely day."

"Yes I know, but I got you a present and I want to ask you something."

He took a box from his pocket and handed it to her.

"Tina, will you marry me?"

She opened the box and looked at the ring inside.

"Oh, Gordon, this is lovely. Yes, I will marry you." He slipped the ring onto her finger.

"It fits," she said.

"Lucky guess." He smiled.

They talked about Gordon continuing to run the business in Leeds and then coming to her each weekend. They didn't set a date for the wedding; he was just happy she had said yes to him.

They returned home very happy and tired. Sally was staying over at May's, so they had the place to themselves. When they got inside, he took her into his arms and kissed her.

Tina slid her arms round his neck and responded. When they made love that night, it had so much more meaning than before. Tina could not explain why.

They slept in each other's arms and she woke to feel him caressing her body with kisses. He cupped her breasts in his hands and let them wander over her body as he kissed her nipples. She moaned as the warm feeling rushed through her. His lips travelled down over her body, stopping at the top of her legs.

She did not want him to stop and urged him to lie on top of her, and as he entered her, she felt as if she would explode with the excitement.

Tina had never before felt this way. She had loved Solly and he was always so gentle with her. She thought he had always satisfied her sexually, but this was a brand new feeling and she never wanted it to stop.

Later when they had dressed and had breakfast, they crossed the yard to May.

"Hello, chuck, did yer enjoy yerselves?"

"I did, May, and guess what? Gordon has asked me to marry him."

"'Bout time too, though yer look a bit peaky. Have yer overdone it with the wine?"

"No, I just feel a little tired."

"Well have a cuppa, that'll do yer good."

"Thanks, that would be nice. Where's Sally?"

"She's out back playin'."

As she said it, Sally ran in, saw Tina, and wanted to sit on her knee. Almost immediately, she squirmed her way down again. "Want to play," she said and ran outside again.

When they had drunk their tea, Gordon said he should make his way back to Leeds and do some work.

"Tek care, lad," said May.

"Thanks, May, I'll be over next weekend."

Tina walked him out to the car and he kissed her. "See you soon. I will ring you every day. Get some rest. May's right, you do look a bit tired."

I will," she said. "See you next week."

She waved as he drove down the hill and out of sight.

Tina had an idea, and she told May she would be back in a little while.

She left Sally with May and went out. When she returned she sat in May's kitchen.

"May, I'm having a baby."

"Is it what yer want? Are yer happy?"

"Yes, it's happened sooner than I wanted. But probably that's why I look tired."

"Well, yer best tek care, lass."

They talked a while longer, and then she collected Sally and took her home. They had spent little time together of late, and Tina felt guilty. They had a lovely day together, and when Sally was in bed, Tina phoned Gordon.

"Hi, was the journey back to Leeds OK?"

"Yes, I came to the office, got caught up in the work. Did you get some rest?"

"No, but I have some news, Gordon."

"Oh, what's that?"

"I'm going to have a baby."

"Are you sure, Tina?"

"Yes, I got tested today."

He went quiet.

"Gordon, are you still there?"

"Yes, sorry, I was just surprised."

"Are you pleased?"

"More than anything. I'm just sorry I'm not there with you."

"I'm OK. I have May."

"Well take care, Tina, and remember, I love you very much."

"I love you too."

She hung up and decided that she would have an early night.

Next morning she and Sally visited Lilly and David.

Lilly was pleased to see them and David was just going into the town and said he would take Sally with him. She loved to see the boats and he always took her down to the harbour.

"Gordon asked me to marry him," she told Lilly.

"That's good. It's about time you settled down again."

"Lilly, I'm having a baby."

"Really, I have said it before, you don't do things by halves do you? Are you happy?"

"Yes I am."

"Then so am I. Congratulations, love." They decided to walk down to the harbour to see if they could see David and Sally.

In the harbour, the tide was out, and the boats were listing to one side in the damp sand. The seagulls were flying round looking for bits of food. They saw Sally; she had a small bag in her hand and she and David were collecting pebbles on the beach.

When they reached them, Lilly slipped her hand into David's and they smiled at each other. Tina thought it was nice that they should feel this way at their age.

"Tina and Gordon are getting married, and Tina is having a baby," she told him.

"Oh good, in that order?"

"No, the baby may come first," laughed Tina.

"Then congratulations are the order of the day," he said.

They all went back to the house and Tina said she ought to be getting back to the farmhouse. They said their goodbyes and she set off for home.

When they got back, Sally said she wanted to play until tea was ready.

"OK, but don't go too far away." Sally was out of the door before Tina had finished speaking.

Ten minutes later Tina called her in for her tea. When Sally didn't show, Tina sighed and went over the yard to May's.

"Hello, chuck, what can I do for yer?"

"Hello, May, I've come to collect Sally for her tea."

"She's not here, luv."

"I wonder where she is then? I told her not to go far."

May told her kids to go out and look for Sally. They all went out, but came back a while later; there was no sign of her.

Albert went up and down the road in case she had wandered off a little way.

"But she never goes anywhere except back and forth between the two houses," cried Tina.

Another hour went by and there was still no sign of her. Tina was beside herself with worry, and May said that they should call the police.

The police arrived half an hour later and she gave them Sally's description and what she had been wearing. They left and told her to wait at home.

Two hours later Gordon arrived. May had called him. He took her into his arms.

"Don't worry, love, they'll find her. She's just wandered a bit too far that's all."

Tina nodded, but she did not believe him. She was so worried. It got dark outside. Where was her baby?

Sometime around midnight, the police returned and said that they were still searching but hadn't found her. They asked more questions about neighbours and had she seen any strangers in the area.

Tina told them about the man who walked his dog. She said she did not know his name or where he lived. All she knew was that he had told her he lived just up the road.

When they had gone Tina said, "You don't think he could be involved, do you, May?"

"Don't know, lass. Have yer seen 'im lately?"

Tina shook her head. "No."

"You should try and get some rest, Tina," Gordon told her.

"I can't until I know."

"We're here," he said. "You have another reason to take care now."

She agreed to lie down and Gordon promised to wake her as soon as there was any news.

Tina woke to feel sun on her face and hearing voices below; she made her way downstairs. The police were there and the doctor. Gordon walked towards her and took her into his arms.

"Have you found her?" she asked.

"Sit down, love," said Gordon.

"They found her; she was in a house up the road. The man and his dog only rented it for a month."

"Where is she? Let me see her."

Gordon cleared his throat, but before he said anything, Tina looked around at the faces that were in the room. She saw May's tear-stained face.

She heard someone scream "Nooooo," and realised it was her. The doctor came over to her and gently gave her an injection. "This will help you, Tina," he said. When he left, he told Gordon he would call later in the day.

Gordon helped her back upstairs and stayed with her until she sank into oblivion.

Over the next week, days merged all into one for Tina. She was unaware of her surroundings; she knew people were coming and going, but she did not speak or cry.

The doctor said it was shock and it was just a matter of time until she came out of it.

The day of the funeral dawned. It was raining and all the neighbours and her friends were there. Tina's face was wet with the rain, but still no tears.

May and Gordon were worried for her and what effect it would have on her unborn baby. They didn't know how long she could go on in this way.

The police found the man. He had not come from Cornwall as he had told Tina. He had met her dad while he was in prison and her dad got the man to agree to do it.

They didn't tell Tina that when they found Sally, there was a note next to her little body and all it had said was PAY BACK TIME! This had been the undoing of her father, because with the information May and Gordon had given the police, it had led them straight to him. He was daft enough to think that if he told them who the man was, that he would not be involved.

It all came out in court, and both men went to jail for the rest of their lives.

Tina and Gordon went to the court to hear them being sentenced. She still had not spoken.

As they left the court, she came face to face with her sister and stepmother.

"Well, you done it this time," her sister said. "Yer've brought this family down with yer stuck up ways. Well yer got what yer deserved."

Gordon shoved her away as quickly as he could. He then took Tina home and helped her to bed, staying with her until she was asleep.

May shook her head. "Eh lad, how much more can she tek."

"I don't know, May. She has taken more than anyone I know; there must be a breaking point.

Over the following week, Tina remained in her catatonic state, not doing anything except sitting in the rocking chair outside the door.

Gordon said he would go to Leeds and find someone to run the office for a while and he would come back in a couple of days' time.

May said she would look after her until he did. When Gordon came back, the doctor told him to take Tina to places she had taken Sally. This was the only thing he could think of to try bring her back to reality.

Gordon took her all over but she remained the same. Finally, he took her down to the harbour and they sat on the beach. A seagull flew by and its shrill cry seemed to startle Tina. Gordon felt her tremble; her body shook and she buried her head in his chest, and he held her as the sobs wracked her body. She cried for over an hour; he just held her until she was still. Then he took a handkerchief and dried her face.

"I love you, Tina, I will be here for you." She nodded her head, but still did not speak.

When they returned home he made her a cup of tea. May came across and she could see that Tina had been crying. She looked at Gordon expectantly, but he shook his head.

May went back to her home and Gordon took Tina to bed and lay with her; again she cried. When he dried her face, she looked at him and said, "Why?"

He took her into his arms. "Oh Tina. Tina, love, I have no answer, but I do want you well. You have to be so strong."

"What made my father hate so much that he had to take away my child?"

"Because he's evil and you are good."

"Hold me, Gordon."

He held her and then kissed her.

"Love me, Gordon, please don't leave me?"

"I won't."

He kissed her and ran his hands over her swelling belly where another life was growing. She asked him to make love to her.

"Are you sure you feel up to it?" he asked.

"I need you to," she said.

At last, she was back.

During the next few months, Tina continued to get better. She talked and acted normal, but the life and sparkle had gone from her eyes.

May would keep an eye on her, but Tina didn't want to do much more than sit in the chair outside her door, and be on her own.

One day when it was quiet, May walked over to her with a pot of tea.

"Here yer are, lass, get this down."

"Thanks, May. I haven't really thanked you for being there and all you have done."

"No need. Yer like one of me own and anytime I can help I will."

"Why me, May, haven't I already paid enough?"

"I'm afraid with a family like your'n, they don't know when enough is enough. Yer've paid a high price. But they'll get their comeuppance believe me."

"I'm not going to marry Gordon, May."

"Why ever not? Yer know he loves yer."

"Yes I know and that's why. I won't have him hurt, and he will be if he's married to me."

"What about the bairn?"

"Gordon can see it, but I don't know how I'm going to look after it, May? I loved Solly and Sally was like him. I can't get it out of my head thinking if she suffered."

"Why torture yerself, lass?"

"I can't help it."

"Yer need a holiday."

"Maybe."

"I got ter go an' make me brood some dinner. Do yer want some, Tina?" She shook her head. "No thanks."

May went home and rang Gordon.

"What's wrong?" he asked.

"I'm right worried, lad. She's not looking after herself."

May continued to tell him what Tina had said.

"I'll come up tomorrow."

"Don't let on I told yer owt? I think she needs ter get away a bit."

"I think you may be right, I won't say anything. Thanks for ringing, May."

"That's alright, I'll see yer when yer get here."

The following morning Gordon arrived and he was shocked at the sight of Tina. She was pregnant, and instead of gaining weight, she had lost it. She had dark circles under her eyes, and when she smiled, it failed to reach her eyes. He knew she was still hurting.

"I'm thinking of taking a week's holiday, Tina. Would you like to keep me company?"

She agreed but without any enthusiasm.

"Where shall we go?" he asked her.

"I don't mind, Gordon. Wherever you want to go."

"What about a trip abroad, we need some sun."

"OK."

He took her into Whitby to the travel agent's and he booked a week in Spain. They would leave in two days' time. It didn't leave them very much time to get ready, but he thought it would be a good thing if she were occupied, and it gave her little time to change her mind.

They returned home and he cooked a meal, but Tina only poked at it.

"Tina, you have to start eating. You have to look after yourself and the baby. It can't look after itself; it needs you."

She looked at him. "OK," she said. Her voice was as flat as she looked.

They went to bed, but when Gordon woke, the side of the bed that Tina had been was empty and cold. That meant she had been up a long time.

He went downstairs and the door was open; he found her outside in the chair. Even though the sun was shining, it was weak and had no warmth in it. She still had her nightclothes on and nothing on her feet. She was cold.

He knelt beside her. "Tina, love, you're so cold. Come inside; you'll make yourself ill. Think of the baby."

She looked at him and let him lead her inside the house. She let him sit her down in the chair and wrap her in a blanket, and then he made her some hot tea.

He loved her and hoped this holiday would be good for her. She looked ill, not glowing as she should be."

The tea warmed her and she went upstairs and got dressed. Tina knew she should be helping herself to get better, but she could not snap out of it. They spent the day doing last minute things and packing, and they went to May's in the evening.

"Just think, Tina, when yer come back from this here holiday, yer'll be tanned and fit, ready for this bairn."

"I hope so. I can't help feeling tired all the time."

190

Gordon took a hold of her hand. "That's understandable, love. You have not been eating properly or sleeping. We love you, and I'm worried about you and the baby."

"I know. I know what I should be doing, but I feel so empty. I might feel a little different after the holiday."

"I hope so, chuck. I'm right worried 'bout you I am."

"I promise I'll try," she said.

"You'll have to. Because that lad there," she said, nodding to Gordon, "is right worried about you and that bairn. Now go and get yerselves away and have a good time."

They went to bed and left early the following morning.

Over the next week, they relaxed and her pale skin turned a golden brown.

One evening while they were having dinner, he took her hand. "Tina, I love you so much and I want us to be married."

Tina shook her head. "I love you, Gordon, but now I'm so afraid that if we get married, I may lose you."

"Why?"

"Everything I love I lose and I don't want that anymore. I can't live through another loss."

"You won't lose me, I can promise you that."

"I'll think about it."

They finished the meal and he suggested that they walk down to the beach. He took her hand as they walked on the sand, the rippling of the water just touching the edge. He turned and kissed her, and for the first time in a long time, she felt she could respond.

They walked back to the hotel. When they were in their room he undressed her and made love to her. When it was over, she cried. Gordon held her until she had finished, knowing that she had to go through this grieving, if she was to ever get back to something like normality. The shock she had been feeling since Sally had gone was now beginning to wear off.

Later he washed her face with a warm flannel, wrapped her in a robe and lay with her. Eventually she said, "I'm sorry, Gordon."

"Don't be, you have every right to feel the way that you do. I think now, you have started back on the road to recovery. I think you needed to feel this way before you can start getting on with the rest of your life."

He wrapped his arms around her; she snuggled into his chest and they slept.

When they woke next morning, the sun was streaming through the window, and even though it was still early, it was hot.

They dressed, had breakfast and headed down to the beach. He looked at Tina and said, "You look lovely this morning."

Her hair was shining, her skin had a healthy glow; she looked a lot better, and her belly was swollen with the baby she was carrying.

As they sat on the sun bed, Tina's hand rested on her stomach and she felt the baby kick. She took a sharp intake of breath and looked at Gordon.

"What is it?" he asked.

"The baby, it just kicked." He placed his hand on her stomach and he felt it too.

"Our baby, Tina, this is our baby."

By lunch time the sun was too hot to sit in and they moved from the beach. When they had changed, they walked down the little narrow streets, looking at all the old shops. She saw an old pipe, and knew that Albert would love it.

She bought a Spanish Flamenco doll for May. Tina thought they were a bit tacky and they were mass-produced, but when May knew they were coming to Spain, she said she would like one. Tina thought it was a small price to pay, considering how good May had been to her.

Outside one shop was an array of Spanish silk kaftans. One was a vivid blue and Tina said she would like it as it would be cool to wear here in the evenings, and she could wear it at home. Gordon said that he would like to buy it for her.

When they changed to go out for the evening, Tina put it on. He told her how lovely she looked.

They were due to return home in two days' time, and they spent that time walking and sleeping and they even ventured out into the water.

On the last night of the holiday, they were in a little bistro and Tina took Gordon's hand.

"Thank you for putting up with me."

"I love you, Tina, and you needed time. I'm just glad to be with you. We have to go home tomorrow, and Monday, I have to get back to the office in Leeds, see how things are doing. I have been away from the office a lot of late; we must protect your interests."

She nodded her head. "Yes and I will have to catch up on the work that will have come through to my office at home."

"There's not much. I kept up to it, knowing you were unable to do it."

"Thanks, Gordon, I don't know what I would have done without you all."

"As I have said before, I love you; it was no problem."

The next day they flew home and May was waiting for them and she had made them something to eat.

"Oh my, Tina, yer do look well, nearly like yer old self again, It's done yer good, but eh, I have missed yer."

After tea, Tina unpacked the gifts she had bought for them. Albert was thrilled with the pipe, as Tina knew he would be. May, she was in raptures over the doll. One would have thought you had given her the crown jewels.

"Oh lass, this is grand, I've always wanted one o' these. She placed it high on an old cabinet she had in the corner. "Pride and place this has." Then she shouted, "If one of you lot so much as runs near this, I'll wallop the backsides."

Then she let out a loud guffaw; it didn't take much to please May.

Tina spent the following day unpacking and washing their holiday things. On Sunday, Gordon returned to Leeds but said he would come back the following weekend.

"I'll call you," he said. "Just remember to take care of yourself and our baby."

He kissed her and drove off down the hill. She watched him until he was out of sight.

Tina told herself that she needed to be organised, and over the next few weeks, she was. Gordon came over at weekends and they went shopping for the baby. She worked from home during the week, but the hardest thing was when she decorated the bedroom that had belonged to Sally for the new baby.

Before they had gone on holiday, Gordon had asked May to clear out Sally's things, so at least Tina would not have to face that chore. May had packed all the things and stored them in the attic space.

Tina painted the bedroom a pretty lemon and white, and when Gordon came at the weekend, he was impressed at her handiwork.

"You've done a good job here, Tina. Just be careful not to do too much. Anything you can't do, just leave it for me. Although looking around there's not much left to do."

Lilly and David came to visit on the Saturday. "You're looking well, Tina. At one time I was quite worried about you, but you seem to be doing fine now."

"Thanks, Lilly, I'm looking forward to having the baby now. At the moment, my days seem so empty even though I have plenty of work to do."

"I understand what you mean, but all that will soon change."

Over the next few weeks, Tina spent a lot of time walking and going to the beach in Whitby. During these times, she thought a lot about Solly, Maurice and little Sally. Oh, how she missed her. She missed them all, but Sally more so.

What had she done in her short life to deserve to die the way she did? Tina still tortured herself wondering what Sally's last thought were.

Did she cry out for her? Did she suffer? Tina hoped not. When she was thinking like this, Tina got quite depressed, and then told herself that it would not be good for the baby, and snapped out of it. She would return home and not tell anyone how she felt.

May made sure she ate every day by asking her to have tea with them, and Gordon was there at weekends. Tina blossomed and started looking like a pregnant woman should.

One Saturday, the first week in December, Tina went into labour. Gordon was there to take her to the hospital. She was only in labour four hours, and when it was all over, Tina could not help but compare it to the last time, when she had given birth to Sally.

They moved her to the ward from the labour room and then Gordon was allowed to see her. His smiled as he walked down the ward, told her he had seen the baby.

"She's beautiful, how do you feel."

"I feel great, just a little tired that's all."

They called the baby Aimee. She couldn't have been more different from Sally. She didn't scream, she only cried when she was hungry, she was so good. Aimee was a very pretty baby with a mass of dark curls, and she looked just like Gordon.

When they took her home a week later, it felt strange taking her into the bedroom where Sally had been before.

May was over the moon with her. "Eh lass, she's right bonny, what a picture."

"I know and she's so good, totally different from Sally, but I wouldn't have swapped her. I did love her, May."

"I know, lass, I know."

Tina's eyes filled with tears. "I won't ever forget her, May."

" I know, how could yer, still, this little 'un needs yer now. It's time ter go forward."

Tina kissed the baby's head and lay her down in the crib. She went back down to the kitchen where Gordon had made her some tea. As she drank it, she said, "Oh, that's good thank you."

"Tina, will you marry me now?"

"No, Gordon. I love you, we're engaged but I'm not ready. Let's keep our relationship the way it is for now, shall we?"

"OK. You only have to say when you're ready."

"I know."

Gordon stayed with her two more days before he went back to Leeds. Tina spent her days getting to know her baby. She was so quiet, that it was no hardship to her. Aimee was so good, that apart from feed times, Tina almost forgot she was there.

May came over all the time and clucked like a mother hen.

Slowly the weather began to turn, and when it was warm enough, Tina would take Aimee in the pram and walk into Whitby. Aimee loved going out, and she was always gurgling and was so content.

Gordon continued to ask Tina to marry him, and she always said that she loved him, but never named the day.

When Aimee tuned eight months old, Gordon came over for the weekend and Tina noticed at once how quiet he was. They spent the day playing with Aimee, and when she went to bed, they sat outside drinking wine.

"What's wrong, you've been quiet all day?"

He looked at her. "Tina, I've been patient. You know how I feel about you and you know I will always be here for you. But are you ready to marry me now?"

She shook her head. "I'm sorry, Gordon. I love you, and we have known each other a long time, but I don't think I am ready to make that commitment. Since Sally died, I feel as if I am going through the motions of living and taking care of the baby. I don't know why I am holding back."

"Tina, we have a baby, surely that's a commitment. I am only human and I want more than just a weekend with you and my daughter."

"I can't give you that at the moment, Gordon."

"Well then I'm sorry, Tina, I think it's best if we don't see each other for a while. Maybe then you will change your mind."

The old stubbornness kicked in. "Fine, if that's how you feel?"

"Tina, I don't want this, but I don't want you part time either. I'm going back to Leeds. Call me when you make up your mind."

He got up, and within ten minutes he had packed his things and driven away.

As always when she felt hurt, she held her feelings in check until he had gone. Then she broke down and sobbed. Why couldn't she marry him, he was a good man, what was wrong with her?"

She cleared away the glasses and went inside. She climbed the stairs and got into bed, but could not sleep.

The next morning as she was feeding Aimee, May came in the door.

She saw at once that something was wrong. She said, "I didn't think yer was in, not seein' the car like."

"Gordon left last night, May. He's gone back to Leeds."

"Oh, is he alright?"

"No not really. He wants us to get married."

"Well it could be worse, I thought yer loved 'im?"

"I do, I don't know what's wrong. Anyway, he said he would stay away until I called him."

"He's too good ter let go, lass."

"I know, but I don't know, May."

May sighed. "Well there's only you can decide. Is there owt I can do?"

Tina shook her head. "No thanks. I think I'll take Aimee out for a while."

"Suit yerself, come an' have some dinner when yer get back."

"I'm not hungry, but I will have a cup of tea. Thanks."

"No bother, some day yer'll find happiness. Yer have to."

May went back to her cottage and Tina got Aimee ready and took her out. She didn't call Gordon that week or the next, and the longer she left it, the harder it was to make the call.

Before she realised, Aimee's first birthday was coming up and it had been four months since she had last seen him.

Unbeknown to Tina, he had rung May on a regular basis to ask how she was coping, and told her not to mention it to Tina. He had rung a few days before and said, "May, I want to bring a present over for Aimee, do you think Tina would mind?"

"No I don't, I think she might like to see yer."

"May, I will be bringing someone with me. She's only a friend, but she's never been to Whitby."

"Eh lad, do yer think that's a good idea?"

"What am I supposed to do? She hasn't called. It's obvious she doesn't need me, and I don't plan to grow old on my own."

"True, but she's stubborn, yer know that."

"Yes, but maybe seeing someone else with me will get some reaction."

"Aye well, we'll see."

Before he arrived, May told Tina that he had rung an he would be coming over with a present for Aimee.

"I thought he might."

"Yer've not been in touch then?" said May, knowing full well that she hadn't.

"No, and I don't know what I want, May."

"He'll not wait forever yer know, Tina."

"I know."

When May looked, she could see the sadness in her eyes. She sat down opposite her and said, "Eh lass, whatever am I ter do with yer I don't know, yer've had enough sadness. Why don't yer tek the happiness?"

Tina nodded, but said nothing.

Two days later Gordon arrived and May saw the woman in the car. He got out and went to May's.

"I wonder if you'd mind giving my friend a coffee while I go see Tina? To prepare her, you know."

"Aye lad, bring her in."

Gordon went outside and soon returned with the woman May had see sat in the car.

"May, this is Julie. Julie, this is May. She's a diamond and if she's your friend, you have nothing to worry about."

"Sit yerself down, lass, while I make a brew," May told her.

Julie felt at ease immediately.

"I won't be long," Gordon said to her as he disappeared out of the door.

May came back from the kitchen with the coffee. "Don't be shy, how long have yer known him?"

"About two months. He handled some promotional work for me."

"He's a good lad."

"Yes he is." May couldn't help noticing her face light up as she said it.

"Are yer fond of him then?"

"Yes, but he's too worried about Tina to notice me."

"Don't be too sure. She doesn't know what she wants that one. I told her she'd lose him."

"I don't want to be used just to make her jealous and force her hand. I really like him, but I won't play second fiddle. She either wants him or she doesn't, and if she doesn't, she has to let him go."

"Aye well, just you hold on, she's leadin' him a merry dance. But I luv her I do, but sometimes I could just shake her. Mind, she's been through't mill a bit."

"Yes he said, though not in detail."

Gordon came back. "Well?" asked May.

"Aimee was asleep. Tina was pleased to see me, but she said she just wants us to be friends. Come on, Julie, I'll take you to meet her."

"Is that such a good idea?" she asked.

"Why not? She's told me where I stand. She had her choice."

They crossed the yard together. He knocked at the door and she opened it. The look on Tina's face told him nothing.

"Tina, this is my friend Julie. I just wanted to introduce her to you."

"Hello, come in."

"We'll just stay a minute," he said.

"I've heard a lot about you," Julie said to her. "I wish I lived somewhere like this, it's lovely."

"Yes it is, would you like a drink?" she asked them.

"No thanks, I've just had one at your friend's across the yard."

"Have some wine."

"No thank you."

"Well I'll have one if you don't mind?"

Gordon looked at Tina. This was so out of character for her. He noticed that she looked thin and gaunt. He would have a word with May before he left.

He had intended to stay longer but decided not to. "This is for Aimee," he said, handing Tina a parcel.

"You will give it to her, won't you?"

"Of course I will, why wouldn't I?"

"Well I don't know."

"She's your daughter, Gordon, I wouldn't deprive you of each other."

"Thank you, we'll be going now, Tina. I'll ring you mid-week, but if you need anything before, please ring."

She nodded. "I will." Then she turned to Julie and said, "Take care of him, he needs someone to love him."

Julie smiled. "Thank you."

When they left Julie said, "I feel awful."

"Why?"

"She doesn't look well. She looks like someone lost. She loves you, Gordon."

"But she doesn't show it. She doesn't know what she wants. We were engaged, but she wouldn't agree to marry me. What am I supposed to do?"

"I don't know. You're a wonderful person."

"I've always been there for her, but I can only take so much. I'm a man and I don't want to be on my own. I want to be loved."

"But she's been through so much."

"Yes, and I can only give her so much. I have needs also."

Julie took his face between her hands and kissed him.

"Let's go into Whitby and find a place to stay."

In Whitby, they found a small B&B that overlooked the harbour. The lights twinkled on the water in the breeze, but what made it more romantic, was that it was December and the Christmas lights lit up the town.

After dinner, even though it was cold, they walked down by the water. There was something magical when water, moonlight and sand came together that could not be explained.

They said little at first and then Julie said, "Where do we go from here, Gordon?"

"We all have to move on. Aimee is my daughter, but Tina doesn't want me. I have to find someone who does."

They came across a small bistro, went inside and sat in the corner by the fire. They ordered a glass of wine and held hands.

Watching the wax run down the bottle from a candle, Julie said, "I love you, Gordon, do you know that?"

"I'm more than fond of you, and I need someone to love me."

"It's me, Gordon, I am here, and I want you to know and I'm ready to show you I'll never let you down. This love will grow every day and I hope it will last forever."

"That's wonderful, Julie, you are just what I need."

"Take me back to the hotel. Let me love you."

They left and walked back to the hotel. They had booked separate rooms, but only used one. They locked the door and their lips met at once.

She loved him so much. She had wanted to be patient and wait until he was ready, but it seemed as if that time had come.

She unbuttoned his shirt and ran her fingers through the hairs on his chest; this just intensified the feelings she had.

He unbuttoned her blouse and let it fall to the floor. Piece by piece they took off their clothes until they were both completely undressed.

Their hands and fingers explored bodies. They were unaware of how they came to the bed, but they were in bed with the covers over them and their naked bodies touched. As they came together, it felt like a shock that fired their passion even further.

Julie ran her hands over his back and he caressed her breasts. She was round and womanly and he loved it. They reached a climax that shook him, and then they lay still waiting for the passion to subside, but wanting it to last forever.

A little while later, he rose above her and entered her and she gave a moan of pleasure. Their bodies moved in unison, until their passion exploded and spilled over.

They lay in the aftermath of their lovemaking, the light from outside reflecting on the walls of the darkened room.

She got out of bed and went to the bathroom. When she returned, he took her into his arms, and that was how they went to sleep.

When she opened her eyes again, it was morning. She looked at his sleeping face and gently kissed him. He stirred and reached out for her. She moved closer to him, and as their bodies touched, she felt the hardness of his manhood.

Slowly they made love without the urgency of the previous night. A little later, they showered and had breakfast.

As they ate he said, "You are wonderful, Julie."

"You're not too bad yourself. Gordon, I love you, but I don't want to spend my life playing second best to Tina."

"You won't have to. I have accepted the fact that she only wants me on her terms."

"Does that mean we're a couple?" she asked.

He kissed her. "Yes, I think it does mean we're a couple."

They packed up and left to make their way back to Leeds, taking a detour to see if they could see Aimee. May told them that Tina had left early that morning to visit Lilly and David.

"Will you tell her I'll ring her?"

"I will, lad, and you tek care."

Over the next couple of months, Tina lost all interest in everything. She was only interested in Aimee, but once Aimee was in bed, she would start drinking, and she was drinking as much as two bottles of wine each night.

She didn't remember going to bed, but would wake up in the morning with a mouth that felt full of sawdust, and her head felt as if she had been hit with a hammer.

Tina always took care of Aimee, but May became increasingly worried about her. She was thin, and had dark circles under her eyes.

May was sitting with her one day, when she asked, "What I want to know is why? Why didn't yer tek the happiness he was offerin'?"

Tina shrugged her shoulders. "I don't know, May. I loved him, still do, but didn't want to be tied to him for life."

"But what are yer goin' ter do, lass? Just look at yer, all skin and bones, women on the streets look better than you do."

"I know and now I have lost him. I have made a mess of my life, and all I ever wanted was someone to love me."

"Gordon did love yer, an' yer pushed him away."

"But there was something missing, May. I don't know what it was."

"Well I know one thing, lass, yer gonna end up old an' done before yer time, if yer don't sort youself out. Leave the bairn with me, and get yerself downtown and smarten up."

"Maybe you're right, May. I'll go tomorrow."

"Good, bring 'er early."

Next day she left Aimee with May and went into the town. She bought some new clothes and things for Aimee and she called into a wine bar and had a couple of drinks before returning home.

"Had a good day have yer?" asked May.

"Yes, not bad."

May could see that she had been drinking.

Tina said, "May, would you be able to keep Aimee tonight? I met someone today and I'm going out tonight."

"OK, where did yer meet him?"

"In the pub."

"The pub? Well I never, it's not the done thing, lass."

"I know, but how else am I going to meet people?"

"Nay, there's better places. The fellas in the pubs are only after one thing, and why are they there? Just drinkin' away the week's pay. But I'll have the bairn, if that's what yer want."

"Thanks, I'll see you in the morning." Tina went to her house and got ready to go out. She made her way back down into the town and the pub that she had arranged to meet him.

He had been in the bar when she had ordered her wine earlier. They got talking and he said he was in town working for a couple of weeks, and asked if she would like to meet him later for a drink.

Tina agreed before going back home to ask May to look after Aimee. Now she sat in the same pub drinking.

The guy turned up and they had a few more drinks, and then things started to blur. She remembered meeting a few people, but wasn't sure that she liked them.

She had no idea how she got home, but the next morning her head felt like lead and she was so sick. May took one look at her and told her to go back to bed.

Later that day she had recovered enough to collect Aimee. May was appalled at her appearance.

"Thanks for looking after Aimee."

"Someone has to, but look at yer. It's nowt ter do with me, Tina, but I've seen women on the streets look better than you at the minute, and where in God's name did yer get them bruises?"

Tina shook her head. "I can't remember; all I know is I feel so sore. I remember having a couple of drinks and then I don't remember anything else."

"Yer shouldn't go ter the pubs. Just look at yerself, yer thin, bags under yer eyes. Yer've lost yer sparkle."

Tina began to spend more and more time away from home, leaving May to take care of Aimee. In desperation, she rang Gordon.

"Gordon, you have ter come an' see her. She's never home, an' she's hit the bottle."

"I'll come and see her, May. But I don't think it's me she wants."

"Be prepared for a shock, she don't look nowt like herself."

Even though May had warned him, he was not prepared for the way Tina looked when he saw her.

"Hello, Tina," he said. "How are you?"

"OK I suppose."

"You don't look it, you look ill."

"I'm fine, you just worry about your own life."

"Tina, I worry about you; after all Aimee is our daughter. We could have been together, but you didn't want that. I don't know what you want. I have to get on with my own life, but it doesn't stop me caring about you. Drinking and going off the rails is not going to help with your problems."

"I don't need help, Gordon, especially from you. So why don't you just go and do what you keep telling me to do, get on with your life."

Gordon sighed and left. He went over to May's. "I can't reason with her. She does look ill; there is nothing I can do at the moment, May, but call me if you need anything for Aimee."

"I will, but I don't know what to do now."

"Just keep an eye on her. Will you make sure Aimee is looked after?"

"Aye, you have no worry there."

"Thanks, I'll see you soon."

Tina sat by her window. She watched him go into May's and a few minutes later, he left. There was no one to see the tears run down her face.

Tina knew she looked a mess. Her hair was lank and greasy. She was thin and gaunt, and her body felt battered and bruised.

Each night she would go to the pub and get drunk, meet different men and let them use her. She did not remember any of their names and had no recollection of how she got home.

The other thing was, the care of Aimee fell to May more. Tina knew she should be looking after her, but she hadn't the energy. She was in a deep hole, and she couldn't climb out.

She felt worthless. Her mind recalled the abuse that she had to endure for the years previously, and the love she had found with Solly.

His death had set her on a downward spiral of despair. After his death, nothing seemed to matter except Sally. Now, she had gone, and even though she thought she had loved Gordon, and certainly Aimee, nothing mattered anymore.

Tina cried openly. She was not a bad person, why had she suffered as she had?

Her head thumping, she went through to the kitchen. Blinded by tears, she took the bottle of pills from the cupboard, and with a glass of vodka, she swallowed a handful of the pills.

She went back upstairs and lay on the bed, closed her eyes, and knew nothing more.

How long she lay there, she did not know. May had seen her about four that afternoon, just before she took the pills. She became worried when Tina did not come for Aimee.

May crossed the yard and opened the door. She saw the half bottle of pills on the table and the vodka bottle.

"Oh my God. What now?"

She heaved her body upstairs and found Tina sprawled on the bed. Her skin was grey and damp with sweat, but she was still breathing. May went back downstairs and called Albert.

"Get the ambulance, silly lass as tried ter do herself in."

The ambulance arrived in minutes and then she said, "Call Gordon. I'll go with her; you look after the bairns."

At the hospital, they put her into a side room. May had to wait in the waiting room where she sat for nearly two hours, and no one came to tell her what was going on.

Gordon came panting through the door. "How is she, May?"

"Nay, lad, don't ask me. She's bin in there two hours and no one has told me owt. It's a good thing I went over when I did. I don't know how long she'd bin there."

A nurse came out to them and asked if they were her family.

"No, she only has us," said Gordon.

The nurse said they could go through and see her. They walked into a side ward where Tina was. There was little difference between the whiteness of her skin and the whiteness of the sheets, she was so still.

Gordon took a hold of her cold, clammy hand. Tina's eyes flickered open. "Why did you do it, Tina?"

Her voice was barely a whisper. "I don't know. I'm fed up at having to cope alone. I can't do it anymore."

"But you don't have to, you never had to, Tina. You had me, you have May."

May was silently crying. She blamed herself, of course, but no one was to blame.

The nurse came back and said that they had to leave, but they could come back later.

Gordon kissed Tina. "I'll come back and see you." Tina nodded and closed her eyes.

As they left, the doctor caught up with them in the corridor.

"She's been lucky," he said. "Another hour, and she wouldn't have made it. She's underweight and very frail. We will have to keep her in for a few days, possibly assess her mental state. Is there anyone we should contact?"

Gordon shook his head. "No, we're all she has. We'll come back later if we can?"

The doctor nodded and left them.

Tina was in the hospital a month. She was so depressed she had a mild breakdown. She couldn't stop crying; she felt she was worthless to everyone, including herself.

The doctor said it was a combination of Sally's death, Aimee's birth and depression, and because she was so stubborn, she would not admit that it bothered her about Gordon.

When Tina left from the hospital, she was still frail and needed a lot of care. Gordon arranged to have some time away from the office and stay with her.

He and Julie were not getting on very well at this time. She was not prepared to share him with Tina, and he was not prepared to abandon Tina.

It took a further month before Tina started looking better and was able to start taking care. One night when they sat outside, Gordon took hold of her hand.

"Tina, I have always loved you. I was the one to leave, but it was you who pushed me away. Now will you let me care for you?"

She shook her head. "You deserve better than me. You're kind and gentle. I'm worthless. You don't know what I got up to these last few months, Gordon. I let men abuse me because I felt unworthy."

He held her close. "You are a beautiful person, and I love you. Why do you constantly put yourself down? Think of all you have achieved, fought hard to gain respect. You don't want to throw it all away and let others think they were right about you."

Her tears began to flow. "Who in their right minds would want me now?"

"I do, Tina, I love you. I want to care for you. I want you and our daughter in my life. Let me in."

He kissed her gently and she realised that here was the one man she could trust. She needed to feel safe and he would never hurt her. His kisses told her that he would be gentle with her and he would take care of her.

He took her hand and led her inside and up to the bedroom. He kissed her and she responded. They lay on the bed and he caressed her. She sighed and ran her hands over his back. As he gently made love to her, she moaned with pleasure.

"I will always love you, Tina, I can't say it enough." As their lovemaking reached a climax and they came together, she realised that only Gordon could make her feel this way. All the men she had been with in the past had left her feeling empty. That is if she remembered them at all.

She had loved Solly. He had always been kind and gentle with her. Gordon was much younger and had a young man's passion, and his lovemaking was more urgent. Tina thought that she would never respond to such feelings, but he made her feel exciting and always satisfied when their lovemaking was finished.

He knew that she would never trust anyone a hundred percent, but she trusted him as much as she would ever be capable of, and he didn't want to do anything to make her think differently.

They went to sleep in each other's arms. When she woke next morning, she felt much better than she had for a long time. She actually made breakfast for Aimee and Gordon.

After breakfast Gordon said, "Tina, I want to marry you and take care of you all the time. I know you turned me down before, but now I'm asking you again. Will you marry me?"

"I don't know. I like having you here, but I like having my own space too."

"You can have all the space you want. Just let me get close enough to show you how much I love you."

"I love you in my own way, Gordon. Don't push me. Let me take things at my own pace."

"OK, if that's what you want. But you know how I feel."

He stayed with her another two weeks before returning to Leeds. He said he had to get back to the business, but he would come back at the weekend. May kept an eye on her and Tina started to look better, but she was still too thin.

Six months later saw great changes in Tina's life. She and Gordon got married in a quiet ceremony in a little church in Whitby, with only May and Albert, Lilly and David as witnesses. There was no reception, just a little tea and cake back at May's.

She made a decision to sell the business. Gordon found work with a local fisherman, and she made some improvements to the cottage and outbuildings, including May's cottage. Aimee also started going to the local nursery.

She changed the office into a study and thought she would try writing a book. She could write about her life. Someone may read it and be able to identify with it. Maybe it could help them. Who knows?

It seemed once again, life was sweet.

Towards the end of the year, Tina was in Whitby doing some shopping, Aimee's second birthday was coming up and she was looking for a present for her.

As she crossed the road, she saw Gordon sitting in one of the coffee houses with a woman. She looked familiar, but Tina could not place where she had seen her.

They were deeply engrossed in conversation and seemed oblivious to their surroundings.

She crossed to the other side of the road, abandoned any thought of shopping and went home.

She was still trying to place where she had seen the woman when Gordon returned home a little later. He obviously wasn't going to say anything, so she did.

"I was shopping in Whitby today."

"Oh, did you buy anything interesting?" he asked.

"No, but I did see you."

"Oh, why didn't you say hello? Where were you?"

"I was walking past the coffee shop where you were talking to a woman. You were so engrossed, you didn't see me."

"Oh yes, that was Julie. You remember her, I brought her to meet you once. She was in Whitby for the day. She walked past where I was working, so we went for coffee and caught up on all the gossip."

"I see."

"You should have come in."

"You were too busy to notice me."

He walked over to her and put his arms around her. "It was nothing, Tina. She's an old friend." His face gave nothing away and she had no reason to disbelieve him.

A couple of days later, he announced that he was going to Leeds. He said there were a few things he needed to do. Tina felt uneasy, but again, she had no reason to doubt him.

When he left he told her he would be home around six that evening. She pottered around all day, and around five o' clock she began preparing a meal in readiness for his return. Six o' clock came and went but Gordon still had not arrived home.

By nine o' clock, she tipped the uneaten meal in the bin. A little while later, he rang and said he had met a couple of old friends; they were having a few drinks so he would stay over and see her in the morning. He asked her if she minded.

She said no, but deep down she did. She locked the door and went to bed, but found it difficult to sleep. She kept wondering if he was being truthful with her. She loved him, and he had put up with a lot from her. She wondered if he was happy living in Whitby or was he missing the hustle and bustle and all that Leeds had to offer.

Gordon did not arrive home until lunchtime next day, and it looked as if the drinking session with friends had gone on most of the night.

She felt better at seeing him, but guilty at doubting him.

"I'm sorry. I only intended on having a couple of drinks, but we hadn't seen each other for a long time, and it just went on."

"It's OK, I understand that you need to see your friends. Just remember, I do love you, Gordon. I may not always show it, but I do."

"I know you do."

From then on, Gordon started to find excuses to visit Leeds more often. At the beginning, Tina didn't worry too much, but when it started to happen on a regular basis, she knew something was not right. He was spending more and more time out.

She had just put Aimee to bed, and when she came downstairs, he was putting on his coat.

"Where are you going?" she asked.

"I thought I might take a walk into Whitby."

"Shall I ask May to keep an eye on Aimee and come with you?"

"No, not tonight. It's cold and you'll be better off here."

She looked at him. "What's going on, Gordon?"

"What do you mean?"

"I mean you're never here these days. You are either going off to Leeds or into Whitby. You haven't made love to me for weeks, and I know when something is not right. I think you owe me an explanation. If I've done something wrong, fine, let me know."

He removed his coat and walked further into the room. He cleared his throat and then said, "You've done nothing wrong. I met up with Julie and things have just happened. I didn't want to hurt you, Tina, but I didn't know how to tell you."

"So what are you saying, Gordon, that you love Julie and this is the end of the road for us?"

"I really don't know."

"Well you can't have us both, it's either her or me."

"I know, I've known you a long time and we have been through so much. You don't deserve to be hurt anymore, but I think I need some space. I don't know what I want anymore."

Tina became angry. "Fine, so while you're finding your own space and making love to Julie, where does that leave me? What am I supposed to do?"

"Tina, I'm sorry. I know you feel hurt, but I have to be honest with you."

"Well I suppose I should be grateful for that at least."

"Look, if it's any consolation to you, it's me who is at fault. You are not to blame."

"No, but I've not been easy to live with. I suppose if I had, you wouldn't be going to her. She has not had to live through what I have gone through, and I am not feeling sorry for myself. When are you leaving?"

"I was going to wait until you had got used to the idea."

"Well don't stay on my account. I don't want you sharing my bed and then going to her," she said bitterly.

The look on his face told her how sorry he was and she knew she was being cruel, but she couldn't help it. In any case, she had cause, didn't she?

"Then I had better go. It's obvious that you don't want me. Julie does love me."

He went upstairs and threw some things into a bag. When he came down again, he said, "I didn't want it to be like this, Tina, but you haven't made it easy for me."

"And I suppose it's been easy for me?"

"No it hasn't, but now you have to let go of the past, otherwise it will eat you up, and you'll never be able to have a normal relationship. It's time to let go, Tina."

"I would expect something like that from you, you being a man."

"I'm going, before we both say things we will regret."

As he walked out of the door and got near the car, he heard a crash. He got into the car and drove away.

Tina had watched him walk out the door. She had picked up an ornament from the table and thrown it at the door where it had smashed into little pieces. Hot tears ran down her face and she fell to her knees and sobbed.

What a mess, first she had put up with her father, then she lost Solly and Sally, and now Gordon. Every time she thought she had found happiness, something happened to take it away from her.

In the days that followed, Tina tried to cope. Some days were hard and some were easy, but she struggled on.

She knew the one person who needed her was Aimee, and she had not been a very good mother to her of late. As before, May had taken over the care of her daughter.

One day Tina decided she had to pull herself together. She went to the bathroom and washed her hair. She changed her clothes and then set about cleaning the cottage. It was a month ago since Gordon had left, and this was the first time she had bothered.

When she had finished, she walked over to May's. She knocked at the door and walked in.

May looked at her and smiled. "Well that's a lot better, chuck, how do yer feel?"

"I'll cope. I think it's about time I sorted myself out and started taking care of my daughter."

"Well, lass, yer can't carry on as yer have bin."

"No, I suppose she will be better for him than I was. I can't love him the way he needs loving."

"Eh lass, he did love yer. All he needed was the chance ter show it, but yer did keep knockin' him back."

"I know. I couldn't help it."

"You know best. I'll help yer, now do yer want a cuppa?"

"No thanks. I'll take Aimee and go into the town. She needs a new coat and some clothes."

"Right, lass, come over when yer get back, have yer tea."

"Thanks, May, I will."

Tina spent the afternoon with Aimee in Whitby. When she had bought the things she needed, she made her way home. By the time they arrived back, it was just beginning to get dark. Tina dropped the shopping off in the cottage and walked over to May's.

"Here yer are. Did yer get what yer wanted?"

"Yes, thank you."

"Sit yerself down, tea's ready."

After tea, Tina said she would take Aimee home, give her a bath and put her to bed.

"Yer sure you can manage, lass?"

"Yes, don't worry, May. I have to start and get my life back together."

That is just what she did. Over the next six months she decorated the cottage, again. Spent a lot of time making sure she did everything she could for Aimee and by the time summer came around, she looked more like the old Tina when Solly had been alive.

She was in the garden one day and heard the telephone ringing. When she answered it, she heard Lilly on the other end.

"Hello, Tina, it's been a long time since we last saw you. How are you doing? Is Aimee well?"

"We're fine, Lilly, and I'm sorry, I should have contacted you. I have been busy, still, that's no excuse for ignoring you."

"It's OK, I understand. Listen, why don't you and Aimee come over for the weekend. David's friend Chris is coming and it would be nice to have someone nearer his own age. We old ones soon run out of conversation."

"Thank you, Lilly, I'd like that, but I hope this isn't one of your attempts at matchmaking?"

"No, it's nothing like that."

"Good, then we would love to come, but I'll tell you this, Lilly, I've had enough of men, and I definitely won't be getting married again. If I did, it would have to be someone very exceptional. By the way, what does this Chris do?"

"He's a teacher. David's known his family for years. He rang and said he could do with a break and David invited him for the weekend. So it wasn't planned."

"Fine, Lilly, when do you want us to get there?"

"Anytime you want. Come Friday afternoon, and then we can spend some time with Aimee; we have missed having her."

"Thanks, we'll see you then. Give my love to David. Bye, Lilly."

Tina told May about Lilly's invitation, and she thought it would be a good idea for them both to get away from the cottage for a few days.

On Friday morning, May looked after Aimee while Tina put some things in a suitcase. She made them some lunch before they left to go to Lilly's. The journey only took a half hour, so they were soon walking up the garden path to Lilly's home.

Lilly opened the door and picked up Aimee. "It's so good to see you both. Aimee, you have grown.

As she put her down David walked through from the kitchen. "Tina, it's lovely to see you, and you look so well. You both do."

As he was speaking, Tina noticed a man standing behind him. He was about five foot six inches, early forties and had fine, sandy coloured hair. He had kind eyes that twinkled when he smiled, and he was smiling when he looked at her.

Lilly saw Tina looking. "Oh by the way, this is Chris. I told you he's here for the weekend too."

She held out her hand. "Hello, Chris."

He took her hand. "Hello to you too." They all laughed and the ice was broken. They had a pleasant afternoon talking and catching up on old times.

Around four o' clock, Lilly said, "I'll make something to eat."

"I'll give you a hand," Tina said.

"No, why don't you and Chris take Aimee for a walk. I can manage better on my own."

"That's fine with me, what about you, Tina?" he asked.

"Yes, that would be nice. I'll get Aimee's coat."

They walked down to the harbour. The boats were bobbing on the water and Aimee ran straight onto the sand. They caught up with her. "I'm sorry if you were asked here to make numbers up this weekend," he said.

Tina shook her head. "No, it's fine really. I haven't seen Lilly and David for a long while. The visit was long overdue."

"Have you known them long?"

"I've known Lilly about sixteen years; she used to work for my husband before he died. I've only know David since they got married."

"I knew David from the time I drove lorries for the firm he used to work for. But he knew my father years before then."

"How long have you been teaching?"

"Three years. I still like to keep up with driving, so I do it during the school holiday."

They walked a little longer before she said, "I think I'll take Aimee back and give her tea. She's had a long day."

While walking back to the house, they talked about other things, small talk mainly. Tina had enjoyed his company. It made a change from the conversations that she had with May. Not that there was anything wrong with her, just that she was not the brightest, and her topic of conversation was limited. Other than May, she only had Aimee, so it had been a change.

Tina found Chris to be polite and he appeared to be genuine and very placid. She pulled herself up short. What was she thinking of? Here was a man she had known for only a few hours and already she was summing him up. *He's got to me already, and I didn't want any more involvement with men*, she silently said to herself.

When they got back, she said she would give Aimee a bath before her tea.

"Do you need a hand?" Chris asked her.

"No thanks, I can manage." She bathed Aimee and sat her in the lounge until she had made her tea. When she went back into the room, she found her sat on Chris's knee and he was reading her a story.

"Well, she seems settled. Thank you for keeping her occupied."

"I enjoyed it, and so did she."

Once Aimee was in bed, they all sat on the porch eating and drinking. There were no awkward moments, no strain and the conversation was flowing. Tina felt so relaxed and was surprised how quickly time went by. Eventually Lilly said she was tired. They all helped to clear up and went to bed.

Next morning after breakfast, they all went into the town and did some shopping, and then returned home for lunch.

After lunch, David went for his afternoon nap and everyone else sat on the porch watching Aimee play. "Why don't you two go off and have a meal on your own this evening? I'll look after the little one."

"Lilly, Chris may not want to," said Tina

"I just thought you might enjoy some intellectual conversation. You won't get that here." She laughed.

"Oh I don't think so," she said.

"I think it's an excellent idea," said Chris. "That is unless you have other plans, Tina."

"No I haven't any plans."

"Good, that's settled then."

Tina had a shower and changed her clothes. She said goodnight to Aimee, then she and Chris went back into town to the tiny bistro they had seen earlier.

"Did I make it awkward for you by asking you to come out tonight?"

"No, I just didn't want you to think you had to agree to Lilly's suggestion."

"I didn't."

"Well I get the distinct feeling that Lilly and David are trying to play the matchmaking game again."

"I think I know you a little bit, and you will only be pushed as far as you want to be."

The meal was pleasant, and she enjoyed his company. Later, they took a leisurely stroll back towards the cottage.

"Lilly told me you've had a rough deal in your life."

"Did she now?"

"Oh, nothing personal, just small talk."

"Yes, I've had my fair share, but I'm back on track again, and this time I intend to stay there."

"I've enjoyed tonight, Tina, thank you. Maybe we could do it again sometime."

"I don't think so, Chris, but I've it enjoyed it too. I shall be returning home tomorrow."

"Can I ring you sometimes, as a friend?"

"Yes," she said. "That would be nice, but only as a friend."

By now, they had reached the house. He gently pecked her on the cheek, thanked her again, and went inside, leaving Tina sat on the porch.

She sat a little while longer thinking about him and how pleasant the evening had been. He was very nice, but she could not allow herself to become involved with him, or anyone else for that matter. Every time she got involved with someone, she was the one who ended up getting hurt.

No it was better just to stay friends, she thought.

Tina left the following morning after breakfast. She thanked Lilly and David and said goodbye to Chris.

When she arrived home, the first thing Aimee wanted to do was go see May. While she went across the yard, Tina unpacked and put the dirty washing in the machine. When she had finished, she walked over to see May.

"Hello, lass, have yer had a good time?"

"Yes I have, it was a nice change."

"We met Chris," said Aimee.

May and Tina looked at each other. "Did yer now, and who is Chris when he's at home?"

"Oh, just a friend of David's," answered Tina. "He was staying with them for the weekend."

"Oh yes?"

"Now don't you go getting any ideas, it was just platonic and that's the way it will stay."

"I never said owt," said May with a glint in her eye. "When are yer seein' this Chris again?"

"I'm not, we've arranged to ring each other occasionally as friends."

"As friends?"

"Yes, as friends."

Tina took Aimee back to the cottage. After tea, they walked along the cliff tops. The sun was just setting and there was a slight breeze. They sat a while and Aimee made a daisy chain. Tina watched the waves gently rolling onto the sand below.

Her thoughts turned to Chris. He was nice and she had enjoyed his company; it would be nice to talk to him again.

They got back to the cottage and she got Aimee ready for bed and read her a story, before tucking her in and turning down the lights.

Tina went downstairs and poured a glass of wine. She sat in the old chair outside the door and the quietness was deafening. There was only the occasional hoot from an owl in the tree, and the cat lay at her feet, asleep. At that moment, it seemed she was the only person around; it was even quiet from across the yard.

The ring of the telephone made her jump, and she answered it. "Hello?"

"Hi, Tina, it's Chris. I just thought I'd ring to ask how you are."

"I'm good, thank you. Where are you?"

"I'm still at David and Lilly's. I'm going back tomorrow. I wondered if I could call and see you on the way?"

"Yes, that would be nice."

"I think there's a little pub just down the road from you. Would you like to meet me there?"

Tina thought a moment. "Why don't you come here, you could have something to eat with us. I don't want to take Aimee into a pub, and if it gets too late, she will be here already to go to bed."

"That's kind of you, but I don't want to put you to any trouble. Why don't I bring something with me and then you won't have to prepare anything?"

"If you're sure, that would be great."

"What time do you want me to arrive?"

"What time are you leaving there?"

"I was going to leave around four tomorrow afternoon."

"Good. It only takes half an hour to get here."

"I'll stop off and get us a meal, shall we say about six then?"

"OK."

"Indian or Chinese?" he asked.

"Pardon."

"Food, what do you prefer, Indian or Chinese?"

"Oh, Chinese please."

"What shall I get Aimee?"

"Oh, don't worry about her, she will have something else."

"If you're sure, I'll see you tomorrow. Bye, Tina."

"Thanks very much, bye."

Tina sat and finished her drink. "I am not getting involved," she said as she went upstairs to bed.

The following morning Tina and Aimee went across to May's. She greeted her with the usual, "Hello, chuck, how are yer?"

"We're having a visitor today, May, would you like to come over?"

"A visitor yer say, now I wonder who that could be."

"Chris, that friend of Lilly and David's."

"Oh aye."

"Don't look like that, May. He's on his way home and he asked if he could call in and see us only as a friend."

"Ay, well, yer need some friends. What about Aimee?"

"She'll have her tea and see Chris before going to bed."

"She can stay here if yer want?"

"Why, we're only going to have something to eat."

"I know, but it would be nice fer yer to have some time ter yerself."

"May, I don't want to get involved in another relationship."

"I know, lass, I know, but just tek a bit o' time, yer never know."

"OK, May, thank you."

Tina polished and cleaned the cottage and then she fed Aimee before taking her over to May's.

"To say he's only a friend, yer went to a lot of trouble cleanin.'"

"It was not for his benefit, I just thought it would save me a job tomorrow."

"I'll believe yer, some wouldn't."

Tina walked back across the yard. She then showered and washed her hair, and she wore the blue Kaftan that Gordon had bought for her so very long ago. She liked it and felt comfortable and the colour suited her.

When she was ready, she poured a glass of wine. As she put the bottle in the fridge, she heard the sound of a car. She opened the door as Chris stepped out of the car.

"Hi, did you manage to find us OK?"

"No problem." He came in the kitchen with food, wine and flowers.

"These are for you," he said, handing them to her.

"They are lovely, thank you," she said as she took a vase from the cupboard and placed the flowers in water.

"Shall we eat before the food goes cold?"

"Sounds good to me," he replied.

Tina laid out the meal and poured the wine.

Throughout the meal, they talked; she told him a bit about herself, but not everything.

He told her about himself and his family. All the time he was there, they were never stuck for something to say; the conversation flowed between them all night. Despite her statement about not becoming involved with anyone, she found him very attractive. They drank the wine, or rather, she did. He only had the one glass; he said he did not drink much and he was driving.

When they had finished, they cleared away and sat in the lounge.

"So what are your plans for the future now?" he asked her.

"I don't have any at the moment. I just want to make sure that Aimee is happy. This is a nice location to live in. I just take every day as it comes."

"Best way."

He looked at the clock and jumped up. "I had better make tracks, I didn't realise it was so late."

They had spent so much time talking, that the time had flown by. Tina was surprised to see it had gone midnight.

"It's a bit late to start driving back now. Why not stay the night and set off early in the morning?" she said.

"If you think it will be OK I would appreciate it."

"Good, in that case, would you like some coffee?" she asked.

"That would be nice, thank you."

She went through to the kitchen, poured the rest of the wine into her glass and put coffee in his cup. Chris came into the kitchen and stood behind her.

"I have enjoyed tonight, Tina, thank you. Maybe we could do it again sometime?"

"I'd like that."

As she poured the milk into his coffee, he put his hands gently on her shoulders and kissed her. As they broke apart, he looked embarrassed.

"I'm sorry, Tina, you have been such good company and I've really enjoyed myself. It's been a long time since I have enjoyed female company."

"It's been a long time since I've had company. Male company that is."

They walked back into the room, and for the first time all evening there was a lull in conversation. They sat close together and he kissed her again.

It had been a long time since she had had any physical contact with a man. Chris kissed her and she responded to his kisses.

After a while, she said, "Why don't we go upstairs where we'll more comfortable."

"Only if you're sure?"

She nodded her head, took his hand and led him upstairs.

There was little light in the room, so she turned on the small table lamp. She went into the bathroom, and when she returned, he was in her bed. She climbed in beside him and he took her into his arms and began kissing her again.

Her body moved into his and she gave a soft moan. His kisses became more urgent. He moved his lips down and kissed her nipples, taking each one softly into his mouth and sucking gently first on one and then the other.

Her hands felt for his hard manhood that she could feel pressing against her and he moaned. His hands moved down to the crevice at the top of her legs. He gently pushed them apart and rose above her. He entered her and became still as Tina moved under him. Slowly their bodies began to move rhythmically until she could feel the passion building up inside her. She wanted it to go on forever and never stop.

As they moved and climaxed together, she felt an explosion inside her head. Tina had never experienced a feeling like that in her life.

As they lay panting in the aftermath of their lovemaking, he said, "Thank you, Tina, you are really something."

"It was good for me too." With little more to say, he wrapped his arms around her, kissed her and they slept that way until morning.

Tina woke early and saw Chris was still asleep beside her. She slipped out of bed and went to the bathroom; she showered and dressed and went downstairs. She put on a pot of coffee, and by the time it was ready, he had showered and dressed, and was coming down the stairs.

"Hi, I thought you were still asleep," she said.

"The shower woke me, which is good, as I have to leave early. I must get back home."

"Right."

"Tina, I want to thank you for last night. I really had a good time."

"I enjoyed it too."

"I would like to see you again, but because of the distance involved, it may be next weekend. Would that be a problem?"

"No, I'd like to see you again too. Next weekend will be fine, if you can make it. But do me a favour, if you don't want to come back, let me know."

"I'll do that, but I don't think you have to worry. Maybe we can take Aimee and do something for the day."

"She'd like that. Here's your eggs and toast, will that be enough?"

"It's more than enough, thank you."

When they had finished breakfast he said, "I hate to cut and run, but I really do have to go."

"I understand."

He kissed her again and went out to his car; he pulled out of the yard and waved to her as he drove away. As she watched him go, May opened her door.

"Mornin', chuck, how was it?"

"How was what?"

"Yer night o' course."

"It was good, May, very good."

"Want a cuppa?"

"Why, so you can grill me?"

"Listen, I don't have no excitement in me life, so if it means bein' nosy to get some, then I will. Now do you want that cuppa or no?"

"Of course, I'm coming."

She walked into May's kitchen and Aimee was at the table eating toast. She kissed her head. "Morning, darling, have you been good?"

Aimee nodded her head and continued eating. May poured the tea and sat down.

"Come on then, I thought yer said he was just a friend?"

"He is."

"But he stayed the night."

"Friends sometimes do that, May."

"Don't be coy with me, did yer sleep with him?"

"May," Tina exclaimed, "what a question."

"Well, did yer? First yer say he's a friend, then he stays the night, so, did yer sleep with him? Though it's really now't ter do with me, I just thought yer might like him that way, yer know?" she said, winking.

"Yes I do, and if you must know, we talked so long last night, it was too late for him to drive home."

"That's alright then, talking eh, so that's what they call it these days."

"May, you have a wicked mind."

"Aye it's bin said afore," she laughed. "Now I have ter get me washing done."

"I'll tell you what," said Tina, "I'll give you a hand and then we could go into the town for a bit."

"I'll not say no to lending a hand with washing. But I don't know about the town."

"Why, what's wrong?"

"Now't but old age. I feel that tired just now."

"Give me your washing and I'll take it across home and do it. You sit and put your feet up."

"Yer a good girl, Tina."

"You deserve a rest." Tina collected all her washing and then said, "I'll come back over later, make sure you rest."

"OK, luv."

For the rest of the morning Tina was busy doing her washing as well as May's. By the time she had got it all on the line it was lunchtime She made herself a cup of coffee, and made Aimee some lunch. She then crossed the yard to see how May was feeling.

"I'm fine, lass, got me a headache, that's all."

"All the washing is done and on the line, so you have nothing to worry about. I'm going out with Aimee, so you take some aspirin and rest. Is there anything you need me to get you while we're out?"

"Nice bit o' fish for me tea, if yer don't mind?"

"No problem. I'll see you when I get back. Bye for now."

"Tara, luv."

Tina and Aimee went off into town. She bought her own shopping, and went to the fish shop for May's fish. She also bought a bunch of flowers for her. Tina thought that they might cheer her up.

They returned home, and while Aimee took off her coat, Tina went across to see May.

"How do you feel now?"

"Much better, lass. That little rest did me good."

"Here's some flowers as a thank you for having Aimee, and here's your fish."

"Ta, luv, we'll have that fer tea."

"Would you like me to cook it for you, May?"

"Nay, lass, I can do it. I feel tons better now."

"If you're sure. Right, May, I'll go and see to Aimee, call me if you need anything."

"I will, thanks."

When Tina and Aimee had finished tea, they went for a walk along the cliff tops. The light was slowly fading so they turned and walked back to the cottage. Aimee got ready for bed and Tina tucked her in. Then she walked across the yard to see how May was.

She was sat in her favourite chair watching TV. "Hello, everything OK?"

"Yes, I just popped over with all your washing and to make sure you were alright."

"I'm fine now, thanks."

"Good, I'll get back to Aimee; she's on her own. Call me if you need me."

When Tina got in, she poured some wine, and the telephone rang. "Hello?"

"Hi, Tina, it's me, Chris."

"Hello, did you get back safely?"

"Yes, I'm back at work tomorrow. I just wanted to speak to you and make sure you were alright."

"Yes, I'm fine. It was nice to have your company, Chris, thank you."

They chatted on about nothing important and then he said he would see her at the weekend.

Tina finished the wine, had a shower and went to bed.

Over the following month, nothing much changed. Tina continued to take Aimee out each night before she went to bed. She had seen Chris two more times and had planted some bulbs in the garden. Then one Thursday Chris called and asked if he could come up the following day after work.

"Of course you can, it will be nice to see you again." She was looking forward to seeing him more than she admitted.

The following day, Tina was up early and set about making sure the cottage sparkled, and all the washing and ironing was done and put away. She then bathed and changed Aimee before doing the same. She also put a steak casserole in the oven for their evening meal. Tina walked over to May's and asked if she wanted to come over for a meal.

"Nay, lass, yer don't want me hanging round. Anyway, Albert is working late, and he'll want his bed when he gets in. I have ter see ter him."

"Well bring him when he gets home. It will be nice for us all to be together."

"Albert won't want to, I know, but if yer sure, I'll leave his tea ready. It'll make a nice change fer me."

"Right, that's settled then. See you later."

Tina spent another hour making sure that things were ready. Then she pulled up. *Why am I making a fuss?* she thought. After all, he's only a friend, but she knew she felt differently about him.

May came over about six. "Not too early am I?"

"No, come and sit down. What will you have to drink?"

"Don't s'pose yer have any whiskey have yer?"

"Yes, as a matter of fact I do."

"Ta, that would be grand."

Tina poured May a good measure, and she sat reading to Aimee.

About six thirty, they heard a car pull into the yard and a door slam. She opened the door and let Chris in.

"Hello again, come and meet May. My very good friend and neighbour."

"Hello, May, nice to meet you."

"Likewise," May said, trying to be posh, but not quite managing it.

"Hi, Aimee, do you remember me?"

Aimee nodded her head "yes."

"Would you like a drink?" she asked him. "Wine, whisky or beer?"

"Beer would be fine, thank you."

They sat around the table making small talk, with Aimee doing most of the talking. May said very little, but she was a thinker.

When supper was over, May said she would go back home.

"Albert should be home by now."

"I'll walk over with you."

"There's no need, lass, I'll be OK."

"I know you will, but I'll still walk with you."

She told Chris that she would only be gone a moment.

"I'll clear away while you're gone," he said.

As May and Tina walked across the yard, May said, "He's a bit of alright."

"Yes he is, and he's genuine. What you see is what you get."

"Go and have some fun; send Aimee over if you want."

"That's OK. You get some rest, May. We're going out tomorrow, would you like to come with us?"

"I'll think about it."

Tina kissed her on the cheek. "Take care then. I love you, May. You're the nearest thing I have to a mother."

May's eyes filled with tears. "That's a real compliment. Now get over yonder before I spill me eyes."

"Night then."

"Night, lass."

May closed the door and Tina walked back to the cottage. As she let herself in, she heard Aimee laughing. She sat beside Chris, and he was reading her a story.

"Well, you two look cosy. I'll leave you a few minutes to put the things away in the kitchen."

"We'll be fine."

While Tina tidied up the kitchen, she heard Aimee and Chris laughing at the story. Tina thought back. Solly had been the love of her life. Gordon had loved her and she had not been fair with him; she hoped he was happy with Julie. Now she wondered where it would lead to with Chris.

She had not heard from Gordon for a while, but then she hadn't treated him very nice the last time she had seen him.

Tina finished what she was doing and went through to the room.

"Would you like another drink?" she asked him.

"Yes please, shall I get it?"

"No, I'll get it."

When she came back with his drink she said, "I think it's your bedtime, Aimee."

"Do I have to, Mummy?"

"Yes you do."

"But I want to stay with you and Chris."

Chris took a hold of her hand. "Do as Mummy says. I will be here tomorrow and we will all go out and have fun."

"Oh good." Aimee got off the settee and made her way upstairs. "I like Chris, Mummy."

"I'm glad. Sleep tight; we'll see you in the morning."

She went downstairs, poured another drink and joined Chris in the lounge. He put his arm around her. "I have actually missed you."

"That's nice. I have missed you too."

They had a good weekend together. They visited all the local places, took Aimee to the fair and made love. By Sunday evening when Chris had to return home, they were all tired, but said the weekend had been fun.

"I have really had a good time," he said as he was leaving. "Maybe next time you could come over to me."

"Yes, that would make a nice change."

For the next six months, either Chris spent the weekends in Whitby, or Tina spent them at his home. They had become very close, and Tina could actually admit that she was in love once again.

He had asked her to consider moving in with him, but Tina held off on that idea.

Even though she loved him, she was financially secure and had her own independence. She did not want to give it up. Maybe she just wasn't ready to commit to him full time yet.

The next six months went by much the same as the previous six months. One weekend he said, "Tina, we have been together a year now. I would like our relationship to become more permanent. You seem reluctant to move in with me. I love you, so why don't I try to get a transfer and move here."

"I do love you, Chris, but I am so scared of making that final move. I like the independence that I have and I'm really quite happy with the present arrangement."

He sighed and cleared his throat. "Well as much as I love you, Tina, I'm not. I want something more permanent."

All the time she had known him, this was the first time that they had disagreed about anything, and the next few hours were very strained.

He took his coat from the peg. "I think I'll head back."

"I thought you were going to stay all weekend?"

"Yes I was, but I've changed my mind. I have things to do and maybe a break will give you a chance to work out what you want."

He kissed her and left, leaving her lost for words.

The door opened almost immediately, and she thought he had changed his mind and come back, but it was May.

"Where's Chris gone? I saw him drive off."

"Oh, he's gone back home."

"Why, you two had a row?"

"Not exactly. He keeps saying he wants things to be permanent between us. I don't want to leave here, so he suggested getting transferred here."

"And?"

Tina sighed. "I love him, but I didn't want that."

"Not enough it seems. Yer gonna lose him, lass."

"I know, but I can't help it, May. I've been through too much to start all over again."

"Yer've bin through too much not to grab at happiness when it comes along."

"I know. I just don't seem to be able to commit like he wants."

"What will yer do if he goes?"

"I'll manage. I have before."

"Yer a stubborn baggage, Tina, but only you can mek the changes."

"I know that too."

"Aye well, I better have a drink while I'm here then."

Chris did not contact her all that week. She tried to call him, but all she got was the answering machine. She left messages, but he didn't return her calls. All that week, she agonised over what she should do. There was no doubt that she missed him, but was that enough?

She was to find out how much when the following week she visited some friends, and she decided to call on Chris on her way home.

She thought she would try to come to some agreement over their present situation. After all, they had been together a year and she did love him. She tried to call him to tell him that she would like to see him, but again, she got the answering machine.

She decided to call on him anyway. When she knocked at his door, there was no answer. The neighbour next door came out to see her. "Are you looking for Chris?"

"Yes, have you seen him?"

"We haven't seen him all week, and he usually lets us know if he's going to be away."

"OK. If he shows up will you ask him to call me? Here is my number," she said as she handed her a card.

Tina caught the bus that would take her home. The journey would take her a while and it gave her time to think.

If Chris was prepared to uproot and relocate, then she should meet him half way and make new living arrangements. She loved him, and if he moved in with her, they need not go as far as getting married. If things didn't work out they could go their separate ways without getting too messy.

By Wednesday, she had still not heard from him and she was beginning to get a little worried.

Then something happened that brought Tina's world crashing down. She went over to May's one morning, and getting no answer to her knock, she let herself in. Albert was not there because he had gone to visit some relatives and he wasn't due to come back until the following day.

Tina went upstairs into her bedroom. At first, it seemed as if she was still asleep, but when she got closer, Tina realised May was dead. She had complained of aches and pains for some time, but she had seemed all right the day before.

Tina covered her and went downstairs to call the doctor, and then she called Albert.

Poor Albert, he would be lost without her. The doctor said she had died of natural causes; she'd had a busy life, and was just worn out.

Albert returned, but he was too distraught to see to any of the arrangements, and he asked Tina if she would sort things out. He took the remaining children back to Leeds to stay with friends.

Tina had to take the responsibility of arranging the funeral. The house was officially hers, so she didn't have to do anything with that. Within a couple of days, Albert and some people who she had never seen before came and cleared out the house. He told Tina he had moved the children into a house near friends and they would help him look after them.

She told him when the funeral would be. Poor Albert, he had aged within days and Tina could not help feeling sorry for him.

The following week was so hectic for her. She had no time to grieve herself, and she was desperate to speak to Chris, and she missed May.

The funeral was to be the following week, and as Albert had left her to do everything, she went through the papers he had overlooked to take with him. She contacted her solicitor and he looked at the papers. He told her that May had put a bit of money into a savings account with the Co-op; this would pay for the funeral.

On the day of the funeral, Albert turned up. "Thank you fer all yer've done. I'm sorry it was left to you, but I don't know what ter do without our lass."

"Don't think about it," she told him, but it was a sad day.

When it was all over and everyone had gone, Tina sat and cried. It was her time to grieve now. A little later, the landlady from the pub down the road came. "Here, I've brought you something to eat. I bet you have not had anything all day. What's going to happen to the cottage now?"

"I own it," said Tina. "I bought the whole lot and moved May in when I came."

"I suppose you'll be looking for a new tenant soon?"

"I don't know yet. I have to think about it." An idea was already forming in her mind.

Maybe Chris would be willing to move into the cottage, that way they could be together, but she would still have her own independence.

Tina called Lilly next day. "Tina, how nice to hear from you."

"Lilly, can Aimee and I come and stay for a few days."

"Of course you can, come whenever you like."

"Is this afternoon too soon?"

"No, would you like David to drive over and pick you up?"

"I'll be fine, I'll be there about three then."

"See you then. Is everything OK, Tina?"

"Not really. I'll explain when I see you. Bye."

Aimee was excited because she was going to see Lilly. She always had a good time, and David would take her down to the harbour and let her play in the sand.

"Listen, Aimee, go to your room and put the things on your bed that you want to take with you. I will come and pack for you when I have finished in my room."

She finished her packing and went to see Aimee. She had toys, books and her favourite doll on the bed. Tina packed, and as soon as they were ready, they walked downstairs and waited for the taxi. Within ten minutes, it pulled into the yard.

She locked up the house, the driver put the cases into the car and they drove out of the yard. For the first time since Tina had bought the property, she got out of the taxi and padlocked the gates. May had always been there to watch the place when she had gone to Lilly's, but that would be no more.

The drive to Lilly's seemed to pass quickly. As they pulled up in front of the door, Lilly and David came out to meet them. David carried their cases into the hall, while Lilly hung up their coats. "I've just made some coffee, Tina, come into the room. How are you? You look a little tired."

"I have been a bit busy this last week."

"Yes, we heard about May. I'm sorry; you must miss her."

"I do, but there's something else worrying me. Have you heard from Chris lately?"

"No," said Lilly. "Have you, David?"

"Not for a week or two. Last time I did speak to him, he said he was taking a few days off and going walking in Scotland. Why?"

Tina told them what had happened between them last time they met. He had left, and she had not been able to contact him.

"I'll make some enquiries," said David. "I have a few contacts."

"Thank you."

"Anything else?" asked Lilly.

"No, why should there be?"

"Because you look tired. Are you eating and sleeping?"

"Yes," said Tina. "I do feel tired, but I put it down to events that have happened in the last week or so. You know, Albert was unable to do anything and I had all the arrangements to make for the funeral."

"Didn't he help you at all?"

"No, he only moved the furniture back to Leeds. He said he was moving nearer relatives, so the children could be looked after."

"I don't think he was very fair; after all, she was his wife."

"He's a broken man. I just got on with it."

"Maybe, but he still could have helped. Why don't you go get a checkup?"

"If I still feel the same next week, I will."

"How long would you like to stay?"

"I'll stay until Monday."

"You're welcome to stay longer, you know."

"Thank you, but now May's gone I don't like leaving the cottage very long."

The weekend was just what Tina needed. They walked down to the beach, talked, laughed at old times and she found it very restful. All too soon, Sunday evening came and she had to think about going home the next morning.

As they sat in the porch Lilly said, "Why don't you leave Aimee here with us. You come back and stay next weekend, then take her back with you."

"I can't burden you like that, Lilly."

"Nonsense, she's not a burden. She likes being here, and we love having her. You could go back, see the doctor and have a rest. You can ring her each day. I think you'll miss her more than she'll miss you."

"I'm sure she'll like being here. I could do with some time on my own. Thanks, Lilly."

Next morning when Tina was packing Aimee came into the bedroom.

"Can we stay a bit longer, Mummy?" she asked.

"You can if you want to, and if you promise to be good for Lilly and David."

"Oh yes, yes I will be good."

"Mummy has to go back home for a few days. I have some things I need to do, and the cat will wonder where we are. But I will call you each day and come back next weekend."

When Tina had finished packing, she said goodbye, kissed Aimee and left for home.

Once she had unpacked, she went across to May's cottage. She still regarded it as hers, opened all the windows and let in some fresh air.

She went back to her cottage and the cat rubbed round her legs waiting for Tina to feed her. She made a cup of coffee and sat outside in the warm sunshine to drink it.

She must have fallen asleep, and the ringing of the telephone woke her.

"Hello."

"Tina, it's David. I made some enquiries and found out that Chris has taken two weeks off school and gone walking in Scotland. He's due to come back next weekend. Maybe he thought it would be a good idea to get away and leave you to make up your mind."

"Thanks very much for finding out for me."

"He's a good man you know."

"I know."

"Lilly said I have to remind you to go the doctor."

"I will and thank you once again."

When David hung up, she dialled the doctor's office and made an appointment for the following day. Then she wondered what she should do for the remainder of the day. In the end, she locked up May's cottage, had a bath and went to bed early.

Surprisingly, she slept through until the sun streaming through the window woke her. She had a shower, made the bed, and had some breakfast. She decided that when she had seen the doctor, while she was in the town, she would do some shopping.

She arrived at the surgery and only had to wait a few minutes to wait to see the doctor. When she had seen him, he asked her to wait outside for a few minutes. Then he called her back in.

"Well, Tina, from now on you will need to get plenty of rest and good food. You're pregnant."

"Pregnant, how could that be?"

"I don't think I need to explain that to you."

"No, but I have been careful. I took precaution."

"Obviously not careful enough. No method is a hundred percent safe."

" I know, it's just a surprise."

"Take care and come back and see me in a month."

She left the doctor's in a daze. She went shopping, but could not concentrate on what she was doing, so she returned home."

When she got home, she made some coffee, and without taking off her coat, sat outside. What will she do now?

She could not do anything about Chris until he returned. She had already decided, that if Chris wanted to move closer, he could stay in May's cottage. If it worked out, they, or rather she, would let things progress further.

For the rest of the week, Tina spring cleaned the cottage and had plenty of rest. She spoke to Aimee every day, and spoke to Lilly and told her that she would be there at the weekend.

On her way to Whitby, she stopped off and bought something as a way of a thank you for Lilly and David for having Aimee all week.

When the taxi pulled up in front of the door, she heard laughter coming from inside. The door opened and Aimee came running down the path, and flung herself into Tina's arms. She had obviously missed her. "Mummy, I love you, I'm glad you came."

"You seem to be having fun."

"We are, and guess what?"

"What?"

"Chris is here."

Tina stopped dead in her tracks. "Is he now?"

"Yes and he's been telling us about his holiday. Come on, Mummy."

Aimee took her hand, pulling her inside.

Lilly looked up. "Tina, look who's here?"

"So I see." She was a little cool towards him. She was a bit miffed about him going off the way he did. The least he could have done is let her know where he was. Now he turns up as if nothing had happened.

David made a fuss of her, but Chris said a cool, "Hi."

"Hello, I understand you've been on holiday."

He cleared his throat. "Yes, I felt I needed to get away for a while. A bit of solitary walking alone gives you a lot of time to think things through."

"Yes it does," was all she said.

They had tea, but Tina felt a little awkward; she had not reckoned on him being there. She knew that she would have to speak to him, but here was not the place.

After tea when Aimee was in bed, the four adults sat in the sunroom with a drink. Tina said, "I think Aimee and I will head back tomorrow, Lilly."

"Are you sure, Tina? I thought you would be staying for the rest of the weekend."

"I need to get back, especially now the cottage is empty. Thank you for having Aimee this week. I know she's enjoyed being here."

"She was a pleasure to have. Well if you're sure that's what you want to do, I hope it's not too long before you come to see us again."

"No, I'll make it soon."

They made small talk for the remainder of the evening until Tina made her apologies and said she was tired and was going to bed.

When she had gone, "Tina was quiet tonight," remarked Chris.

Lilly agreed. "Yes, and she still looks tired. She was going to see the doctor this week, but she hasn't said anything, so I don't know if she's been."

"Is she ill?" asked Chris.

"I don't think so," said Lilly. "I think she's probably overdone it, you know with May dying. It was left to Tina to sort everything out."

They all went to bed after this conversation. Tina was still awake and heard them coming up stairs; it took her a long time to fall asleep. She had been surprised to see Chris. She realised that she still loved him, but she was so afraid of getting hurt again. Still, she had other things to think about now.

She fell asleep and woke to the sound of chatter and the sun streaming through the windows.

Aimee was already dressed and downstairs; she had not heard her get up. She got out of bed, had a shower and went downstairs.

"Morning, Tina, would you like some breakfast?"

She shook her head. "No thanks, coffee will do fine."

Chris was not up yet, so after breakfast, she got their things ready to head back home.

"Did you manage to get to the doctor's this week?" Lilly asked her.

"Yes, he said I was a bit run down that's all."

"Nothing serious then, good."

At this moment, Tina did not feel like telling them what the doctor had really said.

Chris was still in bed by the time they were ready to go. This made it easier for her to say goodbye.

"I'm going now, thanks for having me."

"Go carefully, and come down again soon."

She arrived home and unpacked. Then she and Aimee went down to the beach and collected shells. This practice had started when they had first come to the cottage and had just carried on.

When they got back in, Tina was surprised to see that they had been out nearly three hours. As they were going into the cottage, Chris drove into the yard.

"Hi," he said. "You were out a long time. I came earlier and there was no one in. I drove back into Whitby for a while."

"Yes, we went walking and collecting shells; the time just passed us by. I'm surprised to see you."

"Well, when I got up this morning, you had gone and I hadn't had a chance to speak to you. Would you and Aimee like to go out for something to eat?"

"I don't think that's a good idea, Chris. Would you like to come in for a drink?" she asked him.

"Yes, thank you. "

She walked into the kitchen to get the drinks and he followed her. "Tina, I really need to speak to you and I can't do that if you don't meet me half way."

"OK," she said. "Look, Aimee is tired and I would like her to have an early night, I don't think she's had many this last week. Why don't I make us something to eat here, and then we can talk when she goes to bed?"

He nodded. "It sounds good to me. Can I help?"

"You could read Aimee a story; she'd like that."

Aimee had other ideas, and when Tina went to get them for tea, she found them both in the shed sorting through the collection of shells.

"Come on, you two, tea's ready."

After the meal, Tina took Aimee upstairs to get ready for bed, and when she came down again, Chris had cleared things away for her. He had also washed up and poured her a drink.

They took the drinks and sat outside. "You didn't tell me you would be going away," she said to him.

"I felt I had to. We needed some breathing space, but when I was walking and thinking, I realised just how much I missed you both."

"I missed you too. I was angry that you'd not told me you were going."

"I didn't think you wanted a serious relationship."

"I'll tell you something, Chris." For the next hour, she told him a little, but not all, about her life. When she had finished she said, "That's why I'm afraid of getting into a serious relationship again. I am not an easy person to live with, and that can be a problem. But there is nothing I can do about it."

"But I'm willing to give it a try if you are? I still love you, Tina."

"I love you too, but can you understand now why I said no to you in the first place?"

"Yes I can. You should have told me earlier."

"I have had an idea."

"Go on."

"Since May died, her place has been empty. You could move in there, it would save you having to commute and give us a chance to see how things go between us. At the same time, we will still have our own space. If it works out, then we could look at making our relationship permanent."

"Sounds a good idea to me, Tina. I'll go and see the Estate Agents tomorrow about the place."

"There's no need, I own the cottage."

"You own it?"

"Yes, when I bought the farmhouse it included the outbuildings and the gardens. May had been good to me. Where she lived was no good to bring up children, so I said she could have the cottage."

"That make's things easy. I won't have to pay a large deposit before I move in.

"Does that mean you will?"

"I will go home, pack up my things and move in at the weekend. I still have some holiday left, and I will ask to be relocated to the school here."

"Great, why don't you stay the night and go home in the morning?"

"I will. I do love you and I really hope this works."

"I love you too, and I promise I'll try not to make things difficult."

They had another drink and went to bed. He kissed her and wrapped his arms round her. She had not told him about the baby; she wanted to wait until she saw how things turned out. The other thing was, she didn't know how he would accept the news.

After making love, he kissed her again. "This is how I want us to be, Tina."

"I do too," she said.

Soon the steady breathing told her he was asleep. She so wanted things to work, maybe this time things would work out.

Next morning after breakfast, he got ready to go home. "I'll be back this weekend."

"I'll make sure the cottage is ready for you."

Aimee was excited when Tina told her that Chris would be moving into the cottage. For the rest of the week, Tina scrubbed and polished the cottage ready for him moving in. When she had finished, she spent another two days doing the same to her cottage.

On Saturday morning, the sun was shining and Tina waited excitedly for Chris to arrive. She and Aimee went shopping, and bought enough to stock up her cupboards and provisions for Chris. They were just putting the shopping away, when they heard the car pull into the yard.

For the next few hours, they unpacked the trailer and put things away. By mid afternoon, it was all finished, and they were tired. Chris drove into the town and brought a take away back, so that she would not have to cook.

By the time they had eaten, Aimee was tired and ready for bed. Once she was in bed, they sat outside and had some wine. They, too, were tired, but happy in the knowledge that from tomorrow, their lives may alter for the better.

Chris said he would sleep in his cottage that night. They were both very tired, and as the following day was Sunday, they could relax. On Monday, Chris would have to go to the local school to see about work.

Over the next month, things began to work out. Chris got a job in the local school. He ate his meals with them most evenings and sometimes he would sleep over unless he had work, then he would sleep in his place and work late into the night.

Tina had still not found the right time to tell him about the coming baby. She knew she must soon, as her pregnancy was becoming noticeable; she already had to wear loose-fitting clothes. She decided she would tell him the coming weekend.

On Saturday, they spent a pleasant day on the beach with Aimee. When they returned home, she said she would feed Aimee early, and would make something special for them to have later.

"Good, I have some work to do. I'll finish it and come across later."

When Aimee was in bed, Tina prepared the meal, then showered and changed. Just as she had finished, Chris arrived. Throughout the meal, they made small talk.

"That was a great meal. What's the occasion?"

"I have something to tell you and I don't how you will take it."

"Why don't you try me and see."

"I'm pregnant."

"Oh, I see."

"Do you?"

"I presume the baby is mine?"

"Who else's could it be?"

"I didn't mean it like that. How long have you known, Tina?"

"Three months."

"Three months?" he said, surprised.

"Yes, but I didn't know where you were when I found out. Then when I went to see Lilly, I was surprised to see you there."

"I see."

"Look, Chris, I don't know how you feel about this, but I don't really care. If you're not around, I'll manage."

"No, it's fine really. I was just surprised that you have not mentioned it before now."

"Maybe I was waiting for the right time."

"You mean you were testing me?"

"Maybe."

"It's not necessary, Tina. I love you, and I have told you how I would like things to be. The decision is yours. But I want to care for you, especially now with the baby coming."

Tina did not say anything.

"I know it's not been easy for you, but let's just take one day at a time and see how things go. I'm not going anywhere. I love you."

"Oh, Chris, I do so want this to work out."

"Tina, I wonder if you love me as much as I love you."

Here it was again. She had heard the same thing from Gordon. It must be so obvious to everyone she met, but she couldn't see it.

"I do know I love you. I will try my best."

"That's fine by me. Now I think we should celebrate, don't you? We're having a baby."

They sat and talked well into the night. When Tina said she felt a little cold, they were surprised to see it was gone two in the morning.

Chris took her in his arms and kissed her. "Let's go to bed."

The next day they told Aimee about the coming baby. Then they rang Lilly and David and they said they were very pleased for them both.

Over the next few months, she was blissfully happy. Chris spent more time in her cottage than his. He helped with any heavy work and they drifted into a comfortable, relaxed relationship. It was almost like being married without the ceremony.

He would go to work, and some of the time she would clean his cottage and do his washing as well as taking care of Aimee. They would sleep together most nights, but Tina still kept her own space by not suggesting to him that he move in with her permanently.

Sometimes when they visited Lilly, they would keep Aimee for a few days to give Tina a break. On these occasions, they would spend time relaxing, and visiting different parts of the coast.

When Tina was seven months pregnant, Chris asked Tina again to marry him; she still refused.

One evening, they had just finished their meal, and were sitting outside with a bottle of wine.

"I love you even more than I did before," he told her. He placed his hand on her swollen stomach and felt the baby kick. He kissed her.

"I am so looking forward to this baby. I'll look after you. You do know that, don't you?"

She nodded. He took her hand and led her upstairs where he slowly undressed her and together they got into bed, all the while running his hands over her swollen breasts and down over her stomach. He took one of her swollen nipples into his mouth and sucked, causing her to catch her breath, a feeling of warmth and sensuality sweeping through her.

His hands travelled over her belly down to the soft mound below. She moaned with pleasure and placed her hand on his swollen member. She turned onto her side, and while he continued to fondle her breasts, he gently entered her from behind. She found that this was the most comfortable position when they made love.

They moved together slowly, and moving in unison, they came together. They lay until their breathing returned to normal, feeling satisfied. She went to the bathroom and when she returned he held her in his arms.

"I'm so glad that we can still make love. I only want to love you not hurt you, Tina."

"You don't hurt me. I love the feelings we have together."

Two months on and Tina was counting the days to the birth. By now, she was feeling so uncomfortable. She waddled around, not having the energy to do much more.

"I wasn't as big as this with Aimee," she told Chris.

"It could be that it's a bigger baby," he said.

"Maybe, but my back aches terribly this morning and I don't feel too good."

"Why don't you go back to bed? I'll ring David and Lilly and ask them if they can have Aimee until after you have given birth."

"Do you think they will?"

"Of course they will. Aimee loves them and they love having her there. You go back to bed. If they say OK, I'll run her over there."

Tina went back to bed, and as expected, Lilly said to bring Aimee over. Chris packed a bag. He said goodbye, and said he would be back soon.

She must have fallen asleep, because she woke with cramps running across her stomach. She knew that this was the start of the baby coming.

She rang the hospital and they told her to get herself checked in. In between the spasms, she managed to get dressed and get downstairs with her bag. She was just thinking that she should ring an ambulance, when Chris returned.

"How do you feel?" he asked her.

"The baby's coming. I rang the hospital and they said to go in."

"Come on, let's get you there." He picked up her case and led her to the car.

He got to the hospital within twenty minutes. By now her contractions were coming very regularly.

They took her to the delivery room to prepare her for the birth. Half an hour later, a nurse came and told Chris that he could see Tina for a few minutes. She was well on the way with the baby.

When he saw her, she was in so much pain and could hardly talk.

"Is there anything I can do for you?" he asked.

She shook her head. The nurse returned and told him he would have to wait outside.

He waited outside the room, and worried that she wouldn't be OK. An hour later, the same nurse reappeared.

"Is she alright?"

"Yes, you have a fine healthy baby boy; big one, nine pounds. You can see them in a while."

He nodded and sat down again. Another ten minutes passed and then the same nurse came and said, "You can go in now."

He went into the room and saw Tina looking a lot more comfortable than the last time he had seen her.

"Hi. How do you feel?"

"Tired. Have you seen your son?"

He looked into the crib at the small bundle wrapped in a blue blanket and making noises.

"He's lovely. He's not wrinkled like some babies I have seen."

"The nurse said it was because he was a big baby. Now we have to decide what to call him," she said.

"I don't really have a preference."

"I rather like the name Martin," she suggested.

"That sounds like a good name."

"Why don't we call him Martin Christopher?"

"I like that."

He stayed a little while longer and then the nurse came back and said he would have to go and return at visiting time.

He kissed her. "I'll see you later. I'll ring Lilly and let them know."

When he had gone, Tina and the baby went to the normal ward where she could rest. She slept and was unaware of anything until she heard a bell ring. The curtains opened and Chris was there.

"What time is it?"

"Eight o' clock. I brought you a few things."

"Thank you."

"Lilly and David are thrilled and Aimee can't wait to see him."

"I will be home in a couple of days, and then she will be able to come home."

"You need to take your time, Tina. Get some rest while you can."

They talked some more, mainly about the baby, until the end of visiting time. He kissed her and said he would see her the following day.

Tina settled down. The nurse brought her baby in and she fed him for the first time. She stroked his head. He had a fine covering of downy hair. He was lovely, and Chris had been so proud. When the baby had finished feeding, the nurse took him back to the nursery, and she settled down to sleep for the night.

She was in the hospital for four days. When she returned home, her days were full of caring for Aimee and Martin. She and Chris still had their separate places, but he spent most of the time with her.

Martin was nearly six months old when Chris again asked Tina to marry him.

"Yes, I will."

"Do you mean it?"

"Yes, it's only fair that we become a proper family."

"When?"

"Make it as soon as you want to."

"I'll make the arrangements, before you change your mind," he said.

When they made love that night, it seemed to her that it was more loving and passionate than it had been in a long time. They fell asleep in each other's arms.

Tina woke and it was still dark. Something was wrong. First she tried to focus. She could not breathe, and she was choking.

She suddenly realised that it was smoke from fire. She quickly sat up and shook Chris awake. He sat up coughing and choking.

"Quick, get downstairs!" he shouted.

"The children!" she shouted.

"Get downstairs. I'll get them."

She crawled downstairs out of bed and as she opened the bedroom door, she could feel the heat of the fire. She could see flames coming from the sitting room. She choked and spluttered, her eyes stinging from the smoke.

She crawled downstairs, feeling the heat under her feet. She heard Chris coughing as he made his way to the room where the children were.

In the distance, she heard the sound of fire engines. Chris had managed to ring them as soon as he had realised there was a fire.

Tina crawled past the sitting room and out into the yard. The fire engine was just pulling in.

"Quick!" she shouted. "They're in there!"

"How many inside?" asked the fireman.

"Three, my two children and their father."

By now, she was shivering with the cold. He wrapped a blanket around her shoulders and told her to stay where she was.

An ambulance pulled into the yard. The farmhouse was an old building. The heat and smell and the crackle of burning wood as the fire took hold was intense.

"Chris!" she screamed, but there was no sign of him.

As the firemen entered the burning building, their hoses dowsing the fire before them, she watched and waited for them to return. Eventually one emerged from the building with a bundle in his arms. She made to run forward but was held back by one of the ambulance crew. A nurse took the bundle, and Tina realised it was Martin. The fireman looked at the nurse and shook his head.

Tina remembered screaming and someone took her inside the ambulance. She felt a needle slip into her arm. She lay on the stretcher, seeing, but not saying anything.

Another ambulance pulled into the yard as the one she was in drove away. Tina must have slept, how long she did not know. She became aware of the bright lights of the hospital, and someone talking to her, but she couldn't understand what they were saying.

She thought they were telling her that Chris and her children were dead, but they couldn't be, she saw Chris go for them. She slept some more, and when she again opened her eyes, she saw Lilly and David at her side.

"Tina, we are so sorry."

"Chris, is he OK? The babies, where are they?"

Lilly shook her head. "He couldn't get out, Tina. They found him and Aimee together."

"What about Martin? I saw them bring him out of the building."

With tears running down her face, Lilly said, "The smoke got to him."

Tina heard someone screaming. She did not realise it was coming from her. The doctor came. She felt another needle, and then blackness descended upon her.

They kept her under sedation for a few days, but allowed her to stay awake a little longer each time, so that slowly it would sink in what had happened.

By the fifth day, they allowed her to be awake for most of the day. She sat in a chair looking out of the window like a zombie, unable to take in the fact that she had lost everything she loved and owned. She didn't want to live. How could she carry on?

When the time came for her to leave, Lilly and David collected her from the hospital.

David had made all the arrangements for the funerals. Chris and the children were to be buried in the same grave.

Throughout the following week, Tina slept, ate, walked and talked without any feeling of reality. She was sure that she would suddenly wake up and find it had all been a dream.

On the day of the funeral, when she saw the two tiny white coffins and the larger one for Chris, she realised that it wasn't a dream, but a horrible reality. The day dragged on and people said how sorry they were.

Then she was back home with Lilly and David. She sat on the porch, still unable to take it all in. Lilly came out to her, bringing her a drink.

"Thank you," she said. "You and David have been so kind. I can't go back, Lilly. I will sell the other cottage and they can do whatever they want with it."

"Your cottage was gutted. But David will help with whatever you need to do."

"Thank you."

Over the next two weeks, David salvaged some of Tina's things, but only because they had been in the cottage that Chris had used. There was nothing left of hers.

They put the property on the market, and then they helped Tina find a small place close to them.

"I'll move in at the weekend."

"Take your time. Only go when you think you're ready," Lilly told her.

"I have to face life sometime. It might as well be now as later."

That weekend she moved into the flat, and for the first time in eight weeks, Tina was on her own. She sat at the window and stared down at the harbour. How was she going to cope? she wondered.

Over the next few weeks, Lilly invited her often, but she stayed in the flat, not going out or eating properly; but she started drinking again. She found it helped to dull the pain, and she would fall into bed in a drunken stupor each night.

Lilly came to see her. "Tina, you look terrible. You have to take better care of yourself."

"Why? I have nothing left that I care about."

"Tina, what happened was a terrible thing, but you cannot let it destroy you. You have to be strong."

"I'm tired of being strong, and I'm tired of always losing."

"Will you please try, Tina?" Lilly asked her. "If not for you, then for me."

Tina nodded her head and Lilly left, saying she would come back the next day.

Tina looked at herself in the mirror. She did look a mess. She had another drink, then had a shower and washed her hair. She looked a little better even if she did not feel it.

Tina lay on the bed, aching to feel Chris' arms around her. She wanted to hear Martin cry, feel Aimee's arms around her neck.

She took the sleeping tablets the doctor had given her, and slowly put one into her mouth and washed it down with the vodka, then another and another and so on, each time washing them down with the vodka.

Tina lay down and closed her eyes. She felt herself drifting, and in her mind she could see the clouds. She saw Chris, Aimee and Martin, and they were laughing.

"I'm coming," she said. "Wait for me. I'll be there."

This was her last thought as her mind and body succumbed to the unconsciousness that she would never wake from.

No one would ever hurt her again. Tina would know peace at last.

Printed in the United States
74530LV00002BA/178-273

9 781424 141869